THE
DEED
ROOM

MICHAEL R D SMITH

Weathervane Press

Weathervane Press

Published in 2013 by Weathervane Press

www.weathervanepress.co.uk

ISBN 978 0 9562193 7 4

Cover image © Jon Roscorla 2013
www.jonroscorla.co.uk

Printed by Lightning Source

Eddie Tomlinson thought that to be responsible for harming anyone must be bad enough. But to harm someone you dearly loved, someone whose well-being you would put ahead of your own...

Eddie would always remember every detail of that day. He had been through it again and again, agonising about how he might have avoided not just the moment itself, but all that followed. It was a Thursday, hot and sticky, not long before his forty-third birthday. Each day that week he had promised his wife Julia that he wouldn't work late.

"The kids need to see you more," she said. "Rachel, especially. She's gone right off the rails."

But each day some meeting, crisis or phone call kept him away. Eddie had often told Julia he was no more tied to his work than the next person, no more mistreated by his employer. It was just how things were. He was proud of his job, IT Controller of Reverie Communications, a large company based a few miles from Nottingham. With it came an 'attractive benefits package.' A comfortable house in a pleasant market town. And punishingly long hours.

This Thursday Eddie had assured the family he would leave on time, earlier if things were quiet. In the end it was well past seven before he had any chance to shut down the PC and let tomorrow take care of itself. An all-day workshop on a troubled project started late and, badly managed like the project itself, overran. Collared by his divisional accountant on the way out, Eddie lied that of course he was in no hurry to leave and yes, he did have five minutes to talk about next year's budget. Five minutes became forty. Returning to his desk he found an e-mail asking him to stand in for an unwell colleague and give a 'brief and informal' presentation to a group of directors the next afternoon. By now he was so late it made no difference whether he stayed or not.

And so, feeling too guilty to phone Julia, and already bargaining with himself about the time he would leave tomorrow, Eddie stayed and ground out a few more hours in the vast air-conditioned hangars that served as Reverie Communications' head office.

When he grasped his forehead and ran his hand across cropped hair for the last time, it was past ten. Lost as he had been in a world of service levels and key performance indicators, he had paid no heed to the angry, thunder-bringing clouds which had built up outside. The rain sheeted onto the flagstones and the building's glass front as Eddie

3

stepped from the lift and crossed the reception area. He closed his eyes and shook his head. A day to put behind him.

As he sprinted to the Audi Eddie held his briefcase over his head, but by the time he had fumbled for the keys and collapsed into the front seat, he was sodden anyway. He sat in the car panting for breath and listened to the rain hammering the metal roof. He wiped the water from his face. He loved heavy rain when the weather was warm – real rain which washed away dust and cleared as quickly as it came, leaving the world shining. Despite his nagging sense of guilt, he sat watching violent rapid-forming rivulets sluicing the gullies of the car park under the fluorescent lights which the company thoughtfully left on to allow employees to come and go twenty-four hours a day.

The Audi felt snug, the drumming rain soporific. Moments like this were rare. Throughout the day Eddie's mind had acted as a dam, holding back his numbing tiredness. Now the dam burst and he drifted close to sleep.

He was roused as his head jolted forward. Confused, he looked round and rubbed his eyes. Then he started the engine and headed for home.

If Eddie had known what Rachel was doing that evening, he could only have agreed with Julia's assertion. Whatever your interpretation of being on the rails, his eldest daughter was nowhere near them.

As Eddie pulled out of the car park, Rachel was leaning against the wall of a classroom at her school. Her stomach was swilling with a cocktail of strong cider and cheap red wine, whilst a boy a year older than her attempted, with more enthusiasm than skill, to put his hands in her knickers and his tongue in her ear. She was laughing, trying all at once to sway to the dance music coming from the school hall nearby, keep some control over the boy's fumblings and drag on a cigarette. This all coincided unhappily for the boy as she let the cigarette rest on his shoulder. It burnt through his shirt and into his skin. He yelped.

"Bloody hell, Rachel. That hurt. You didn't have to do that."

She leaned forward, long dark hair falling around her face, and laughed again.

"Come on, you," she said, straightening up. She made an effort to smooth her skirt, then tottered across the room, veering to pick up a bottle from the desk. "I'm too rat-faced for this. Let's find the others."

Still clutching the bottle and leading the boy with her other hand, Rachel meandered down the corridor. When the two of them reached the school entrance the doors of the main hall opened, releasing a blast of loud music and a group of four or five other teenagers. The girl leading the way saw Rachel and shrieked her name in greeting.

"Ali, hi!" Rachel shrieked back. "Come on, let's dance."

"We can't," laughed one of the boys. "We've been naughty children and we've been thrown out."

"There's always a few who have to spoil it for the majority," said another one of the group, mimicking a teacher's voice. "Do your parents know you're turning up here with more alcohol on-board than a brewery delivery lorry? You don't have to get off your faces to have fun, you know."

"Yes you do, TOSSER!" Rachel shouted in the direction of the hall. "Stuff this. Who's coming to the Nelson with me? I bet we'll get served in there."

Eddie was driving on country roads. The windscreen wipers were working fast, the headlights on full beam, as he struggled to make out the bends and the dips ahead of him. His enthusiasm for summer rain had been washed away by the stuff itself, and he was driving at speed. To keep himself awake he had the window down as far as the weather would allow. The radio was on loud, playing the most mindless music Eddie could find.

When he was ten minutes from home the phone rang. He expected it to be Julia, and prepared himself for a complaint about his lateness. But on the illuminated display he saw a number he didn't recognise. He pushed a button.

"Eddie Tomlinson speaking," he said to the hands-free microphone.

"Eddie. Lewis Cooper," a deep voice replied. "I knew you'd still be in radio contact. What are you up to?"

"I'm on my way home actually. How can I help?"

"I won't keep you long. I just wanted to run through the things I think the guys will want to hear when you present to them tomorrow."

Lewis Cooper was Reverie's Chief Operating Officer. A younger man than Eddie, he had joined the company twelve months ago, and one of his first significant actions had been to remove Lesley King, the old IT Controller, and replace him with Eddie. People working on Lewis Cooper's projects expected to receive calls from him at any time of the day or night. Despite his exhaustion, Eddie felt flattered and important.

The two men chatted for a few minutes about the next day's meeting. Once Cooper was comfortable that Eddie understood his message, he brought the call to an end.

5

"Thanks for that, Eddie. I'll see you tomorrow. Drive carefully now."

There were a number of pubs around the small town square, but at each one they tried, Rachel and her ever more bedraggled band of friends were refused service. The repeated humiliation of trooping from bars under scornful adult gaze had combined with the rain to undermine their buoyant mood. Whilst the others tried their luck in one last place, Ali stayed outside with one of the boys and vomited in a shop doorway.

A few minutes later they were all back on the street again, and for the first time someone suggested they go home.

"No way," said Rachel. "There's got to be *somewhere* we can go, even in a dump like this."

She herded the group out of the town centre, and they headed instinctively back towards the school. Rachel's shoes had become uncomfortable and she had taken them off. She moved in front of the rest of the group, singing and skipping through puddles like a three year old, turning every now and then to look at her friends.

They neared the last bend in the road before the school. Rachel noticed some more teenagers on the far side of the road.

"Hey look, everybody," she shouted. "They've got booze. Come on."

She turned and ran towards the group, calling their names and whooping, waving her shoes above her head. As she ran, she looked back over her shoulder towards Ali and the others.

"Come on, you lot. What's the matter with you?"

Powerful, quiet and heavy, the car rounded the bend. Dazzled by the headlights, Rachel brought her arms across her face, as if all she needed to do was to protect her eyes from the light. There was a grotesque thud as metal hit flesh and bone and the car ploughed into her. She bounced off the bonnet like a doll, and twisted back into the road. A split second later there was a crash as the car hit a wall, and then for an instant only the sound of the rain. Rachel lay motionless in the middle of the road.

The door of the car opened and the driver climbed out. He started to walk towards Rachel. He looked round and Ali caught a glimpse of his face.

"Oh my God," she said to herself. "It's her dad."

ONE

Maria Cracolicci bit her lip as she typed. She breathed deep, willed herself to stay in control. *Don't let anyone see how upset you are*, she told herself. *Don't let anyone know.*

Around her was the hushed activity of Yates and Wood, a firm of solicitors in Nottingham. It was a Friday morning in autumn more than two years after the Rachel Tomlinson accident, and in Maria's ears a voice droned on. With her secretary's efficiency she transformed the words she heard into characters on the screen in front of her. But she had no idea what it was that she was typing.

Maria was a slim woman in her early thirties who was usually either smiling or just about to. But today she looked serious, perplexed. At times like this she hated working in an office with a passion that should have been spent on better things. She hated the pretence of being maverick Maria who made everyone laugh, big-hearted Maria who fought everyone's battles. All she wanted was to be on her own.

The phone rang. Maria started and looked at it with foreboding. If this were another dose of stinging abuse like the two she had already suffered that morning, she wasn't sure she would be able to hold her tongue. It would be too difficult to pretend that it was just some routine conversation. For a moment she wondered whether she should ask one of the other girls to take the call. But that would be silly – it would require an explanation she wasn't ready to give. She picked up the phone.

Fortunately it was just some routine conversation – a client wanting to make an appointment with Maria's boss, Guy Leighton. She dealt with it, trying hard to sound chirpy. Then she put the phone down, and breathed a long, controlled breath. Panic over, for now at least. But how long would it be, she wondered, before the next call from the lunatic woman who said she wanted to kill her?

Ten minutes to go…

Toby Malkin sat at a desk in the same building. Malkin could have seen Maria through the glass front of his office. But he wasn't looking at her. Nor, for once, was he looking at the legal documents spread out before him. He was looking at his watch, counting down the seconds.

7

Nine minutes to go. Malkin wanted those minutes to pass, but he also wanted to savour each one. Although he felt nervous, a much stronger feeling was a thrilling excitement, something almost sexual. This might be the best day of his life.

There was a knock at the door. Malkin frowned, and glanced at his watch again. Before he could say anything, the door opened and a woman with shoulder-length hair the colour of chocolate put her head into the room.

"Are you busy, Toby?" she asked, a little hesitantly.

Malkin's boyish features twisted into a grimace.

"Not if you're quick, Ruth. It won't take long, will it?"

Malkin watched as she placed some papers on his desk and explained briefly what they were. Even with his mind so definitely on other things, he couldn't help noticing, as he had before, that her skirt was a little tighter, and her shoes a little more dressy, than most of the junior lawyers risked in this environment.

Ruth finished her explanation, and looked at him, seeking approval. Malkin said he was pleased with what she had done, and she smiled and turned to leave. As she closed the door behind her, his eyes moved from the bouncing curls of her hair to the loin-stirring smoothness of her legs. *Who knows*, he thought? Now that he would have a little more time for himself...

He put these thoughts to one side, and looked at his watch.

Six minutes to go.

Maria couldn't bear to be at her desk any longer. She had to be on her own, even if for just five minutes. Grabbing some documents, she made her way by corridors and stairs to a storage area in the building's basement known as the Deed Room. She passed through a heavy fireproof door and then down a spiral cast-iron staircase to the lower of two levels.

This was a place of dust and shadows, where racks of ramshackle wooden shelving stretched in every direction. With its countless wills, trust deeds and conveyances, many of them handwritten in spidery script on thick dry paper, this room was a link between the modern legal profession and its more pedestrian, more prosaic past.

It was also a bolt-hole for the distressed and today Maria was in luck – there was no one else there. She sat down at a desk at the front of the room and buried her head in her hands.

She knew she had made mistakes in the past. She would be the first to admit it. But what was happening today was undeserved. She really hadn't known.

"You scabrous whore," the woman said when Maria took the first call that morning. The tone was flat, but Maria was shocked as much by the submerged fury she could detect as by the words used.

"He's always had a thing about dirty little slags. And no doubt you fit the bill perfectly. But please be very clear about one thing – you were just a shag. That's all. Didn't you realise? There's no way some pissy secretary could ever have meant anything to someone like him."

Maria's astonishment must have been apparent, because one or two people working nearby glanced at her. She ducked her head down, the only way she could find even a scrap of privacy.

"Who are you?" she asked. "What are you talking about?"

"Oh, like you don't know. My name is Stephanie and I am the girlfriend – the long-standing girlfriend – of the man you've been *doing* for the last three months whilst I've been working in New York. Do you know something? Do you know what I feel for you? Pity, that's what. Women like you have only one thing..."

As the string of invective went into a crescendo it all became clear to Maria. His evasiveness at the outset, the occasional mysterious weekend when he said he was watching motor-racing, the embarrassed suggestion last week that they take things a little easier. She could already imagine what lies he might select if ever she bothered to let him explain.

Same old, same old.

Maria interrupted and ended the call.

Ten minutes later, the phone rang again. The lovely Stephanie had now forgotten her professed compassion and had worked herself into a foul-mouthed frenzy. Maria sat tight-lipped, saying nothing. When Stephanie screamed that she would kill her if ever she laid hands on her, Maria rang off.

Now she sat in the lonely basement and made herself believe that it was funny – the thought of her clearly ex-lover spending any part of the rest of his life in the clutches of this demented harridan was as satisfying as any revenge she might extract herself. But this didn't last. In truth she was devastated, not so much by what she had lost as by the feeling that life wasn't fair. It was a feeling Maria knew far too well.

She stood up to return to her desk, eager now to escape the concealing shadows of the Deed Room but wondering just how she would make it through the seven long hours of being at work that lay

9

ahead of her today. Even more harrowing was the thought of the thirty-five long years that stretched ahead after that.

Two minutes to go.

Toby Malkin stood up from his desk, eased himself into the jacket of his brand-new Italian-tailored suit, and checked his swept-back hair in the reflection in the window. On the way out of his office he paused and looked at the scene in front of him. He felt like the son of a Victorian industrialist surveying his inheritance. This was it. His moment. Before long the rumour mill would start its work, and soon all these people would know. There would be different reactions – some would be surprised, some envious, some would feel inadequate. But all of them would be impressed.

And so they should. This was history in the making.

He crossed the open area of the Corporate Department as if in procession, smiling or nodding at the people he passed. On the next floor down he walked to the door of a meeting room. He adjusted his yellow silk tie, straightened his jacket and knocked.

He entered without waiting for a response. His tall frame filled the doorway as he stood looking into a large light-filled room, immaculate, with polished table and imposing line drawings of Nottingham's landmarks on the walls. At the table sat three male lawyers – Hugo Sanderson, Yates and Wood's senior partner, and two others. They all looked serious. *Quite right*, thought Malkin, letting a smug smile fade. *It may be a triumph, but it's a serious moment as well.*

He sat down. Hugo Sanderson – a grey-haired, distinguished-looking man whose eyes burned with the ambition of one much younger – moved some papers on the table in front of him.

"Thank you for making time to see us, Toby," he said. "I know you're very busy."

"Never too busy, Hugo," said Malkin. "I've been a big fan of these annual reviews ever since you introduced them."

"Quite. Well I'd like to start by going into a bit of detail on the finances, if I may. It's been another impressive performance."

Typical of Hugo, thought Malkin. *Playing it by the book. If that's how he wants to do it, it's fine by me.*

But after more than an hour discussing billing targets, business plans and budgets, even Malkin's ability to appear interested and charming at all times had been tested. Just as he was beginning to wonder whether he should try to change the subject, Sanderson closed his file and folded his arms.

10

"And of course, it's only right that you should be rewarded for all this," he said. "You're a special case, Toby. I think you know that. And I have some very good news. Your salary will increase by twenty thousand pounds next year. Be proud of yourself – that's the biggest single rise anybody other than a partner has ever had. Well done."

Sanderson turned and said something to one of the colleagues who flanked him. The two men laughed. Malkin sat looking quizzical and expectant. Then he saw Sanderson begin to collect his papers and his expression became one of concern. *Twenty thousand pounds?* There must have been a mistake.

TWO

As the other men packed up their papers and prepared to leave, Malkin stayed in his chair, knowing he should say something, or at least move, but unable to do either. He was stunned – gripped by a feeling of being outrageously cheated.

Hugo Sanderson stood up, but then noticed the young lawyer still sitting on the other side of the table. He lowered himself back into his seat, and told his colleagues that he would catch up with them later.

"You were hoping for a different message, weren't you?" he said when they had gone.

Malkin twisted his face, the normal composure wrung from his features.

"Hugo, I've achieved so much. I qualify on any grounds you can think of. In your own words, I'm a special case."

"But we're offering you a lot of money."

"That's not the issue."

Sanderson shrugged, a languid movement.

"You know how we do things here, Toby. We're not like other law firms. We're not trying to expand outside Nottingham or into new areas of law. We concentrate on what we know and we keep the number of partners very small. That means you have to wait longer. At the moment there's just no room for another partner, and I can't tell you when there will be. But when you do make it – and, Toby, you will – it will be all the more worth it for waiting."

Sanderson's tone was firm. It pierced the intensity of Malkin's disappointment, telling him it would serve him ill to argue further. The two men continued to talk, and with great effort Malkin's demeanour began to soften, making it appear that Sanderson's gentle encouragement was gradually having its effect.

Ten minutes later, on his way back through the building, Malkin passed Maria Cracolicci at her desk. Unknown to either of them, at that moment he had something profoundly in common with the unhappy secretary: a fervent longing to be somewhere else. He sat in his room, fighting the temptation to drive to the coast, maybe, and watch sunlight glistening on the sea, or to go home and spend the rest of the day lying on his sofa immersed in the music that was his only passion outside work.

From his desk, Malkin could see the office of Guy Leighton, the partner in charge of the Corporate Department. Suddenly he realised how much this man stood for everything he despised – an old-style lawyer sitting on a partnership in this most special of law firms and devoting more energy to some outside interest than to the business of Yates and Wood. Guy Leighton took a phone call, and Malkin watched as he listened for a while, then laughed. It seemed to Malkin that Leighton glanced in his direction. Was he talking about him? How dare he? How dare anybody regard his ambition as ridiculous?

With another supreme effort, Malkin put aside the injustice that threatened to engulf him, and like Maria he resolved that no one would see how he felt. Closing his mind to any thoughts of walking out, and the door of his office to the world, he did what he had done several times nearly every day for the last seven years. He went to his cabinet and fetched a file.

By four-fifteen, Maria's built-in optimism had done its work and she was feeling more upbeat. She had heard nothing more from the abusive Stephanie, and hoped that little episode was behind her. Better still – much better still – in forty-five minutes she would be out of this place for two whole days.

It had been a busy afternoon, but Maria had finished everything she had to do. She could have eked out some last bits of filing to fill the remaining time, but instead she helped the girls around her, to make sure that they would all be finished by five.

When there were about twenty minutes to go, Maria became aware of a presence at her shoulder. She turned and saw Tom Elliott, a trainee solicitor.

"Hiya," she said, smiling. "How can I help?"

"I've just got a few letters that need typing." He handed her some papers. "But there's no rush, if you're busy. They can wait until Monday."

"No worries," said Maria. "I'll make a start now."

As Tom retreated to his desk, Maria caught the glance of the woman who sat opposite her.

"What?"

There was no answer, just a smile.

"Don't be silly," said Maria. "He's not my type. Far too serious."

"If you say so," said her colleague. "Gorgeous eyes, though."

When five o'clock came, most of the secretaries left on the dot. Maria lingered, realising now the moment was here that it had never

13

deserved her longing. She had no one to hurry for, nowhere to go. With unneeded care she cleared everything from her desk, and then she went through her e-mails deleting anything out of date. When at last there was nothing else she could think of to do, she switched off her computer and picked up her bag, ready to make her way to the door. Then she started. In the margins of her vision she had seen a dark figure standing in the door of an office, looking in her direction. It was Toby Malkin.

Maria looked away and headed off. But then she heard his voice, speaking slowly.

"I need you to stay."

Maria stopped. There was no choice. She took off her coat and sat down at her desk. Malkin appeared beside her a few minutes later with an armful of files. He said that he had found something on one of them which was in the wrong place, and he wanted her to check them all and make sure everything else was where it should be.

This apparently simple task ended up taking Maria nearly an hour. As she looked through the files, it was clear that something was very wrong – every single document seemed to be misfiled. There were even letters which looked as though they had been unpicked and re-stapled with the pages in the wrong order. It was bizarre.

She became aware of the office emptying around her. As people left, they switched off desk lamps and office lights, allowing darkness to spread from the corners of the room. Maria glanced in the direction of Malkin's office. The faster she tried to work, the less progress she seemed to make. She flicked her fine hair from her face and watched anxiously as the last person in the open area packed up and left.

At last she was finished. She looked again towards Malkin's door. It remained shut. Through the blind which covered the glass front of the room she could just make out the lawyer's shadowy figure, stooped over his desk. She picked up the files and took a deep breath.

Malkin made no response to her tapping on his door, and carried on studying the document in front of him when she went in. Maria put the files on the edge of his desk and hurried out.

"Not there," he said when she was nearly through the door. "On the chair."

She went back and moved the files.

"It's all in order?" he said, still not looking up.

"It's all in order. But it was in a right mess. Like someone had done it on purpose."

"Really?" Now he was looking at her, smiling with colourless lips. "That seems hard to believe. I thought it would only take a few minutes. I do hope I haven't messed up your evening."

Now Maria wasted no time tidying her desk. She left the building as quickly as she could.

THREE

Toby Malkin stayed in his room for another hour. When he emerged into the car park of Yates and Wood's lavishly refurbished canal-side warehouse he noticed that his classic MG was now the only car there. He waited whilst the automatic security gates swung open in front of him and then he drove out into the night.

His route took him through the city centre. It was beginning to come alive with the Friday night party crowd. People moved around in large groups, girls in split skirts and clicking heels, men in shirts with no jackets, fortified against the autumn chill by their own high spirits only. Waiters in pizza restaurants scribbled orders and re-laid tables as soon as they were free. Each arriving bus and taxi brought more revellers, and outside cavernous pubs, bow-tied bouncers preened themselves, exchanging cocky remarks and flirting with the women. Synthesised dance music boomed from bars and cars, and everything was optimistic of the night ahead. No thoughts now of the tears and tantrums, rows and regrets that would end the evening for so many. The town was starting to rock. The place was alive.

Malkin was young, single and affluent, but had rarely ever been part of this. He would not be tonight.

In one of the bars past which Malkin drove Maria Cracolicci sat with Tom Elliott, the trainee solicitor she had spoken to earlier. Her eyes were red and although it was warm she still wore her coat. In the ashtray between them lay a pile of cigarettes, each one of which had its filter ripped from it.

As Tom crossed the Market Square on his way home he had noticed Maria standing at the front of a bus-stop queue. Although he had never spoken more than the odd sentence to her, he smiled and tried to catch her eye. She didn't notice him until he was level with her, when she raised a cigarette to her lips and pulled on it hard. She was miles away and struggled to recognise him. She gave him a pathetic little half-smile as he walked past.

After about ten paces Tom stopped and walked back.

"Are you alright?"

"I'm fine." She pulled hard on the cigarette again. "Honestly. I'm fine."

16

"Are you sure? You look upset."

She sniffed. "It's nothing. Just ignore me."

He stood and looked at her for a moment. She tried to smile again, with no more success than before.

"Do you fancy a drink?"

She shook her head, and this time the smile was real.

"You're very sweet, but there's really no need."

Tom paused, looking as if he were about to walk away. But then he reached out and took her arm.

"Come on," he said. "I was going for a quick pint anyway. It will be nice to have someone to talk to."

"You won't make a very good lawyer," she said when he brought the drinks to their table.

"That's a bit worrying. I've incurred enough debt to last me a lifetime getting this far. I was sort of planning to make a success of it."

"Well you won't. At least, not at Yates and Wood."

"Why not?"

"You're not enough of a bastard."

"I may be an absolute monster."

"No you're not. You're sweet. Thanks for the drink." She smiled and raised her glass, the tears now gone. "Do you mind if I smoke?"

Tom shrugged.

"I've upset you, haven't I?" said Maria, lighting a cigarette and looking at it with distaste. "I'm sorry. I don't mean to be rude. I'm sure you're hard-working and you're intelligent and you're all the things lawyers are meant to be. But I'm serious – all the people who make it at Yates and Wood are bastards."

"Something's obviously upset you."

"Or someone. It's nothing. It all just gets to me sometimes." She looked again at her cigarette. "But this is no answer. I only smoke when I'm depressed."

She stabbed the cigarette out in the ashtray and then proceeded to take the others out of the packet, tearing the filters off one by one.

"Let's not talk about work," she said. "There are so many better things to talk about. What are you doing this weekend?"

"Nothing much this evening. I've got to be up early tomorrow – I'm driving down to Exeter to see Caroline, my girlfriend. She's a doctor – works in a hospital there."

Maria rested her chin on her hand and leaned forward, relaxing visibly.

17

"That's nice," she said. "What does she look like? I bet she's beautiful."

"I think she is, but then I'm biased. She's about five feet five, blonde hair…"

"Nice figure?"

"Pretty much."

"Blue eyes?"

"Indeed."

"Which football team do you support she said changing the subject," said Maria.

They both laughed.

They talked for another forty minutes – about how he had come to the legal profession late after a few years working for a local authority, about Caroline and about some of the people in the Corporate Department. They shared another drink, and then Maria said that she should go. Tom walked her to the bus-stop. The bus was there waiting and before she climbed on she turned to him.

"Thank you for being so gallant," she said in a little girl voice, smiling and looking hard into his eyes.

"It's no problem. I hate seeing people upset."

She stepped forward and hugged him, holding her head against his chest. Feeling a little awkward, he embraced her loosely and ruffled her hair. When she had boarded her bus, he walked home across the pulsating city centre. He wasn't quite sure how he felt.

Success to the Malkins was what love was to happier families – assumed, a hub around which much else revolved, but something rarely spoken about. From his parents with their eminent academic careers to his venture capitalist brother and his novel-writing sister, it was taken as read that life for a Malkin was a constant process of accumulating evidence of achievement, then politely playing it down. But Toby's successes had never been effortless. He had always been the one who had to run to keep up.

And so, although he would never have admitted it, when he had looked forward to this day – the day on which he had been certain he would become Yates and Wood's youngest ever partner – he had pictured not the reaction of his peers, nor the thoughts of the money. He pictured the moment when he would make an apparently nonchalant call to his parents to tell them his news.

This evening there was no such call, and this evening Malkin fell asleep on his sofa in his executive riverside apartment, surrounded by his solitary comforts – a glass of malt whisky on the table in front of him, the sound of classical music playing on his hi-fi. He woke when the disc came to an end. For a moment there was confusion, then a powerful realisation. As his thoughts found some stillness – like water settling after the impact of a stone – he summoned up every last ounce of resolve. He couldn't be defeated. Making the sacrifices he had made, only to receive nothing in return, was a fairly good definition of stupidity. He wouldn't let it happen.

FOUR

What Eddie Tomlinson found hardest was the suspicion that no one at Reverie Communications believed his illness was real. He thought this poor reward for his years of uncomplaining service. And they cut his sick pay to the minimum at the first opportunity, despite their comforting words at the time of the accident.

But in the days after it had been confirmed that Rachel would survive the freakish collision, everything seemed fine. Once the doctors had dealt with the embolism which was the most serious of her injuries, his daughter's young body repaired itself, and soon she was home. Julia bought a cake, put up balloons, made an occasion of her return. The next day Rachel's friends started calling round again, and soon life for her was as it had been before.

Everyone told Eddie to rest, that his recovery was as important as Rachel's. Reverie Communications told him to take as long as he needed. But he started to worry about what was going on in his absence, even more that his absence would be unnoticed.

"I'll just go in for a couple of days to get on top of things," he told Julia one evening. "I can always take more time off later if I need to."

"Yeah, right," she said.

And so Eddie went back, and his colleagues marvelled at how little it had affected him. Eddie smiled through this, but beneath the surface he was struggling. It wasn't so much the trauma of what had happened, more the appalling thoughts of how much worse it could have been. He found driving difficult – if it was wet or dark he often imagined a young figure in front of him with long hair holding her arms up to protect herself. And he slept badly, his dreams vivid and disturbing.

This went on for weeks, with no sign of improvement. Something had to give, and eventually it did. One evening towards the end of summer he came home in tears. The journey had been difficult, a driver behind him becoming so irritated with his caution that he started to flash his lights, trying to make him go faster. Eddie snapped. He stopped the car and turned off the engine. It was only when someone pointed out, amongst the shouting and blaring of horns, that there would be an accident if he stayed where he was that he agreed to move.

The next day, Julia sent him to his doctor, who signed him off work and referred him for counselling. Here the system broke down – the counsellor was off sick with stress – and Eddie was left largely to recover on his own. This process was slow and hard. Part way through Julia said that she was struggling too, that she couldn't cope with keeping the family going and working full-time as well. They talked long into a fretful night and agreed she should find a less stressful job and reduce her hours.

In all Eddie was off for almost nine months. When finally he went back to work, he went back not just angry and bitter, but poorer as well. The loss of Julia's money, and the months of sick pay, cut deep.

It was a chance comment made by Ollie, his youngest, that really brought home how much things had changed. They were discussing their next holiday, and Julia was explaining to the children that this time it would not be to Florida or the Mediterranean, but to Cornwall or the Isle of Wight.

"Which country is Cornwall in?" asked Ollie.

"It's in this country, darling," replied Julia.

Ollie looked confused. "But you can't go on holiday in this country."

The statement was made innocently, as if he believed that it was something prohibited by law or made impossible by physics. But Eddie took it personally. There was a lot he could do to hide the difficulties they were suffering, but when it started to affect the kids, it was all too much. He couldn't bear the thought that they might be teased at school. Sometimes he found it difficult to accept that one moment of misfortune, one cruel combination of coincidence, could have led to so much change. He felt himself starting to tread once more the road to depression.

But then, a couple of days later, another chance occurrence set him on a different course. Reverie Communications sent him to some dreary conference about security in London. He didn't want to go, and the day started badly. As he walked up the station platform to the standard class compartments, he saw an immaculately presented Lewis Cooper standing outside first class, a mobile phone pressed to his ear, an expensive leather briefcase in his other hand. Eddie had spoken to him only a couple of times since their conversation minutes before he smashed into Rachel. He knew that Lewis Cooper had seen him, and also saw him pretending that he hadn't. Eddie made a point of catching his eye and smiling broadly.

When he arrived in London it was all just as dull as he had feared. Unable to face making small talk over lunch, he walked the streets and ate in MacDonald's. He was late back to the conference, and almost didn't go back at all.

If he hadn't, he would have missed hearing the speaker trying to liven up the difficult after-lunch slot by telling an anecdote. It was a little story of corporate life that was of passing interest to most people in the audience, which served its purpose and was then forgotten.

But it sounded a note in Eddie's brain, and during the rest of the afternoon this note developed into a tune. And then the tune wouldn't go away. Over the next few days, Eddie found himself coming back to it time and again. The idea it represented was simple. It was also dishonest. But, Eddie asked himself, did that matter? Did it matter if it helped his bruised and buffeted family hold on to a standard of living that was surely theirs by right?

From his idea Eddie conceived a plan. And soon he felt so confident about it that he told Julia that when he was in London he had bumped into someone senior from work on the train. Although he didn't want to raise her hopes, this mystery bigwig had hinted – had more or less said – that Eddie was in line for a big promotion and a lot more money. Their problems might soon be over.

This was just the first of many, many lies.

FIVE

The main bedroom in Toby Malkin's apartment faced the river, and being two storeys up was not overlooked. This meant you could have sex during the day with the curtains open and almost no chance of being seen. Normally he liked this. Normally he enjoyed what natural light and a little sense of daring could add.

Patricia Andrew – Professor Patricia Andrew – came back from the bathroom and climbed into bed next to Malkin. She put on her reading glasses, and lay with her arms folded across her small breasts studying him. When she looked at him in this way, he felt like a specimen in her pathology lab.

"Do we have other things on our mind, Mr Solicitor?" she asked, frowning. "Some client refusing to pay our extortionate bill?"

"I'm not with you."

"You weren't your normal attentive self. Perhaps you've fallen in love with someone? It must be either love or money."

"I have absolutely no idea what you mean."

"I hope you do, Mr Solicitor," she said. And then, more quietly, "I can get second-rate sex at home."

She turned away, and from a briefcase beside the bed took a sheaf of papers. Aware that for the time being she regarded him as simply not there, Malkin picked up a remote control unit and pointed it at a small stereo system on the far side of the room.

Toby Malkin had met Patricia Andrew a year before, at a dinner party given by Guy Leighton, his Head of Department. The Leightons and the Andrews lived near each other in The Park, an exclusive area of Nottingham which spread out from the rocky outcrop of the Castle, and which housed those who filled the ranks of the local movers and shakers, and those who thought they did. The buildings were elegant and impressive, with high ceilings and imposing windows. The streets were quiet and lined with executive saloons.

Patricia was a slight woman in her late forties with short dark hair. She was married to a senior director of one of the largest local companies, an important client of Yates and Wood. As Patricia sat down beside him at the dinner table, Malkin had noticed that her dress, make-up and jewellery all had the simplicity of classic good taste, but

23

little else about her. They had chatted throughout the meal in a rather formal way. She had not paid him any unusual attention.

It was therefore a complete surprise when, as they got up from the table, with supreme disguise and her husband less than four feet from her, she slipped a card into his pocket and said under her breath, "Call me."

He had waited two or three days before his curiosity finally led him to dial the number on the card. Professor Andrew answered, and told him to meet her for lunch the following day in one of the city's most expensive restaurants. Finding the whole thing intriguing, but with little idea where it was leading, he followed her instructions, and arrived to find her already sitting at a table, talking on her mobile phone. She raised her eyebrows almost imperceptibly in recognition when she saw him, and motioned to him with her pen to sit down.

"This is all very mysterious," said Malkin, when she finished her conversation.

She ignored this, and gave him a look which he couldn't interpret and a heavy leather-bound menu.

Throughout the meal they talked in much the same way as at their first meeting. Patricia was serious, and offered very little conversation, requiring him to make all the effort. She studied the menu with careful concentration before making her choice. Malkin felt that he also was being studied.

But when the meal was over, she leaned towards him with her hands clasped in front of her. She spoke in a low voice, her eyes flitting around from time to time to make sure they were not being overheard.

"I wanted to meet because I have a proposal to make. If it makes you uncomfortable, let me know and this conversation will never have happened."

"Go on."

"I won't spend time on unnecessary detail. Put simply, I have been married for more than twenty-five years to a man I met at university. The marriage generally works well, but not these days in all areas. I need an arrangement with someone – how shall I put this? – to supplement its flagging intimacy." She paused to allow her words to sink in. "I wondered if this might interest you?"

The only response Malkin could think of was to ask exactly what sort of arrangement she had in mind. As soon as he spoke he felt foolish.

"An arrangement for sex, of course."

He had heard hardened business leaders deliver proposals for corporate joint ventures with more emotion. Nevertheless, the situation was utterly enthralling.

"So what's the proposal?" he asked, swallowing.

"I should have thought that was obvious. If today we find that we..." Again she paused to consider the right phrase. "...get on, I will contact you when I am free to meet – say a couple of times a week – and we will have sex. You will be discreet, and there will be no more to it. No frills. No commitment. No love affair."

He looked at her for a moment or two, trying hard to appear as poised as she did. Around them was the bustle and subdued noise of the restaurant and he waited as a couple on their way out passed close to their table.

"Why me, if you don't mind me asking?"

"Because of what you've told me. You're unattached, so no guilt. You live on your own, so no fussy practical arrangements. And I think that like me you would rather spend your time on your career than developing relationships in a conventional way. You're more or less ideal. Well?" she asked, looking him straight in the eye.

He swallowed hard again. "Let's suppose I'm interested. What happens next?"

"You write down your address for me, and drive home. I wait here for ten minutes, call a cab, then come and join you. Or, if it's my lucky day..." And for the first time there was a barely detectable smile, a hint of the demure. "...join you and..."

Malkin didn't remember what had been said next, but he did know that Patricia had to remind him to deal with the bill, and that less than five minutes later he was driving home in a state of excitement comparable to his most memorable teenage experiences. He paced the flat until Patricia arrived, and when she did, he led her straight to the bedroom, half expecting that at some point she would laugh at him for falling for her joke. But she followed him, as if she did this every day.

When they reached the bedroom he kissed her, and with trembling hands removed first her suit, and then her underwear to reveal a body that was more pert and youthful than he had expected. All the time she stood still with her eyes closed, saying nothing, the strength of her breathing the only sign of her arousal. He lifted her slender frame onto the bed. Still believing that she might stop him at any point, he removed no more of his own clothing than necessary and, after easing himself into her with as much tenderness as he could muster, he took her quickly and intensely. She reached her climax shortly before him, with a concentration of noise and passion that was sudden and almost violent in contrast to her previous acquiescence.

"It looks like it was your lucky day, Professor," he said afterwards, his head propped on one hand and grinning like a schoolboy.

"Do we have an arrangement?" she asked, lying on her back and looking up at the ceiling.

"I think we have an arrangement."

The music came to an end. The only sounds in the room were now the occasional noise of Patricia turning a page, and the distant hum of traffic from outside. Malkin was lying with his hands behind his head.

"You know the Leightons reasonably well, don't you?" he said.

"We see them socially."

"Doesn't his fitness thing bore you rigid?"

"You mean all the running and going to the gym? It is a little tiresome sometimes, I suppose."

"It's all he ever talks about. Isn't he involved in children's sport as well?"

"He coaches the juniors at the tennis club. At least, I think he still does. Why the interest?"

She turned and looked at him over her glasses.

"No particular reason."

She dropped her papers to the floor and moved closer to him. She started to draw small circles with her fingers on the dark hairs of his chest.

"Mr Solicitor, always brooding, brooding, brooding," she whispered. "There's never no particular reason with you."

The lightness of her touch was, for Malkin, one of the most delicious things about her, and very slowly she widened the circle of her stroking, taking in first his stomach and then his thighs, alternating between a feather-light caressing with her fingertips and an infinitely delicate scratching with her nails. She stopped any attempt by him to fondle her and teased him with exquisite skill, running her fingers closer and closer to his most sensitive parts, but delaying any actual contact with them until his whole body ached with anticipation. When at exactly the right moment she took him in her hand he felt that he was going to explode, but knew also that it would be a long, long time before she let that happen. Running her whole hands now over his body, she straddled him and pinned his shoulders down. Then with an intense concentration, made faintly comical by the reading glasses she still wore, she began slowly to ease herself up and down on him, wringing every possible droplet of pleasure out of each movement.

"This time with feeling," she demanded. "With real feeling please, you dark, dark horse."

SIX

It was early morning and there was mist on the river, a low mist which hung over the water. The mist concealed the plastic bags and other debris caught in the bushes at the water's edge, so enhancing the beauty of the scene in the strengthening light. In the fields, frost touched the grass and leafless hedgerows, and farm animals huddled together for warmth.

Near the water was a car park. It was below the level of the road, hidden from passing vehicles. If on this morning there had been anyone about – a fisherman or dog-walker, perhaps, tramping the path on top of the bank which led downstream to a thundering weir – they might have thought it unusual to see an old BMW 7-series pull off the road and follow the unmade track down a slope to the car park. They might have thought it strange that when it reached the riverside it stopped and that its engine was turned off, but that none of the three men inside got out.

If this person had walked the half-mile along the river to the weir and then turned back, on his return he would have seen that another car had arrived. A sports car. If he had stopped and looked carefully he would have noticed that this car was empty, and that there were now four men in the BMW. He may have concluded that their conversation seemed animated. If he didn't mind the cold, this solitary observer could have stood and watched for another ten minutes, noticing perhaps that the fourth man – the man from the sports car – did most of the talking, and that at one point one of the other men wrote something down and passed it to him. Eventually he would have seen this man emerge from the BMW, adjust his tie, then climb back into the other car, before starting the engine and heading off in the direction of Nottingham.

The day of this riverbank rendezvous was a busy day for Malkin. His diary was full with meetings, and in between there were calls to be made, e-mails to respond to, documents to be written. Maria scurried backwards and forwards all day, bringing messages, drafts and water. Trainees and assistants reported to him on the tasks he had given them, in fear of his reaction if anything they did was not to his liking.

Malkin adored days like this, when chargeable hour led effortlessly into chargeable hour. He soaked up the pressure like a sponge,

28

remaining completely in control throughout, with never a hint of a rolled-up sleeve or a loosened tie. These were the days he lived for, the days that set him apart from the crowd.

He spent a lot of the day with Ruth Braebrook, his assistant, working on the early stages of a deal based on the purchase of an Irish company, rather predictably named Project Shamrock by the client. Late that afternoon, he asked Ruth to prepare a note summarising some key legal issues, and to let him see it before she went. At about half past seven, she completed this and brought it through to his office. She stood by his desk as he read what she had written. When he had finished, he made a noise of grudging approval and placed the document neatly on a file.

"Is there anything else you want me to do?" she asked.

"No," he said. "That's it for today. I've just a couple of things to finish myself and then I'll be packing up. You run along and warm Dominic's slippers, or whatever else it is you do for him."

She stuck her tongue out at him and pulled a face.

A few minutes later, Malkin watched Ruth pass the front of his office. Although she had spent nearly eleven hours in the building, she still looked – in pin-striped trousers that fitted snugly around her hips and a white blouse – every bit as good as she had when she came through the door that morning. As she left, she gave Malkin a little wave with her fingers.

He returned the gesture by raising one hand. If he were to be honest with himself, Ruth was a surprise. He wanted to believe that she was an airhead, eye-candy only, but he had to admit there was more to her than that. Her husband, Dominic Braebrook, had been a trainee solicitor with Toby Malkin at Yates and Wood several years ago. They had qualified at the same time, and the rivalry between them had been intense. But then Dominic had left to take his chance as a lawyer in London. He had done well, and whilst he was away, he had met and married Ruth. Now he was back in Nottingham, the conquering hero returned, working for Loxleys, one of Yates and Wood's local rivals.

Ruth passed through the doors at the end of the room and disappeared. Contrary to what he had said to her, Malkin in fact had no intention of leaving for some time yet. He rearranged the papers on his desk and prepared for another long night in the office.

On her way home, Ruth stopped in at a pub near the office where a work night out was already in full swing. It was a birthday celebration for a colleague and she had promised to call in for a quick drink.

She was followed into the pub by Tom Elliott and his girlfriend Caroline, the medic from Exeter. As he stood in the crush at the bar, Tom looked round and caught Maria Cracolicci's eye on the far side of the room. She smiled and waved, and made her way over to him.

"Maria, this is Caroline," said Tom.

"Hiya," said Maria, smiling her widest smile. She grasped Caroline's hand, leaned forward to kiss her on the cheek and looked her up and down, still holding her hand. "You're just as I thought you'd be. Are you here for long?"

"Just a couple of days. My team really can't do without me for much longer than that at the moment."

The three of them chatted for a while, and then found a table together at the back of the pub.

"I really am impressed that you manage to keep your sanity, sitting in an office day in day out," said Caroline to Maria, looking round the room. "Doesn't it get horribly boring?"

"No way," said Maria. "It's never boring in an office. There's always so much going on, if you know how to look for it."

"What do you mean?" asked Caroline.

"Offices are fascinating," said Maria. "You spend so much time working with people you know so little about, and all the while they're trying to show you what they want you to see – what they think will impress people and help them get on. But you can't keep that up all the time. If you watch carefully you pick up all sorts of little clues."

"Clues about what?"

"About what they're trying to hide. Nearly everyone's got something they don't want people to know. I love it when we have something like a department meeting. You look round the room at all these people trying so hard to look important and in control, and you know that most of them have got at least one thing they'd rather keep buried away."

"Such as?"

"All sorts of things. Love affairs, jealousy, laziness, addiction, incompetence, dishonesty. You name it."

"Sounds like the Seven Deadly Sins," said Caroline.

"Like I said, it's fascinating."

"Excuse me, we are talking about Yates and Wood here?" said Tom. "Everybody seems so straight."

"You'll learn," said Maria. She leaned forward, and lowered her voice. "Just look round this place now. See the guy at the bar with the red face?" She indicated with her eyes a man of about fifty, a partner in the Property Department. "He's a member of Rotary, and a church warden as well. But every other Wednesday he goes off to a hotel with those two mumsey-looking secretaries over there. I'm not absolutely certain, but I think there's spanking involved, as well as the sex. It's not a pleasant thought, is it?"

"You're joking," said Caroline.

"Not at all. And the guy he's talking to – Roger du Pre. His wife got bored when the kids left home a couple of years ago, and she got into online gambling. Now he's having to borrow money to cover her losses, even though he earns more in a year than I do in ten. And the woman at the end of the bar – blonde spiky hair, looking like she owns the place. Everyone says she's one of the rising stars, even though she's had three negligence claims against her in the last two years. Why? Because her uncle's the chairman of one of our biggest clients. I think there are some things she's good at, though." Maria's eyes twinkled.

"How on earth do you know all this?"

"I just keep my eyes and ears open. You see e-mails, and documents left on printers. You hear snatches of conversations. Most lawyers just don't think anybody could possibly notice what they're up to. Especially a secretary."

"What about your boss? You must have loads of stuff on him," said Tom.

"Guy Leighton's the exception that proves the rule. Straight as a die. Believe me, I'd know if there was anything."

"Actually, I meant Toby Malkin."

"He's not my boss." She looked offended at the suggestion. "I work for Guy. I just seem to end up filling in for Toby whenever his latest secretary's had enough and walked out. It usually happens after three or four months."

Maria continued to entertain them with her stories of office life until the party began to head off to a restaurant. Tom and Caroline were going somewhere else to eat on their own. They stood on the pavement outside the pub and said goodbye to Maria.

She hugged each one of them in turn. "You two go so well together," she said. "Have fun."

"She's great, isn't she?" said Tom as he and Caroline walked off arm in arm. " A real breath of fresh air."

31

"She's certainly entertaining." Then she stopped and looked at him. "You find her attractive, don't you?"

"Of course I don't. I find *you* attractive." He leaned forward to kiss her on the forehead.

She pulled away, not letting him.

"I think I've decided you should stay away from her," she said. "It's not a good idea to get too friendly with people who work for you. And anyway, she's a tart."

SEVEN

Although he didn't know it at the time, the event which Tom Elliott witnessed the next day would not only shock and disturb him. It would alter the direction of his whole life.

The day started when he woke shortly before the alarm clock sounded. He felt tired. He and Caroline had stayed up too late the previous night. In the restaurant he found himself returning to the subject of Maria, challenging Caroline's view, and from that a whispered row developed. When eventually they went to bed, Caroline said that she was too tired for anything but sleep. Now he would have given anything to have been able to turn over, snuggle up to her warm body and stay there until she woke, so that they could forget their differences and make love.

But his diligence prevailed over his yearning, and he dressed quickly, taking care not to disturb his sleeping girlfriend. Before he left for work, he kissed her on the forehead. Although she would be gone by the time he returned, heading back down the motorways to the West Country, he knew she would be annoyed if he woke her now. If your work was as important as hers, she'd often told him, sleep was essential.

When Tom walked into the office at just after nine o'clock, with his hair a little disordered and with a polystyrene cup full to the brim with coffee in his hand, he looked anything other than Yates and Wood's most promising trainee. He made his way to his desk in the Corporate Department, switched on his computer and shuffled a few papers around. The coffee was too hot, and it scalded his mouth. The papers did nothing to inspire him. Five o'clock seemed a lifetime away.

He would have chosen any day other than this to find that he had an e-mail from Toby Malkin and he swore under his breath when he saw that the message had been sent before seven that morning. It said that Malkin wanted to speak to Tom as soon as he arrived.

Ten minutes later, Tom returned to his desk from Malkin's office with a pile of documents and an instruction to prepare a briefing paper for a meeting later that day. He spent the morning skimming a file, ploughing through as much as he could of a joint venture agreement which ran to more than a hundred and fifty pages, and writing notes. He spoke to nobody, and when the office emptied at lunchtime he began to compose the paper, studying his computer screen with intense concentration. By half past two he was finished, and he sent Malkin an e-mail letting him know.

He received no response, but at about five to three Malkin appeared at his desk.

"Have you finished?" he asked.

"Yes, it's all here, I think," said Tom. "But there are one or two points I need to explain."

At this point a secretary came over.

"Mr Malkin, your clients have arrived."

Malkin looked at his watch.

"Tell reception I'll be down in a minute or two," he said to the secretary. "I have to make a quick phone call."

"You can use my phone if you like," said Tom.

Malkin shook his head and strode off to his office.

Tom was left holding the paper. He decided to use the extra minutes before Malkin returned to check through it again. When he had finished, he leaned round the partition screen next to his desk to look to see if Malkin was off the phone. To his surprise, Malkin's office was empty. He must have forgotten about the paper, but Tom was sure he would need it. He picked it up, together with the contract he had been working on, and set off towards the door.

When he walked into the reception area at the front of the building, he saw Toby Malkin standing at the far end, talking to his clients. At that moment two men came in through the main entrance. Tom thought they looked out of place the minute he saw them. They both had cropped hair, and were dressed in identical blazers and flannel trousers. Each man wore sunglasses. Tom stood to let them pass as they strode up to the receptionist.

"We're here to see Guy Leighton," one of them said.

"Do you have an appointment?" the woman asked, smiling and looking at a computer screen in front of her. "I don't think I've got anything for Mr Leighton this afternoon."

Tom moved away and walked towards Malkin. One of the clients was telling a story, and Tom waited at Malkin's elbow for a suitable moment to interrupt.

Before he had chance to speak there was a sudden eruption of noise from the reception desk.

"Listen, lady," one of the two men shouted, slamming his hand down onto the desk, "it doesn't need to be this difficult. Just get him to come down. We're not leaving until we've seen Guy Leighton. In person."

34

Everyone looked round. Unsure of what she should do, the girl at the desk peered furiously at her computer screen. As he watched, Tom felt somebody brush past him.

"Is there anything I can do to help, gentlemen?" Malkin asked, approaching the two men, his voice calm and authoritative.

"Who are you?" snapped the man who had shouted.

"My name is Toby Malkin. I am a senior lawyer in this firm. Is there a difficulty?"

"No, it's very simple. We have some documents for Mr Guy Leighton. And we need to see him in person."

"Why, in particular?"

"For Christ's sake, can somebody please get Leighton for us."

Malkin stood for a moment considering the request, and then leaned over to speak to the receptionist. A moment later she reached for her phone and spoke quietly to the voice which answered. When she put the phone back down, Malkin turned to the two men and smiled.

"He'll be straight down. Now would you gentlemen like to take a seat?"

He guided them towards some chairs, and walked back across the reception area, taking the briefing paper from Tom when he reached him. Feeling difficult and out of place, Tom sidled off towards the Deed Room, with his contract under his arm. He glanced at the two men as he passed them, and then away again when one of them met his eye.

He came back into the reception area a couple of minutes later just as the lift doors opened and Guy Leighton emerged. Tom watched as he stepped forward, all smiles and enthusiasm, like a vicar at a youth club. The receptionist indicated where the two men who had demanded to see him were sitting. Leighton turned, still smiling, and moved towards them with bounding strides, his hand extended in a pathetic and trusting gesture of welcome.

As he neared them both men stood up. One of them took a purposeful step forward so that his face was only inches from Leighton's. The other positioned himself so that he could see everyone else in the room.

"Are you Guy Leighton?" the first man snarled, any semblance of politeness gone, his demeanour oozing danger.

Leighton stepped back.

"Yes," he said. "Why?"

With a short stabbing motion, the man hit him in the stomach. Leighton doubled up and the man hit him again, hard in the face. The lawyer stumbled sideways, retching and crashing into a table.

"Pervert!" the man shouted. "Lowlife! We know all about you, you fucking pervert."

Everybody in the room froze. The receptionist was the first to react, reaching instinctively for her phone. A second later, Malkin was striding towards Leighton's attacker, shouting. The other man stepped forward and there was a flash of metal. Malkin stopped dead in his tracks.

"Leave it, bitch," the man yelled at the receptionist, pointing the knife at her. He turned towards Malkin. "You! Sit down! Now!"

Malkin backed off. Guy Leighton had picked himself up from the floor, and was half standing again. There was blood on his face, and pitifully, rather than trying to get away or defend himself, he was reaching down for his glasses.

This time the man kicked him. The blow was delivered with crushing force, leather boot smashing into fragile face. Leighton sank to his knees and rolled over in submission, trying to stem bursting blood from exploded nose. But the man kicked him again. Then he turned round. With a look of hatred, he addressed the whole room, barking like a sergeant-major.

"This man is a filthy pervert. This man plays around with little girls and tells their parents he's teaching them tennis. This, pal..." The comment was addressed direct to Leighton. "...is just a warning."

He nodded at his partner, and suddenly the knife was back in a pocket and the two men were gone.

EIGHT

The attack on Guy Leighton rocked Yates and Wood to its foundations. The whole firm was in shock. In the hours and days that followed, lawyers who had no idea how to deal with something like this sat uncomfortably in meetings, wondering if their clients knew what had happened, and praying to whatever gods they worshipped that the subject did not come up. Partners discussed the incident behind closed doors, their grim expressions visible through the glass fronts of their offices.

Two days after the attack, the senior lawyers who made up Yates and Wood's Management Committee gathered around a smooth polished table in a meeting room. The mood was sombre. There were five people present.

Hugo Sanderson opened the proceedings.

"Before we start to make any decisions, I want to go over the salient points. There have been all manner of rumours and stories doing the rounds since Tuesday, but we need to stick to what we know to be true."

"I don't agree, Hugo," said John Bayley, the Head of the Property Department. "It's rumours and stories which cause the most damage."

"I hear what you say, John, but I'd like to continue. The facts are that Guy Leighton has some connection with young children – aged between ten and sixteen – at the tennis club. He has had for years and it's no secret. On Tuesday afternoon, as we all know, he was the subject of a premeditated and vicious attack, during which very clear and distasteful allegations were made about his personal life. There were eight witnesses to the attack. Three of those were our people. The others were representatives of clients, and other law firms. Guy went straight home on Tuesday. I have spoken to him since, and, against my strong advice, he has specifically requested that the police should not be involved."

After a pause, Gillian Hedges, another Head of Department, began to speak.

"I've given this a lot of thought, Hugo, and I know that one can't imagine something as dreadful as this happening without a reason – no smoke without fire, if you will – but somehow I just can't see G being involved in anything like … what he's been accused of…"

Sanderson held up his hand to stop her. "On Tuesday I would probably have agreed with you, Gill. But there's more." He looked at each of the faces around the table, and wondered how many of them knew what was coming next. Yesterday afternoon one of the Corporate Department secretaries went into Guy's room to look for something, some papers from the Law Society, I believe. She had to dig around to find what she was looking for. Amongst his things, hidden in a corner of a cupboard..." Sanderson began to open an envelope in front of him. "...were these."

He slid the contents of the envelope into the middle of the table. There were gasps from at least two of the other lawyers. Strewn before them was a collection of photographs and magazines. The photographs were graphic and obscene. Some of the girls in them were obviously very young. The magazines were similar, with titles like 'Teenage Babes' and 'Young Flesh'.

Sanderson sat with his hands folded in front of him, staring at the table and saying nothing.

He then looked up at the people he had worked alongside for more than half his life and said almost inaudibly, "I've never had to deal with anything like this before."

There was a long silence. Simon Harrison, the firm's senior litigator, reached out and picked up one of the magazines. He flicked through its pages and then tossed it back into the middle of the table.

"Damn him!" said John Bayley suddenly. "Damn his eyes." He stood up and started to walk round the room as he spoke. "Do you need to see anything more, Gillian? Any more lingering doubts? Would it help if we brought in some weeping teenagers from the tennis club so that we could all cross-examine them?"

Gillian Hedges made no reply. She turned to Sanderson.

"Hugo, how much of this..." She indicated with a disgusted gesture the material in the middle of the table. "...is general knowledge? Who was it who found it?"

"Theresa Jacques."

"Oh, fantastic!" John Bayley was shouting now. "Only the biggest gob north of the Trent. Well one thing's for certain, it will be round ⌐   firm in the city by now, if it wasn't anyway. They'll be
            faces."

                        ⌐nce. Bayley's perambulations took him to the far
                        ⌐ he stood with his back to the rest of them, his
                        ⌐ets, whilst he stared out of a window. One or
                        ⌐oodled on the pads in front of them.

Eventually Simon Harrison broke the silence. "We obviously need to be extremely careful about the way we handle this. Do you have any thoughts, Hugo?"

John Bayley spun round to face the room again. "We should take the stupid bastard out into the Market Square and cut his balls off in public."

"John, please," snapped Gillian Hedges. "Can't you be a little more constructive?"

"Well what the hell do you suggest we do? This is going to destroy our reputation. We're going to be seen as That Firm With The Sex Offender. That Firm Where Deviants Get Beaten Up In Reception. It's taken decades to build this thing up and I for one am not going to stand by and see it all thrown away. The first thing we need to do is to drum Leighton out of here and make sure he never comes back."

The group naturally looked to Hugo Sanderson for guidance. He spoke slowly, choosing his words with care.

"I don't see that we have any choice. Although it's unfortunate, Guy can't possibly have any future here, however this all turns out. It's destroyed his reputation. He must therefore leave the partnership. For the sake of appearances, I would suggest that this shouldn't happen immediately. I would propose that we ask him to sign himself off as sick, and that he retires on the grounds of ill health, quietly and without any fuss in six months. If anyone asks in the meantime, we say nothing other than that we are taking appropriate actions internally. With a bit of luck – and assuming nothing else comes out – this may just blow over."

Nobody offered any further comment or dissent. And so, in the time that this meeting had taken, a career which may have been steady rather than sparkling, safe rather than scintillating, but which had spanned twenty-five years with no previous hint of impropriety, came to an end.

Twenty minutes later, Toby Malkin received a phone call. He responded immediately to the request that he should join Hugo Sanderson and the others. When he arrived he sat down at the far end of the room, looked at the collection of photographs and magazines which still lay in the middle of the table, and frowned.

"Toby, thanks for joining us," said Sanderson. "As I'm sure you can imagine, we've had a difficult morning."

Malkin's only response was a half-smile.

Sanderson continued. "The up-shot is – and this will be explained to all the partners in due course – that it is unlikely that Guy Leighton will be taking an active role in the management of the firm going forward."

"What Hugo's trying to say, with uncharacteristic reticence," John Bayley interrupted, "is that we're chucking him out of the partnership before he does any more damage."

Sanderson ignored the comment. "That leaves us without a Head of the Corporate Department. We have to have somebody to fill that role. You are the obvious choice. We would like you to take over with immediate effect." He was clearly not finished, but hesitated before he spoke again. "Of course, that also means that you will be invited to become a partner."

Malkin's response to this was a long time coming. When it did, it caused everybody in the room to question what they had heard.

"I can't accept that."

Sanderson looked askance at Malkin.

"Sorry?"

"Please don't misunderstand me," said Malkin. "Obviously the Department needs a leader, and I am happy to take on that role. I'm also very flattered that you should ask me. But not partnership as well. It just wouldn't be right – me profiting from something as … well, disturbing as this, I guess. I hope you can all see that."

"I'm struggling at the moment, Toby."

"How can I explain? If ever I become a partner in this firm, I want it to be because I've earned it, not because it's fallen into my lap as a result of someone else's weaknesses."

Most of the people in the room were still trying to recall if anyone had ever turned down the offer of partnership before. It was Hugo Sanderson who broke the silence.

"You've rather surprised me. But if that's how you see things, then this is not the time for me to interfere. Perhaps we can talk in a little more detail in a few days' time."

There seemed to be nothing more to be said, and so Toby Malkin left the room.

"I'm impressed," said Gillian Hedges once he had gone. "You don't often see that sort of integrity in a young lawyer these days."

If any of the lawyers on the Management Committee had felt any fleeting sense of guilt at the decision they had reached, they might have drawn comfort from knowing they had done no more than finish the work which the rumour mill within Yates and Wood had started. This had already dealt Guy Leighton blows every bit as vicious and damaging as those which the thugs in reception had visited upon him. Against these blows there was no defence.

From the moment that Leighton's assailants had fled, the rumours spread like a disease, a disease carried down telephone lines, via e-mail messages and through stolen conversations at coffee machines. Elements of the story which began as speculation were reported to the next listener as established fact, and then embellished in their onward transmission. Within hours the nature of the attack, and the things Leighton had done to provoke it, had been magnified to utterly implausible proportions. And although they had previously never seen fit to express a single word of suspicion, half the people in the firm now revealed that they had always thought there was something odd about him.

Later that same day, Tom Elliott came back from a photocopying session of Herculean proportions, and stopped at a desk near to Toby Malkin's office to drop off the fruits of his labour. Malkin's door was closed and through the glass front of the office Tom could see Maria Cracolicci standing with her hands placed on her hips, engaged in what was clearly a confrontation of some sort with Malkin.

Tom was intrigued. He had never seen anybody disagree with Malkin, let alone stand up to him. He stood transfixed, watching the way Maria shook her head and flashed her dark eyes in anger. It was an impressive sight. Suddenly she made a dismissive gesture and marched to the door.

Tom scuttled away. Maria strode to her desk and packed away her things noisily. She tossed her hair back defiantly and left the building without a word to anyone.

Shortly after leaving the boardroom Malkin called Patricia Andrew, summoning her to meet him that evening.

From the moment she arrived at his flat, she was powerless before him, unable to exercise any of the control she normally enjoyed when they were together. As soon as she walked through the door, he marched her to the bedroom, where he pulled her clothes from her like an ill-mannered child ripping open a birthday present. He was as urgent, and the act was over as quickly, as on their first afternoon. But there was none of the delicious tension of that occasion, nothing of the precision and refined mutuality she had taken such care to instil in him since. He was demanding, insistent, insatiable. He seemed intent only, in the words he had used on the phone, on rogering her senseless.

41

A little later, he took her again, with no more finesse than the first time, and afterwards they dozed. When Patricia woke, she lay still for a while, and then prepared to leave. But as she climbed out of the bed he reached over, took hold of her wrist and hauled her back, kissing her and running rough hands through her hair, then over her neck and breasts. He manoeuvred her onto her front, lifted her hips and, with a private sense of triumph, penetrated her for a third time. He thrust his way towards his climax, eyes closed, face straining with effort as if he were running a race he had to win at any cost. When finally he collapsed, sweating and panting over the finishing line, he pushed her away and fell forwards onto the bed.

"Mr Solicitor," she said, after they had both regained their breath, her eyes wide and mocking. "What's got into you? Have they given you a nice big pay rise?"

He rested his head on his elbow, and looked her up and down.

"It's better than that," he said. "Much, much better than that."

NINE

THAT EVENING

Toby Malkin

After Patricia Andrew had gone, he dressed – dark trousers, white shirt – and walked through to his lounge. From his most expensive bottle he poured himself a larger glass of whisky than normal, and then he assaulted the night with his music. He chose Bach – Kennedy's Led-Zeppelin-meets-the-Baroque version of the A-Minor Violin Concerto – and he played the manic third movement over and over again, standing up sometimes to conduct furiously with an imaginary baton or to play an air violin, and then stretching his arms wide as if to embrace the music. For him the searing, twisting notes of the soloist and the galloping rhythms of the orchestra were the reach and the drive of his ambition.

Later, he stood by the window and looked out at the lights of the city. He found himself looking in the direction of The Park, thinking not of Patricia Andrew, and certainly not of Guy Leighton. He thought about Ruth Braebrook.

He felt strong. A success. He was about as pleased with himself as it was possible for anyone to be.

Ruth and Dominic Braebrook

Ruth left work soon after five. There were no extra hours for her today. Although it was only Thursday, it had been a long week already. She had worked hard on Project Shamrock, and although she was little more than a bemused observer of the Guy Leighton goings-on, the tension within the firm was taxing.

She would have given anything to be able to spend an evening in front of the television with a glass of wine. But in the middle of the afternoon Dominic left her a message saying he was bringing some potential clients home for a bite to eat. They were a couple from London – entrepreneurs he knew from his days in the City – and as they happened to be in Nottingham he wanted to talk to them about the lawyers they used.

Dominic said they wouldn't expect anything special, but Ruth swore when she picked up the message and literally threw the phone down. After she left work, she rushed to Sainsbury's, and spent a manic hour cooking, tidying up and cursing her husband.

Ruth hated the evening. The conversations about London made her restless, and she didn't like the guests. She couldn't help imagining that her husband's attention to the woman – a sports-car blonde in leather trousers – went a lot further than professional courtesy required.

Lewis Cooper

As the winter's evening settled down in Nottingham, Reverie Communications' Chief Operating Officer arrived at Newark airport, New York, on an internal flight. He was on his way home from a visit to the company's American headquarters, and two days of wall-to-wall meetings. Ever the opportunist, Lewis Cooper had timed the trip to coincide with a meeting of the organisation's Global Board. He had thus had plenty of chance to rub alongside some fairly important shoulders and to squeeze some pretty senior palms.

Maria Cracolicci

Maria danced. She bopped till she dropped. She whirled and she twisted and she spun.

After storming out of the office following her encounter with Malkin, Maria wandered the shops. When her anger had subsided a little, she went home to her flat and sat on the sofa for an hour, listening to her most melancholy music.

But then, as was her nature, she snapped out of her mood, and called some friends. Like every office girl, she knew that Thursday night was the night to party, so that you felt bad on the firm's time and not your own. She changed quickly, and took a cab into town. That night she was wild. She laughed and she screamed and she flirted. She led her friends from pub to pub, and on to one of the city's biggest clubs.

And then, to bury her anger, she danced. She was a dancing queen. She could have danced all night.

Tom Elliott

Spent his evening thinking about himself and Caroline.

Hugo Sanderson

Breaking the news to Guy Leighton was one of the hardest things that Hugo had ever had to do. He could have written, or phoned, or asked someone else to bear the message. But he was a decent man, and he felt that it was something he had to do in person.

He walked the half-mile from the office to the Leightons' house. Catherine Leighton let him in. She looked distraught, and he suspected she had been crying for most of the last two days.

Hugo explained the decision that the Management Committee had reached. He chose not to mention the material discovered in the office cupboard. Leighton seemed to accept what he said without question. It was as if the most important thing for him was to make sure that Hugo didn't feel uncomfortable.

Guy Leighton
After Hugo left, Guy told Catherine what had been said. He couldn't face the prospect of another evening of her tears, and so he changed into his tracksuit and pushed himself to exhaustion on the multigym he kept in his garage.

Patricia Andrew
Patricia had a long bath and an early night. She told her husband she was feeling, quite literally, shagged out.

The Tomlinsons
Eddie enjoyed his evening. He took the family out to eat in an American-style diner, and he left the waitress a large tip.

When they arrived home, he and Julia watched television for a while. Then she said that she was going to bed.

Eddie waited until the sounds of his wife moving around upstairs stopped, and went to the corner of the dining room which served as his study, closing the door behind him and drawing the curtains. He switched on his computer and opened a carefully hidden file. He made some slight adjustments to a document on the screen, changed a date, and printed it off. After taking the result from the printer, he scribbled an illegible signature at the bottom and placed it in a pocket of his briefcase, which he then locked using a combination of numbers known only to himself. He switched off the computer and went upstairs.

This was something that Eddie had done once every month since attending the conference in London, more than a year ago. The first two or three times he had felt so nervous he could hardly hold the pen when he added the signature to the document. Even now, his heart beat faster every time he did it.

As he climbed into bed in the comfortable house in the pleasant market town, and snuggled up to Julia's warm body, Eddie couldn't help feeling pleased with himself.

And why not? At this moment he had every reason to think it was all under control. By taking matters into his own hands, he had overcome the problems which Rachel's accident had caused, and it had all been so easy. At this moment Eddie couldn't possibly be aware – simply didn't have enough information to be able to know – that what he had chosen to do would lead to murder.

That night, Eddie slept peacefully.

TEN

As the room filled, the noise level grew. So did the sense of excitement. People began shouting to make themselves heard, and waiters carrying trays of cheap sparkling wine returned for new supplies ever more quickly. Women hugged each other and compared little black dresses. Men in dinner suits told jokes and peeped down the fronts of the dresses. Festive music filled the rare gaps in the noise, and all the time the throbbing crowd edged nearer to the double doors at the end of the room.

Behind those doors was a dining area festooned with streamers and balloons. Crackers and party hats lay on tables, and on the stage was a disco, with light show and mirror ball. When finally the doors opened they released into the room the pressure not just of the last half hour, but of the whole of the previous twelve months. There was an undignified scramble as laughing, happy people hurried through, filling the room with their chatter, trying to make sure they sat near friends, and away from bores and slimeballs.

This was Yates and Wood at play. This was the annual Christmas party.

The event was held in a suburban hotel, and every year the firm's newsletter encouraged staff to bring spouses and partners. Hardly anyone did. When a whole year's worth of debauchery had to be squeezed into a few hours – in the way that some of the women had to be squeezed into their dresses – the result was not something you would inflict on anyone you loved.

Tom Elliott didn't know this. The party which took place a week after Guy Leighton's downfall was his first at Yates and Wood. If she hadn't been working, he would have brought Caroline. By the end of the night, for more than one reason, he was glad he hadn't.

During the meal which opened the proceedings – with its food fights and drinking contests – he sat with his fellow trainees, knocking back the wine and joining in the raucousness. As the evening progressed he was surprised by a number of things. By the speed and lack of shame with which people paired off. By the open and self-satisfied whispers of cocaine being snorted in the toilets. And most of all by the three stunning-looking women – one blonde, one dark, one red-head – who

47

sat fawning over three of the most geeky-looking senior lawyers from the Property Department.

"Who are those women?" he asked one of his colleagues. "I've never seen them before. What the hell are they doing with blokes like that?"

"Get wise, Tom. Let's just say that unlike all the lawyers in the room those girls will be putting in a few chargeable hours tonight."

From time to time Tom bumped into Maria. She was in full party mode, equipped with Santa hat and spray can string, dressed in an impossibly small frock. She was perpetually in motion – dancing, singing, laughing, flirting – as if it were her personal mission to have enough fun for the whole firm. For half an hour or so in the middle of the evening he lost her, until, on his way back from the Gents, he saw her in a dark corner, sitting on the knee of a lawyer. She was snogging him as if she wanted to remove his tonsils.

"You seem full of the joys of the season," Tom shouted above the sound of Slade when he found himself next to her at the bar soon afterwards.

"You've got to. IT'S CHRISTMAS," she yelled back, in a passable impression of Noddy Holder. "And the firm's paying. What's the matter – aren't you having fun?"

"It's not really my scene," he said, having to put his mouth right up to her ear to make himself heard, and feeling her hair brush momentarily against his face. "I think I might sneak off soon."

Maria smiled at the barman, took a sip from her drink and fumbled with her purse. Then she leaned towards Tom.

"Can I come with you?" she asked. "Let's go and have a chat somewhere quieter. Perhaps come back later. I'm not really having as much fun as you might think."

Toby Malkin attended the party for half an hour only. By the time he arrived, the lights were down and the room was filled with ghostly silhouettes, moving to the pounding music, or entwined in the shadows, or engaged in intense conversations which would be lost to them in the morning.

Malkin stood by the bar, and ordered whisky. There was no single malt, and when he sipped the blended variety on offer, he winced and asked for more water. Occasionally he exchanged a nod or a few words with other visitors to the bar. But generally he stood and he watched. He frowned with amused curiosity when he noticed Maria Cracolicci and Tom Elliott slip out together. For a moment, as they passed through the doors at the end of the room, they were bathed in light, and he saw them link arms.

He stood by himself for a while longer, his eyes flitting between the scenes around him. Then suddenly the light in the room increased as the DJ announced that it was time for some old Christmas favourites and urged everybody onto the dance-floor. Malkin noticed Ruth Braebrook, dancing with a group of other women, and caught her eye. She looked ravishing. Her dress was more classy than most in the room and fitted her voluptuous figure perfectly. She was wearing long black gloves, a black choker round her neck and red tinsel in the tumbling dark ringlets of her hair.

Malkin sipped his whisky and looked across the dance-floor again. Ruth was coming towards him, swaying her broad hips to the music, singing along and waving her arms above her head. He held her gaze as she approached. When she reached him, she stopped, put her hands on her waist and cocked her head to one side. Then she leaned forward and took hold of his tie.

"Come on, you," she said. "Let's see you dance."

She turned and, still holding his tie, led him away from the bar. He just had time to reach back and put down his glass.

They danced, her movements enthusiastic and deliberately exaggerated, his more graceful and restrained. Occasionally he took her hand in his, to guide her to move in the way that he wanted. They danced only briefly. After a couple of numbers the DJ announced The Birdy Song and of this Malkin wanted no part. As people around him began to perform the actions to the music, he bowed and kissed the back of Ruth's hand, his lips lingering on her skin, his nose searching for and remembering her perfume.

Then he turned and headed back to the bar. He ordered another whisky, and drank it quickly. Ten minutes later, he was gone.

The cold air in the car park made Tom feel even more drunk than when he was inside and the sound of the disco still throbbed in his ears.

"OK, party girl," he said to Maria. "Where are you taking me?"

"Oh, I don't know," she replied. "Let's just walk."

"Not with you dressed like that. You'll freeze." He took off his jacket and placed it round her shoulders.

"My hero."

"If you're going to take the piss, I'll have it back."

They left the car park and started to walk the quiet suburban streets, arms linked once again. As they strolled, they chatted about the party.

Tom was still incredulous about the escort girls. Maria seemed unfazed by this and everything else.

"You'll get used to it," she said. "It's no big deal. It's bound to happen when the rest of the year's so joyless."

They came to the river, and began to follow a dark path along the embankment.

"Did you see the great Toby Malkin slither in?" Maria asked. "Did you see how he just stands there, taking everything in, storing everything away? God, he makes my flesh creep."

"What do you mean? And anyway, you can talk. About storing things away. I bet you've got all sorts of gossip on him, just like you have on everybody else."

"Nothing," she said, turning her head sharply towards Tom.

"But you seemed to be having a right old ding-dong with him the other day in his office. I've never seen anyone stand up to him the way you were. What was all that about?"

"When was this?"

"The end of last week. When all that stuff about Guy Leighton came out."

"Oh, that." She stopped and turned so that they were both looking out over the wide blackness of the water. "I can't remember. But it all ended up getting out of hand. As usual."

Maria shivered and pulled the jacket round her. They started to walk again. They reached a bridge and climbed up away from the water, and headed back along a main road in the direction of the hotel.

"I bet you wish Caroline was here."

"Of course. But I'm enjoying being here with you." Tom reached over with his free hand and ruffled her hair.

"You're really in love with each other, aren't you? You're so lucky."

"I guess we are."

"What would she say if she could see you now? Wouldn't she mind?"

"Mind about what? We're just talking."

"If I were her, I'd mind."

When they arrived back at the hotel they stood in the car park listening to the muffled sound of the music coming from inside.

"Do you want to go back in?" Maria asked. "There's at least another hour to go."

"I'm not really bothered. What about you?"

"Let's go. I'll drive you home."

50

Maria led the way to a small Renault parked at the back of the car park. As they pulled away, she switched on the radio. A song she knew was playing, and she sang along as she drove, leaning forward to wipe the mist furiously from the windscreen from time to time. Her mood became lighter by the minute, and as they pulled up at a large roundabout, she turned and looked at Tom.

"Listen," she said. "I've changed my mind. I don't feel like stopping the evening now. Come back to my place and have a drink. We can listen to some music."

Before he could answer, she drove round the roundabout and headed back towards the river and the city centre beyond.

Her flat was near the Arboretum, close to the new university. When they drew up outside, Tom found that he couldn't open the door of the car. He struggled with it, imagining that he was hiding his drunkenness until he noticed that Maria was watching him and grinning.

"It sticks sometimes," she said. "You won't be able to open it. I'll need to do it from the outside."

In the flat, she showed him into the front room and went into the little kitchen. She found wine and made coffee. Still wearing his jacket, which was far too big for her, she brought the drinks through to the sitting room. She stood in the middle of the room, warming her hands on her coffee, swaying from side to side.

"Don't just sit there," she said. "I feel like dancing again."

"You said you didn't want to go back to the party."

"I know I did. But now I want to dance. And to some real music."

He watched her as she put down her cup and started to look through a pile of cassettes. She selected one and put it into her ageing stereo system. Then she turned to face him, reaching up and running her fingers through her hair. For the first time in his life he felt he understood what people meant when they talked about come-to-bed eyes.

But then he started and sat upright, spilling some of his drink, a look of horror on his face.

The music was on as loud as it would go. Tom had to shout to make himself heard.

"You cannot be serious. Mr Postman? You think the Carpenters is real music? Give me strength."

Singing along to every word, she shimmied across the room, took his hand and hauled him up from his chair.

"Come on, you. Let's see you dance."

51

Tom was no dancer, but she gave him no choice. She was a great dancer, and she was everywhere, one minute in front of him, the next minute behind, spinning him round, pulling him this way then that, gliding, teasing, mimicking.

When the track finished he collapsed laughing onto the sofa.

"No more," he said. "I surrender. I'm knackered."

She stayed on her feet, turned the music down but continued to dance to the next song. Her movements were now more restrained, more sensual. She kicked off her shoes, then removed his jacket and threw it at him.

"You could be quite good if you relaxed a bit."

"I'll stick to drinking," he said, and drained his glass.

He watched her for a while longer. He started to feel that he could watch her all night. When one song finished and another began, she stopped dancing and sat down next to him.

"I love this track," she said, her voice barely audible. "My dad used to play it all the time."

"I must admit, some of this is better than I thought. Didn't the singer die very young?"

"Karen Carpenter? She was thirty-two. Same age as me. Much too special for this world."

Maria lost herself in the melody and sang along quietly. Tom stared at the floor in front of him, stealing occasional glances at his hand, which lay inches from Maria's leg. By minute degrees he moved it so that it was touching the outside of her thigh, and then, very gently, he began to caress her with his fingertips. Her only response was to sigh and to carry on rocking herself to the music. He became bolder, and started to stroke her legs, feeling his way more firmly now. Then he took hold of her hand and squeezed it.

She opened her eyes and reached out to touch his hair. She moved her face so that it was next to his. They kissed – tentatively – and looked for clues in each other's eyes. Then he pulled her towards him, his hands seeking out the intimate places of her body, his mouth greedy for hers. She responded, but as he began to pull at her clothes she stopped him, pulling away, gripping his wrists.

"No," she whispered. The effort she was making to control herself was obvious. "We mustn't. It wouldn't be right. Think about Caroline."

She waited until their breathing subsided. Then, still holding his wrists, she leaned towards him and kissed his forehead, with tenderness rather than passion, before easing herself away. She tried hard to smile.

"I'll fetch you some blankets," she said. "It's time we got some sleep."

At about four in the morning, Tom stirred, craving water. The effort of finding his way to the kitchen woke him completely. On his way back, he looked in through the doorway of the bedroom. By the light from the hall he could make out the shape of Maria's face as she slept, and he stood and watched for a while. He could also see the crumpled dress lying where it had fallen on the floor.

Taking great care to make no noise, he found his jacket and let himself out. Then he walked the three miles home across the city in the freezing night air.

ELEVEN

Eddie Tomlinson felt hot and his mouth was dry. As they worked their way down the list – and as they neared the letter M – he found it harder and harder to concentrate. He took off his glasses and rubbed his eyes. Then he took a deep breath and looked at the list again.

"Langdale Developments?" asked Tom Elliott.

"Consultancy work," said Eddie. "We hardly use them these days. Five k maximum."

"LML?"

"Software support. And some hardware. The annual spend is a fixed amount."

"Are you sure?" said Tom. "It seems to vary, according to what I've got here."

"Sorry? Oh, we're talking about LML, aren't we? You're right. I'm getting confused. There's a small fixed charge, and then we pay more if we call them out. My mistake. Sorry."

He watched Tom write a note after they had discussed each name. They were sitting in one of Reverie Communications' meeting rooms, reviewing a list of the company's computer suppliers. There were only two more to go before they reached the Ms, and Monte Cristo Software was the first of those. To Eddie, the name stood out from the rest as if it were written in letters six inches high. It now seemed such a ridiculous name.

As they dealt with another company, Eddie forced himself to calm down. There were only the two of them in the room, after all, and the young lawyer sitting opposite him had no reason to be suspicious. Very soon this would all be over.

The last company before Monte Cristo Software took several minutes to deal with. Just as they were finishing, the door of the meeting room opened and Toby Malkin came in. Lewis Cooper – his enormous frame filling the doorway – was with him. Malkin was in the middle of an anecdote, and when he finished both men roared with laughter.

"How are you chaps getting on?" Malkin asked.

"Quite well, I think," Tom replied. "We're about halfway through."

Malkin looked over Tom's shoulder at his notes.

"What's the next one? Monte Cristo Software." He read the name slowly. "I bet you can always *count* on them." He looked up and grinned.

"Pathetic, Toby," said Lewis Cooper. "Come on then, Eddie. What do they do for us?"

Everyone looked at Eddie.

"They're not... I mean, you probably won't... It's not easy to explain."

"Are you alright?" Lewis Cooper asked. "You look dreadful."

"No, I'm fine." He took a drink of water, spilling a little down his chin. He wiped it away with the back of his hand. "Monte Cristo. They're a very small outfit. Very specialist software."

"And what do you pay them?" asked Tom.

"Three thousand a month."

"It's always the same?"

"Yes. Why wouldn't it be?"

"Jolly good," said Lewis Cooper. "Anyway, Mr Malkin. We'd better go and celebrate this promotion of yours. The table's booked for twelve thirty."

Malkin looked at Tom and Eddie. "Keep up the good work," he said.

As the two men left the room, Malkin allowed Cooper to go first, and then turned in the doorway. He studied Eddie for a second or two, then disappeared.

Toby Malkin owed Reverie Communications a lot. His rapid progress as a lawyer had much to do with his being the company's trusted local adviser. This in turn relied on his relationship with Lewis Cooper, and on his personal control over every piece of work Yates and Wood did for the company. True to this, he checked with Tom Elliott later that day that he had reached the bottom of the list, and asked how Eddie Tomlinson had been.

"Fine, most of the time," said Tom. "Although he did seem a little strange around the time you came in. Maybe he's frightened of Lewis Cooper."

Malkin considered this as he returned to his office. It seemed to make sense – most people feared Lewis Cooper's occasional but spectacular losses of temper. He shut the door, sat down at his desk and touched the mouse on his laptop. The screen flickered into life. He checked on the diary system what Ruth Braebrook was doing the next day. She had two meetings, and had simply put "keep free" against some time in the middle of the day. Lunch with Dominic, perhaps? Whatever it was would now be rendered irrelevant. He picked up the phone and dialled her number.

"Ruth, it's Toby. I need you to come with me to London tomorrow. It's to do with Project Shamrock. I'm going to drive down. I'll pick you up at home at six-fifteen."

They spoke further about what Ruth would need to bring with her and then he put the phone down. He thought about her making hurried calls and offering flustered apologies. That he could cause her to have to do this pleased him enormously.

TWELVE

Ruth made sure she was ready well before six-fifteen. She had avoided telling Dominic in any detail what she was doing, only that she would be out early and back very late. She was glad that he was still asleep when Toby Malkin pulled up outside the house. She had a fairly good idea that her husband would not think the sight of her climbing into his old rival's car, dressed in a brand new suit – the skirt of which was shorter than it had seemed in the shop – was an ideal start to his day.

The purpose of the trip was to carry out the *due diligence* on the company at the centre of Project Shamrock. In Ruth's experience, the reality of this rather grand-sounding process – the process of assessing the legal health of a company prior to its purchase – was generally a tedious day trawling through box after box of arid legal documents.

On the way down to London they talked easily. Ruth explained how she planned to renovate the house she and Dominic had bought in The Park. Malkin gossiped about colleagues.

"This is beautiful," Ruth said, referring to the music playing in the car. "I'm not sure I've ever really listened to a whole opera. What is it?"

"La Bohème," said Malkin. "Puccini. It's very popular, but still worth hearing."

"It sounds romantic to me. Does it have a happy ending?"

"Hardly," Malkin replied, laughing. "The poor little heroine dies."

Their destination was the offices of a firm of City solicitors, where they were to be given access to a data room. This was as Ruth had expected, a poky little place with no windows, stuck at the end of a basement corridor. In order to reach it, she and Malkin walked past cleaners' cupboards, store rooms filled with stationery and anonymous little alcoves with no obvious purpose.

"My God," she said. "Sometimes the glamour of this job is enough to turn a girl's head."

They established themselves in the room, and worked hard until mid-afternoon, examining contracts and leases, taking notes and making lists of anything they wanted copying. Mindful of the need to make progress, they spoke little. The building was constructed directly above a tube line, and at regular intervals the distant rumbling of an approaching train grew dramatically into a climax of noise and rattling which shook the whole room before fading into quiet.

Towards the end of the day, Malkin told Ruth that he had arranged to see the lawyer who was acting for the other side. Before he went upstairs to meet him, he gave her a list of items he wanted her to research whilst he was gone.

Left by herself, Ruth became aware of just how isolated this little room was. She looked around, and wondered if the fire alarm worked, or whether anybody knew she was there.

Then she forced her mind back to her work. She was starting to feel tired, but she made herself ignore this. In the silences between the noise of the trains she listened out for Malkin's footsteps in the corridor.

An hour and a half passed, and still he hadn't returned. Ruth found the answer to the last question on his list, reread the notes she had made and put down her pen. It was warm and the room was becoming uncomfortably stuffy. She needed some air. She stood up and went over to the door.

She pressed down on the handle. At precisely the same moment, someone opened the door from the other side, pulling it away from her hard. Ruth stumbled forward and gasped. The person grabbed her wrists, making her squeal.

"Careful. Are you alright?"

"My God," said Ruth. "I had no idea you were there."

Malkin relaxed his grip on her wrists and stood looking down at her. It was difficult for her to see him in the shadows of the corridor. He guided her back into the room and pushed the door shut behind him. Then he waited for her to calm down.

"OK now?"

She nodded and then frowned. "Were you waiting there? I didn't hear…"

Gently he lifted one finger and placed it on her lips.

"That's enough. Shhh." He moved his finger away and then, with the lightest of touches, began to stroke her face. "You look so frightened," he whispered. "There's no need. Why would I frighten you?"

She had frozen the moment he touched her and now she looked down.

"Please don't, Toby. Please."

He put his finger back on her lips and pressed. "Don't say anything else," he said.

58

Suddenly Malkin was the thorough and diligent professional again, charming and bustling, as if what had just happened between them never had. Ruth looked at him once or twice, scrutinising him for some trace of emotion. But there was none. He simply applied himself to the legal work, and she followed his lead.

An hour and a half later he closed the file on which he was working and looked at his watch.

"We'll stop now. Do you feel hungry? I certainly do. After everything we've done today, I think Yates and Wood should treat us, don't you?"

"I'd just as soon grab something quick and get back to Nottingham," said Ruth as they packed their bags.

"Don't be silly. All work and no play..."

It was dark outside, and although the rush hour was now over, the main thoroughfares of the City were still busy with the yellow and red lights of the ever-moving traffic. The shadowy side streets and dimly lit courtyards through which Malkin led Ruth were quieter. They passed the odd late worker heading for the tube, the occasional couple walking arm in arm or gripped in a last illicit kiss before returning home to husbands and wives.

They arrived at a small and exclusive-looking restaurant, tucked away in the corner of a tiny close near the river. They were shown to a table in the semi-darkness at the back.

Whilst they ate, Malkin was attentive and charming, and Ruth began to relax, wondering if she might have imagined what had taken place in the basement office. But when they had finished their meals she took a deep breath and leaned forward.

"Toby, what happened between us back there..."

"Nothing happened."

"You know what I'm talking about. I'm very flattered. But it mustn't happen."

"Why not?"

"Because I'm married. That's why not."

"That's good."

"What is?"

"Your answer."

"I don't follow."

"You're saying that if you weren't married something could happen. And so all we have to do is overcome your rather touching adherence to the outdated promises you've made to Dominic, and...well, who knows?"

She rolled her eyes. "Don't try catching me out. You know what I mean."

"Do I?"

He didn't respond to this, but suddenly his expression became intense. "You do realise it's pointless," he said. "Totally impossible."

"What is?"

"The idea that you're going to stay faithful to Dominic."

"No it's not. How can you say it's impossible? That's ridiculous. I should be very offended."

"No you shouldn't. It's not a comment about you. It's a comment about the lifestyle you've chosen. You and Dominic will spend the next twenty or thirty years doing all sorts of crazy hours, constantly being in very close contact with other successful people – attractive people, people driven by money with lots of it. Are you seriously telling me that neither of you will ever give in to the temptations? Think of all the weekends you'll spend in the office, the nights in hotels, the trips abroad. Think of all the people you know who've had affairs."

Ruth sat saying nothing for a while.

"I don't think it necessarily has to be like that," she said eventually. "Not for everybody."

"Well now, Ruth Braebrook!" he said, leaning back in his chair. "The passion and forcefulness of your arguments overwhelm me. How can you deny it? There's both opportunity and motive. If you don't give in to lust or curiosity, you'll give in to loneliness. And if somehow you manage to resist all those, there's always revenge."

"Revenge?"

"You're not seriously telling me you don't know what Dominic's like? Surely you must have compared notes about the times before you met."

"Not really. Why should we?"

"I would have thought that was a sensible precaution. Especially with someone like Dominic."

"For God's sake, what do you mean, *someone like Dominic*?"

He didn't answer. She thought back to the blonde with the leather trousers and drew a pattern with her fork in the congealed film of sauce left on her plate. When she looked up again, there was a resigned smile on her face.

"Why do I feel that this is all some way of trying to talk me into the sack? Which won't work, by the way."

"It's nothing of the sort. Try me."

60

"Try you?"

"Yes. Ask me to sleep with you and see what I say."

She studied him for a long time before saying anything, looking for clues in his expression. There were none. She drained her glass slowly. Then she shook her head.

"All these mind games, Mr Malkin. It's much too much for a girl. I'm going to powder my nose."

They finished their meal and made their way back to the car. They drove away from the City with its curious mix of history and modernity, and into London's far less glamorous sprawl, heading for the motorway and the route back to the Midlands.

"Listen to this," said Malkin as they drove. "Tell me what you think."

He pushed some numbers on the phone in a hands-free cradle.

"Hello. This is a message for Mr Toby Malkin. It's Eddie Tomlinson from Reverie Communications. We met yesterday." There was a long pause. "I ... wanted to talk to you about ... Monte Cristo Software ... one of the companies on the list we went through yesterday. Well, you and I didn't, but I spoke to your assistant. The thing is I've not been very pleased with them ... Monte Cristo, that is ... and so we'll be getting rid of them. And I just thought that you should know so that hopefully you can take them off the list. I wouldn't want you wasting your time. Hope all this makes some sense. You can call me, I guess, if you need any more information."

The line went dead.

"How bizarre," said Ruth. "He sounds so frightened. What's it all about?"

"It's just an insignificant little matter I'm doing for Reverie," said Malkin. "A review of their contract terms with their suppliers. That's what makes it so strange."

Soon afterwards they hit the motorway. The road was quiet and Malkin drove fast, flashing his lights aggressively at anyone who blocked his progress, and veering into the middle lane to overtake on the inside whenever necessary. He put on some gentle music and Ruth dozed at first and then fell asleep.

She woke soon before they pulled up in front of her house.

"Sorry," she said. "Have I slept for long? I didn't mean to. It's been a..."

Malkin had stopped the car and now he turned towards her. He put his finger on his own lips this time to quieten her.

"Ruth, make no mistake. It is entirely inevitable that you will be unfaithful to your husband."

He put his hand on her knee and then ran it up under her skirt. This took her by surprise and she was slow to react. Ignoring her protests, he squeezed her firmly, as if claiming her, and felt her gasp.

"And," he whispered, "when it happens, I'd love to be there."

He laughed and took his hand away. As she got out and walked towards the house, he revved the growling engine of the car as loudly as he could and pulled away with screeching tyres.

THIRTEEN

No one in the Tomlinson family had any idea they were being watched, let alone how closely. The man was professional and discreet. He had been told that money was no object, that there was no need to rush, no need to risk making mistakes.

Over the first few days he gathered basic information. He followed Eddie and Julia to work and the children to school. Taking care to change the car he used, he sat outside the house for long hours, building up a picture of the comings and goings, surreptitiously taking photographs. He found out about property prices in the area, and about the value of the cars the Tomlinsons drove. He made phone calls and talked to people, pretending to be a long-lost relative, or a solicitor hunting missing beneficiaries. Like a scavenging fox, he even rooted through the dustbins.

By this process he worked out that the house – a substantial Victorian semi in a quiet residential street – was likely to be empty every weekday morning. To his delight, he also noted that the children let themselves in and out using a key left under a flowerpot by the back door.

These discoveries made the rest of his task much easier. He took nothing away, but spent several mornings in the house, looking through anything of a personal nature he could find – letters, computer files, diaries, photographs. Above all, he looked at financial information – bank statements, bills, credit card details, receipts. He took extensive notes as he worked and was careful to leave everything undisturbed.

Finally, he spent a couple of days in York, tracking down Rachel at the university, following her and taking more pictures.

When he was finished, he was pleased with his work. Although he had found no obvious evidence of anything salacious or spectacular – no love affairs, hidden cruelty or secret vices – he had been thorough, and that was the most important thing. Detail, detail, detail. He had been told to concentrate on detail.

One miserable mid-week evening, someone rang the doorbell of the house where Tom Elliott lived. One of his housemates answered. The wind caught the door, and he struggled to keep hold of it. It was sleeting heavily and a blast of icy air invaded the warmth of the house.

On the doorstep stood a woman, dressed in jeans and a dark leather jacket, which she had pulled up over her head to protect herself from the weather.

"Come in, come in," the housemate said. "How can I help?"

"Is Tom here?" the woman asked, removing the jacket from her head. She shook her hair and tried to straighten it.

"He certainly is."

He opened a door off the entrance hall and leaned into the room behind it.

"Tom, mate. Visitor for you." Unseen by the woman in the hall, he winked and leered as he spoke.

Tom appeared and stopped in the doorway.

"Hello," he said. He blinked in disbelief. "This is unexpected."

The woman smiled a deliberately forced smile.

"I'm sure it is," she said. "I just thought that as you seem to have been ignoring me at work since you crept out of my flat in the middle of the night three weeks ago, this was the only way of getting to talk to you."

Maria turned and walked past Tom into the room from which he had emerged. He glanced at his housemate and then followed.

Maria was already sitting at one of the chairs by a table.

"Would you like some tea?" Tom asked.

"No. Just an explanation."

He sat down at one of the other chairs and folded his arms. He looked up sheepishly, and then away again.

"Maria, I haven't been ignoring you," he said eventually. "I was away over Christmas and it's been crazy since New Year. I've been meaning to talk to you, but I've just been too busy."

"Crap," she said. She smiled, but the smile failed to reach her eyes. "Try harder."

"What do you mean?"

"I mean come up with something that's at least half-believable." She paused and rolled her eyes in exasperation. "Look, despite your best efforts to persuade me otherwise, I know you are different from the artless arseholes I normally run up against in this job. How can you be *too busy* to talk to someone who sits yards away from you all day? If I've done something to upset you, please just tell me."

He studied her as she spoke. The words and the body were those of an adult, but the child in her was very pronounced. He imagined that if you saw a photograph of her as a five year old, you would recognise her immediately. The dark eyes and the shape of her mouth – which

64

was a little too big for her face and which curled up at the corners as she talked – would give her away.

"You've done nothing to upset me," he said, after a pause. "Far from it."

"So what's the problem?"

He took a deep breath. "I was embarrassed. I didn't know what to say. I don't have much experience of situations like ... you know, and I guess I didn't know what you were thinking."

"What are you talking about?"

"That night when we were walking by the river, we seemed to be close, and then you just drove me back to your flat. And the dancing and the way you were dressed ... I thought you were trying to seduce me. And I suppose I felt you expected me to make a move, and when you said no I didn't know if you meant it, and then I woke up and it just sort of felt better that I didn't stay all night and... Oh, I don't know, Maria. Does it all have to be so complicated?"

"No. It fucking doesn't."

The strength of her expression surprised him. They looked at each other for a while. Then she screwed her face up and clenched her fists.

"Ahhhh," she said through gritted teeth, the noise one of pure frustration. "Will you stop looking so sorry for yourself. I did not try to *seduce* you. You're a sweet guy and I thought we could have a laugh. I've met Caroline and I like her. I'm not into breaking up happy couples. It's really not my style."

There was a long silence. Tom looked uncomfortable, and stared at the table.

"I've acted like a right prat, haven't I?" he said.

"Yes."

"It's probably because I'm just an artless arsehole."

For the first time there was some thawing of Maria's mood, a hint of her relaxing.

"No you're not. That's the whole point. Look, I don't mind what happened at my place – I've done enough stupid things in the past to know when to keep my knickers on. You were drunk; I'm totally irresistible to any man. These things happen. It's the ignoring me ever since that upsets. Surely you can do better than that. I just want to be friends. God, how cheesy does that sound? But there's no other way of putting it. And, Tom, I need a friend at the moment."

"Why? What's happened?"

She paused. "Toby Malkin wants rid of me."

"In what way?"

"He wants me to leave. Find another job."

"How do you know?"

"It was either my feminine intuition, or when he called me into his office and said, 'Maria, I think it would be best if you found another job.' One of the two."

He ignored the sarcasm. "When did this happen?"

"It's happened twice. The first time was when you saw us in his office the day they sacked Guy. I didn't tell you before, but that's what the arguing was about. And he said it again today. He says it whenever I piss him off. I try so hard not to, but I just can't help myself."

"Why would he want to get rid of you?

"He's always hated me. Well, for years anyway. And now he's flexing his Head of Department muscles."

"Are you sure?"

"Of course I am. It's so unfair – nobody else pays the same as Yates and Wood. And anyway, I don't want to leave. Why should I?"

They sat holding eye contact. Maria looked as if she had something more to say.

"There's another reason as well," she said eventually.

"What's that?"

"He knows I'm suspicious."

"What do you mean?"

She chewed on her bottom lip, and then shrugged. "Guy Leighton's never touched any young girls. He didn't keep pornography in his office."

"Yes he did. Everyone knows what happened."

"No they don't. Toby Malkin set the whole thing up."

Tom looked shocked. "You're joking. How?"

"Very easy, really. He paid a couple of thugs to carry out the attack and he planted the magazines in Guy Leighton's room when he was working late one night. Then he made sure that somebody like Theresa Jacques found them."

"How do you know all that?"

"I've worked with Guy for years. I know he's been set up."

"And is that it? That's your only reason – that you've known him a long time?"

"No – think about it. You were there that afternoon, weren't you? Toby Malkin just happens to be in reception when the attackers walk in. They ask to see Guy, but of course there's no appointment, so Tanya on the front desk won't call him down. She says that when it

66

started to get nasty, Malkin came over and told her to call Guy. He told her that the quickest way to stop it getting out of hand was to do what they wanted. She did what he said, and – surprise, surprise – Guy gets his head kicked in, and Toby Malkin gets his job. If Malkin hadn't been there, apparently to smooth things over, Guy would never have gone down to reception."

Tom stood up and walked to the window, his hands pushed into the pockets of his jeans. He gazed out into the darkness. After a while he turned round to face Maria again. There was part of him that wanted to agree with her, for reasons he hadn't worked out. But everything logical about him – and there was plenty – said the opposite.

"Maria, Toby Malkin is a brilliant lawyer. I can't believe what you say. It's all circumstantial."

She shook her head. "I'm right," she said. "Trust me, I'm right."

They carried on talking, going over the events of that day again, thinking hard about whether anyone could have hidden the pornography in Guy Leighton's room without Maria knowing. Nothing Maria said persuaded Tom she was right.

"You've not told Malkin what you think?" asked Tom.

"Of course I haven't. I'm not that stupid. But I'm going to tell someone – I thought Hugo Sanderson would be best." She paused and looked a little nervous. "I know it's a lot to ask, but I wondered if you would come with me."

He wished so much that she hadn't asked him this.

"I can't do that, Maria. I'm just not convinced that what you're saying is right. And anyway, why go to Hugo?"

"Because Toby Malkin knows I suspect him, and if Toby Malkin is prepared to do what I know he did to Guy, what would he do to me to shut me up?"

"Oh, come on! Even if I could be persuaded that Malkin frames people as child molesters, there's no way I'm going to believe that he'd do anything to you just because he might think you're a bit suspicious. You're getting it way out of proportion."

"Am I?"

"Yes. You've got no proof. You're feeding off scraps."

He could feel her disappointment and it pricked him. He desperately didn't want her to leave in this frame of mind.

"Look," he said, "let's think about this some more. You're always saying there are clues about all sorts of things to be found in the office. I promise you, if you can find any real evidence to support what you're saying, I'll come and talk to Sanderson with you."

If Caroline had heard this, he thought, she would have despised his weakness. Maria smiled, with real warmth.

"Well, I am at least right about one thing. You're definitely far too nice to be a lawyer."

When Maria came to leave, the weather was every bit as atrocious as when she arrived. She stood at the door, looking out at the sheets of rain sweeping through the parts of the night which were illuminated by street lamps.

"I'm right about Toby Malkin," she said. "And I've got this image of him waiting for me when I get home, ready to cut me into little pieces or something. I couldn't stay here, could I?"

She saw the look on his face and winked.

"Joking," she said. She kissed the end of her index finger and pressed it to his forehead. "Sweet dreams," she whispered.

She pulled her jacket over her head and stepped out into the weather. Then she ran with little steps, in shoes not made for running, down the path and along the pavement to her car.

FOURTEEN

On a grey winter's morning when the light struggled to make itself noticed, the man who had carried out the surveillance of the Tomlinson family sat in Toby Malkin's open-plan lounge.

His name was Donal Stark. He was about forty, and was dressed in casual but expensive clothes. On the table in front of him he had placed an old-fashioned lighter made of brass, a packet of cigars and a number of envelopes and folders. He sat back in his chair, the ankle of one booted leg resting on the knee of the other, his hands held behind his head, as he looked round and tried to work out just how many hundreds of CDs the shelves on the walls contained.

Stark was a Dubliner who had come to Nottingham pursuing a woman and had never left. He was a trier, a man who would turn his hand to anything if he thought it would help turn him into a pillar of the local business community. He had sold cars, owned betting shops, run bars, provided hired muscle to pubs and clubs, dabbled in private investigation. All this with some success, but without ever finding the real Midas touch, although he hoped his 7-series BMW might persuade people otherwise.

Malkin came through from the kitchen carrying two mugs of coffee. He placed them precisely on coasters, and then made himself comfortable at one end of the long settee, a notepad and a pencil on his lap.

"Well then. What can you tell me?"

Stark began with the basic details, and went through them methodically. As he spoke, Malkin made an occasional note or stopped him, by raising one finger, to clarify a point or ask a question. When he opened a file of photographs of the family, Malkin leaned forward and picked it up.

"Quite a striking-looking girl," he said, looking at a picture of Rachel.

"And she knows it," said Donal. "Little vixen. I reckon she's got at least three guys on the go. Mind you," he added, "Ma Tomlinson's not bad for her age either."

Malkin studied the pictures for a few moments longer, then closed the file and placed it back on the table.

"Go on," he said.

Over the next forty minutes, Donal created a picture for Malkin of the Tomlinson family, detail by detail, painting by numbers. When they discussed Rachel's accident, Malkin asked question after question, until he was satisfied that Eddie had been responsible, and that there was a link between this incident and Eddie's breakdown.

At this point, Malkin looked into the distance and thought carefully for a moment. He then wrote several notes on his pad.

"OK," he said. "Tell me about their finances."

The Irishman reached for another file of papers, and at the same time picked up his cigars and began turning the packet over and over. "I've got quite a lot of detail here, but I'm not sure I've got the whole story."

"Tell me what you have got," said Malkin.

"Well, Tomlinson earns about fifty thousand. Mrs T a lot less, about twelve. She used to earn much more, but as you know she changed jobs and went part-time a couple of years ago."

"Around the time of the accident?"

Donal thought for a moment. "Yes. Fairly soon afterwards. Anyway, even when she was working full-time, they were living right up to their means. Relying on credit to keep up appearances. The mortgage is big, takes a good chunk of Tomlinson's income. They've got car loans, and in the past they were carrying big, big credit card balances. There's not much in the way of savings, and they live very well. Everything in the house, from the hi-fi to the kids' mountain bikes, is more or less top of the range."

"OK. I've got the picture. What else?"

"When she changed jobs and he got ill, the whole thing started to creak. They missed a mortgage payment, paid the minimum on the cards, cashed in an endowment. But they didn't stop spending. Didn't do anything that would have made it obvious they were struggling. But I reckon it was getting pretty serious, because they had the house valued around that time. But then suddenly, a month or two after Tomlinson went back to work, it all gets better. All the problems disappear. And the thing is…"

"Wait," said Malkin. "Let me think." He sat in silence for several minutes. Then he wrote something on his pad, and looked up. "I think you're going to tell me that suddenly, as an answer to all their problems, the family start receiving an extra payment every month. Something not obviously linked to their jobs. Something they hadn't ever received before. How am I doing?"

Stark looked a little deflated. "You're spot on," he said. "That's exactly what happened."

There was a tearing sound as Malkin removed the top piece of paper from his pad. "And," he said, folding the paper and sliding it across the polished surface of the coffee table, "unless I'm very much mistaken, the amount they receive every month is this."

The other man picked the paper up, unfolded it and read what Malkin had written.

"Right again. I'm not sure you need me, Toby. You seem to know it all already."

Malkin leaned back and folded his hands in his lap. He looked up at the ceiling and smiled.

"Interesting, Tomlinson," he said. "Very, very interesting."

Although Maria Cracolicci's flat was less than a mile from the city centre, the surrounding area was quiet. She had the upstairs of a crumbling semi, covered in ragged, dusty ivy, which clung to the peeling window frames and worked its way into holes in the brickwork. The flat on the ground floor had been empty for months, since the lonely death of the widower who had owned it, and the walls of the building were thick. It was rarely that Maria heard any noise from her neighbours. The house stood at the end of a road which was no more than a track and which led nowhere – a country lane which had been smothered many years ago by the creeping embrace of the city. There was very little passing traffic – the odd car turning round, the occasional person on foot heading towards a forgotten little park which the house overlooked.

Maria was alone in her flat. On this grey winter's day, she stayed in bed until gone ten. She had no particular plans beyond a vague idea she might wander into town with a friend that afternoon, and after watching children's television for an hour and drinking coffee, she decided to pamper herself.

She unplugged a portable tape recorder in the kitchen, placed it on the floor just outside the bathroom and put on her favourite Carpenters album. As the music began, she filled the bath, pouring scented oil into the swirling water which gushed from the taps. Around the edge of the tub she placed a number of tea lights, which she then lit, as well as a larger candle which began to release a heady perfume.

Maria pulled her white cotton nightdress over her head, and dropped it to the floor. She studied herself in a mirror on the wall, cupping her small breasts in her hands and turning to look critically at her bottom. Feeling more or less satisfied with what she saw, she tested the water with her toes and climbed in.

71

She lay there for a long time, rereading a letter she had received from a friend in Australia the day before. Whenever the water started to cool, she topped it up. The flames around her trembled as an occasional draught disturbed the air, and from time to time one of the tea-lights burnt down and died. The music came to an end and the only sound was the dripping of a tap. Like one of the expiring flames around her, her attention started to struggle and flicker. Eventually the letter fluttered to the floor and she dozed.

She was woken by the sound of knocking. It came from the front door downstairs, and was insistent, demanding attention. Maria wondered if she might not have heard an earlier, less urgent noise. Although the bathwater had become tepid, she decided to stay where she was and to ignore the door. She wasn't expecting anyone. She couldn't be bothered to move.

But her caller refused to give up and almost straightaway knocked again, thumping the door this time, and banging the letter box as well. Maria could see from where she lay that the light in her front room was on, and she cursed. On this grey morning, the light would be visible from the road, and would suggest she was in. But still she stayed where she was. *Please go away*, she thought. *I want to be alone.*

She heard nothing for a few moments, and relaxed again. Suddenly she sat up and gripped the sides of the bath. Her eyes were wide, her mind alert. A bang from downstairs told her that her visitor had tried the handle on the door and had found it unlocked. She remembered that when she came in the night before she had been thrilled to see the letter from her friend. Distracted by this, she must have left the door open. *How stupid. How unbelievably stupid.* The person was now starting to climb the stairs.

Maria pulled herself out of the bath. She grabbed a towel and dried herself as best she could. By this time, the intruder had already reached the top of the stairs and had stopped outside the flat. Whoever it was now stood only a couple of yards from her. Maria couldn't be sure whether the door which separated them was locked or not. For a moment there was silence, then another loud knock which rattled the door in its frame.

She glanced at a bread knife on the kitchen table. *You're over-reacting*, she told herself. *Better just to stay quiet.* Instinctively, she stepped away from the door. As she did her foot caught against the tape recorder on the floor and she stumbled. Still believing against all logic that she might not have been heard, she reached out to steady herself, grabbing at a small table. A vase which had been resting on it crashed to the floor.

"Hello," called a voice she didn't recognise. There was more knocking. "Open the door."

Maria pulled the towel round her and stepped forward.

"Who is it?" she said, trying to sound confident.

"It's a surprise. Just open up."

She took a deep breath and then turned the lock slowly. As she did she kept her foot wedged against the bottom of the door. She tried to peer round to see who was there, but as she did something was pushed at her face, obscuring her vision. She raised one hand to protect herself, and struggled to stop her towel from falling.

"My God," she shouted, her tone a mixture of anger and incredulity. "What the hell are you doing?"

The door was now wide open. Maria was staring at the gormless, grinning features of a delivery boy, partly hidden by what he was carrying – one of the biggest bouquets of flowers she had ever seen. Still smiling, he pushed them towards her again.

"Stop it," she snapped. "Don't push them in my face like that."

The youth stopped.

"What's the matter? Aren't you pleased?"

She fought to control her emotion. "Yes, I am pleased. But you shouldn't have come in like this. What do you think you're doing? Why couldn't you have left them on the doorstep?"

"I thought they might get stolen."

Maria's anger started to recede, and she reached out to take the flowers.

"I'm sorry. It's just you frightened me. Would you mind going now? I'm not wearing a great deal here, and it's sort of getting cold."

The youth turned and, looking crestfallen, retreated down the stairs. Feeling guilty at the way she had talked to him, Maria shouted an apologetic thank you at his back and then closed the door. The bouquet was vast, and it was a struggle to hold on to it. She leaned back against the wall and tried to collect her thoughts. Then she looked down and read the message card attached to the flowers.

A peace offering. Are you free tonight? Your friend, Tom. Xxx

"Do you need anything more from me, Toby?" asked Donal Stark. "There's more I can tell you, if it's of any interest."

"Oh yes," said Malkin. He eased himself out of his chair, and walked to the large window at the end of the room, where he stood looking out at the battleship grey of the sky. "Tell me it all. I want to hear everything."

They talked first about the extra money, and then covered a lot more ground about the family. When it appeared that they had dealt with everything, Malkin asked one final question.

"Tell me, from all that you've found, does the name Monte Cristo Software mean anything?"

Stark shook his head. "No," he said. "I don't think so."

"Really? Perhaps we ought to give Tomlinson some credit. At least he's kept that hidden."

Malkin thanked the Irishman for his efforts and asked him to leave the papers and photographs. He showed him out, then returned to his sitting room and selected a Wagner opera from one of the shelves of CDs. He listened to the whole work – all four hours – from beginning to end, and whilst he did he worked intensely and without a break, referring often to the material his henchman had left. Sometimes he paced the room muttering to himself, sometimes he sat at a desk in an alcove off the living room, writing notes, making lists and revelling in the detail he had at his disposal. When the music came to an end, Malkin carried on working. By the time he had finished it was nearly dark, and he stood by the big window watching the lights coming on all over the city.

He then walked over to the sofa, sat down and picked up a packet of photographs. He laid out in a small pyramid pictures of Rachel, Julia and Eddie Tomlinson, the two women on the bottom, the husband and father on top. He studied them for several minutes, then smiled, shook his head and placed the pictures back in the packet.

FIFTEEN

She looked everywhere. In files, in archives of e-mails, in Toby Malkin's desk, briefcase and diary. And she asked everyone – the secretaries of all the partners, anyone she could find who knew anything about the tennis club. For days on end she thought about very little else.

And through this she turned up things she thought significant. There were e-mails which had passed amongst the partners in the days before the attack. These hinted at something murky about Guy Leighton, and as far as Maria could work out began with a conversation over lunch between Hugo Sanderson and Toby Malkin. *Malkin could easily have started rumours such as this*, she thought, *so that the allegations which followed reached receptive minds*.

Sitting in her flat late one night, Tom said that he wasn't persuaded. Weren't they just as likely to be evidence of Guy Leighton's guilt?

But then there were the whispers that Malkin was now pushing for partnership, using the excuse that it was what his clients expected. Surely this exposed his earlier refusal as a sham?

"Hardly," said Tom as they strolled round the lake in Wollaton Park on a Saturday afternoon. "Clients will find it strange that he's not a partner."

But despite their failure to agree on this, the two of them grew close. Caroline had exams, which kept her occupied for weekend after weekend in Exeter, and Tom reasoned with himself that there was nothing wrong with him spending time with Maria, now they had established the ground rules. They developed a way of talking which mimicked the dropped consonants of Karen Carpenter's accent – *waitin', hopin', lookin', thinkin'* – and Maria was effusive with her affection. But although there was hand-holding and there were hugs, each of them took great care – self-conscious, almost embarrassing care – not to do or say anything which could be construed as a step towards anything more.

Tom was frequently surprised by things Maria said. She would make observations about people at work – identifying troublemakers, spotting relationships develop – from only the smallest of clues. She also had a good understanding of the legal files on which she worked, and she was happy to use her knowledge to help him do well. He told her one evening as he lay on her sofa that she should have gone to university.

"I nearly did." She was sitting on the floor, with her back to him. "I had a place at Manchester. To do law, would you believe?"

"Why didn't you go then?" he said, sitting up.

"Because of Dad, I suppose. I was fifteen when Mum upped and left, and he needed me there too much. It wasn't just the *cookin'* and the *cleanin'* – he had no one else to turn to. He never actually said he didn't want me to go away, but it was obvious."

"That's such a shame. So where's your dad now?"

She leaned forward and hugged her knees.

"He's gone. Just like Mum, chasing his own happiness, and ruining mine. He got in touch with a roly-poly widow in Padua through some family connection, and then he told me one day he was going back to Italy to live with her. I don't blame him, but by that time it was too late for university."

"It's never too late. You could go now."

"No I couldn't. I can't afford it. And I guess I've just got used to this as a way of life."

There was one thing about Maria that Tom would have changed if he could, one thing which touched him far more than he ever told her. Twice when they were out with other people from work, he found, just as he had at the Christmas party, that suddenly she was all over some man she hardly knew. Kissing and fumbling and giving all of herself. He knew he had no right to feel jealous, but each time he left early and never mentioned what had happened.

When eventually Maria did come across something of real value in her mission against Malkin, it happened in an unexpected way. She was out with Tom in the city centre one Saturday evening. They met in a bar in the Lace Market.

"I just can't think of anything else you can do," said Tom, when inevitably the conversation turned to Malkin. "Except admit you're wrong."

Maria narrowed her eyes and shook her head. "No way. One day you will see that I'm right. And then you'll understand why I can't let it go. Can't you see how Malkin is these days – swaggering around, ordering people about for kicks, showing off to Ruth Braebrook all the time?"

"I see somebody running a department extremely well – a dedicated, professional lawyer." Tom took a swig from his beer. "And I also see somebody who's going to work out that you're spying on him."

The muscles in Maria's face tightened in an expression of embarrassed defiance.

"Come on," she said. "Let's go and eat. This is depressing me."

As they walked along the side of the Market Square, Tom asked a question about someone at work. Maria turned to him and opened her mouth to answer. But before she could speak, Tom gripped her arm and pulled her with him as he veered off at a right angle.

"What's the matter?" she asked. "Where are we going?"

"Don't say anything," he said. "Just keep walking. I'll explain in a minute."

He walked fast with his head down, looking at the ground. She had to skip to keep up. Then he stopped. He glanced over his shoulder and led Maria into a pizza restaurant.

"Tom, are you please going to explain what's going on here?"

"I will, I promise. Just give me a moment. Come on – let's sit over there."

He headed for a table which looked directly out of the front of the restaurant. It was still covered with the leavings of its last occupants. They sat down, and Tom looked round at the other diners. He moved some of the debris in front of him and leaned forward, his face close to Maria's.

"OK," he said, in a low voice. "You're never going to believe this, and I know I'll regret telling you, but if you look across the Square, you'll see three doormen outside the pub next to the bank. Can you see them?"

"Two tall guys and a smaller one? All wearing bow ties."

"That's them."

At that moment a waitress appeared and began clearing the table. They sat in silence, waiting for her to finish.

"Go on," said Maria when she had gone.

Tom leaned forward again. "The smallest one, the stocky chap – I only saw him from the side, but I'm sure I'm right. I'd bet my mortgage on it, if I had one. He's the man who beat up Guy Leighton."

The expression on Maria's face changed instantly and she spun round, peering across the Square.

"You're not serious."

"No doubt about it." Tom was pretending to study the menu as he spoke. "Hey, where are you going?"

"I'm going over there. To smack him in the mouth, probably."

"Oh for Christ's sake, sit down!" He gripped her by the wrist and held her back physically.

They struggled for a moment, and then Maria relented and sank back into her seat. One or two people looked round.

"What do you suggest we do, then?" she said. "Just sit here and eat pizza and forget about him? How can you be so detached all the time?"

"So you think clattering over there and giving him a hand-bagging is going to deliver a fatal blow to Toby Malkin's ambitions? I'm not detached. Just sane."

"But you can tell he's a nasty piece of work. How much do you think Malkin had to pay him?"

Tom put his head in his hands, staring down at the table. Then he looked back up at Maria.

"I don't think he paid him anything. All this tells you for certain, is that the person who attacked Guy Leighton works as hired muscle. So what? Anyone could have paid him."

When their food arrived they ate and spoke very little. Tom tried to talk about other things, but Maria paid no attention and answered in monosyllables. She spent most of the time staring at the three men. Eventually Tom gave up trying to make conversation, and watched them as well.

At one point, they saw the man Tom had picked out holding his hand up imperiously to stop a group of people from entering the pub. He talked to them, and as he waved them past, his attention was diverted. He reached for a mobile phone clipped to his belt and put it to his ear.

Maria stopped chewing and put her knife and fork down. She frowned and watched as the man continued his conversation. Then she turned and looked at Tom, her eyes wide.

"I've got it!" she said, clenching her fist. "I have got it! How could I have missed it?"

Without saying anything further, she eased herself out of her seat and headed off to the Ladies.

Two minutes later, she came back and stood in front of Tom. The difference in her appearance was noticeable – she had brushed her hair, and put on lipstick and blusher. She had also unfastened at least two buttons on her blouse.

"How do I look?"

"You look good. But what's all this in aid of?"

"Get ready to be impressed," she said.

"Don't do anything stupid, Maria."

"Trust me."

She blew him a kiss and walked away. He watched as she left the restaurant, expecting that she would head across the Square. But she

78

didn't. Instead she turned to her left and disappeared. Tom sat for a few minutes trying to work out what she could be doing. Then he saw her approaching the pub from a different direction. In her jeans and her heels she appeared nonchalant, and as she neared Guy Leighton's assailant she said something and Tom saw her laughing. But that was all – she didn't stop to remonstrate or argue, she just walked past the man and into the pub.

Nothing happened for ten minutes. Then Maria emerged again. Her movements were more deliberate now, and she looked over her shoulder as she walked. She strode up to the stocky little doorman and started to speak to him, pointing back into the pub and waving her arms. They talked for some time. At one stage Maria turned round and lifted her jacket up and they both seemed to examine something just above her bottom. After that she appeared to relax, and Tom could see her smiling. The doorman offered her a cigarette, and she held his hand steady as he lit it for her. They carried on talking, until the man reached into a pocket and handed her something. Maria took it and then walked away in the direction from which she had first come, her hips swinging and her head held high.

When she slipped back into the restaurant and sat down opposite Tom, she was beaming.

"I presume you're going to tell me what that was all about."

"Absolutely. Look."

From her pocket she took a card which she placed on the table in front of her, turning it round so that he could see it. It was tacky, obviously home-made, and it simply read:

JEZ BRADLEY
FREELANCE SECURITY SERVICES

Tom picked up the card and studied it. He turned it over and looked at the telephone number printed on the reverse, then glanced up at Maria. She was still smiling broadly.

"And?" he said.

"07. It's a mobile number, you tit. I've got his mobile number."

"How does this help?"

Maria leaned forward and lowered her voice. "Because of what happened that morning. Just before he went down to reception, Malkin was in his office making a call. If I'm right, that call would have been to the two thugs. Yes?"

"Maybe."

79

"At the same time a call came through to me from Lewis Cooper at RevCom. A call for Toby Malkin. Now, here's the important bit. When Lewis Cooper came through to me he was annoyed – he's got an awful temper. He'd used Malkin's direct number and it had rung several times without anyone answering. Amongst all the swearing he told me how unusual that was. If Toby had been using the phone on his desk to call my new friend Jez Bradley, that wouldn't have happened. Cooper's call would have been diverted straight to me. But it wasn't. And the reason for that was that Toby Malkin was already talking to someone, *using his mobile*."

She paused, her expression encouraging Tom to speak.

"You say that as if all this should suddenly become clear to me," he said.

Maria held out her hands in a gesture of feigned despair. "You're supposed to be the intelligent one here. If Toby Malkin's mobile bill shows that he called Jez Bradley's number ten minutes before the attack, we've got the connection we need. Can't you see?"

He studied her still-smiling face. "Just as a point of minor detail, I assume that you have full access to all Toby Malkin's mobile phone bills. No problem getting hold of those?"

"No problem at all," she said. She winked and nodded her head. "You wait and see."

Tom frowned and shrugged. "If you say so."

They finished their meal and when they came to leave, Maria made a point of paying her half.

"I insist," she said, looking round with mock nervousness, and deliberately raising her voice so that half the restaurant could hear. "I wouldn't want anyone to think I fall into bed for the price of a pizza."

Tom was getting used to this sort of thing and he ignored it. But as they stood up and prepared to leave he stopped.

"I've got to ask you this," he said. "What exactly *did* you say to Jez Bradley?"

She smiled. "Easy. I just told him I'd had a row with a woman in the pub." She fluttered her eyelashes, and spoke in her little girl voice. "Silly cow. Just because she thinks I shagged her boyfriend. I think she tried to burn me with a cigarette as I walked past. You couldn't have a look for me, could you?"

Maria turned round in the way that Tom had seen her do earlier. She pouted and looked down at her bottom, stroking it, as if she had been hurt.

"Hussy," said Tom. "Come on, let's go and listen to the Carpenters."

SIXTEEN

Corporate law – the buying and selling of companies – is the most macho area of legal practice. It attracts testosterone-fuelled male lawyers, who measure their manhood by the size of the documents they draft, and their virility by the length of their late-night hours. It isn't exclusively a man's world, but women who make it to the top are rare, and the men who more generally do are the legal world's hard men. Expensively suited, with silk ties and Jermyn Street shirts, perhaps. Carrying exquisite fountain pens and sporting immaculate haircuts, maybe. But hard men – street-fighting bruisers from the front row of the scrum – nevertheless.

The lives of corporate lawyers revolve around deals. Mergers, acquisitions, joint ventures, disposals, hivings-up, hivings-down, restructurings – these might have different exotic-sounding names, but they are all deals. Deals to Malkin's breed are like kills to packs of lions, periods of intense and vital activity, preceded by stalking and preparation, followed by gorging and preening. Deals are the stuff of life.

The deal at the heart of Project Shamrock was now well advanced, and in an attempt to bring it to a close, Malkin was due to spend some time in Dublin. Here he would lead the negotiations with the other side, supervising the development of the voluminous documentation in which the details of the deal would be recorded. Being based in Dublin had two distinct attractions. He could bill the client for every waking hour. And he could insist on being accompanied by Ruth Braebrook.

They were booked on an early morning flight. Once again, Malkin arranged to pick Ruth up from home. This time, when he pulled up outside the house, she wasn't waiting for him and he had to walk up to the front door and ring the bell.

"Sorry, I'm not quite ready," she said as she opened the door to him. "Do you want to come in?"

He stepped into a high-ceilinged hallway, and as Ruth ran upstairs he stood taking in the detail of the house, with its polished wooden floors and heavy wallpapers. He could hear her moving about, and so he peeped casually into the large front room.

"Dominic not about?" he asked as Ruth came down the stairs, her shoes in one hand and a suitcase in the other.

"No. He's away on business. Somewhere near Leeds, I think."

She turned towards a large bronze-framed mirror which hung in the hallway, and made some adjustments to her hair. Malkin caught her eye in the reflection and raised his eyebrows. Ruth turned back to face him.

"He was working till late last night. He called me from the meeting."

"If you say so." He picked up her suitcase, and moved to the door. "Come on, Mrs Braebrook. Leave your hair alone – you look great already."

"Wait a minute," she said, her expression becoming serious. "I want you to be honest with me. Do you know something definite about Dominic? If you do, I want you to tell me."

"Anything definite? No, I don't think I know anything definite. But we haven't got time for this – if we don't go now we'll miss the flight."

He opened the door and walked to the car. Whilst he struggled to fit the suitcase into the back seat, Ruth scurried around the house before setting the burglar alarm, closing the door and pulling on her shoes all at the same time.

She climbed into the passenger seat of the car, took a couple of deep breaths to compose herself and wriggled in an attempt to straighten her skirt.

"Allow me," said Malkin, reaching and smoothing the material for her.

There was something unconvincing in the way she pushed his hand away and very little resolve in the way she told him to stop it.

When Malkin and Ruth arrived in Dublin, they hit the ground running, going straight from the taxi into a negotiating meeting in a city-centre hotel.

The two of them appeared seriously out-gunned. They had the support of Geoff Duval, a senior executive from their client company, who met them in the hotel foyer. But facing them across the large dark-wood table of the meeting room was an army of lawyers, financial advisors and corporate managers under the generalship of William Southern, a partner from the London firm Malkin and Ruth had visited previously. This army was also able to draw on the resources of a firm of Irish lawyers. Ruth and Malkin would be relying on laptop computers and mobile phones. It looked like boys against men, bows and arrows against tanks.

Toby Malkin would not have had it any other way. His favourite deals, the deals on which he excelled, were those where he was the underdog, where he had to call on his full range of skills just to stay in the game. From the moment the meeting in Dublin started, he was consummate, and it was clear that his performance on Project Shamrock would be one of his best ever. Within an hour of arriving, he had deliberately picked a fight with William Southern over an obscure point, and when he didn't get his way he walked out.

It took hours of pleas and pandering, concessions and cajoling, to make Malkin return, and when he did he took control. He punished the other side by setting a furious pace, rattling through point after point, overwhelming everyone with his detailed knowledge of the deal. As afternoon turned to evening, he kept going, with never a hint of a break. Eventually, someone on the other side suggested that they stop and reconvene the next morning.

"I don't think the timetable we've set ourselves allows for that," Malkin replied, and moved on to the next discussion point.

And so they worked into the night, and by the time Malkin finally let them stop, Ruth's wrist ached from the countless pages of notes she had taken. As they collected their papers together, Malkin told her she should order some food from room service for herself, as he had to make some calls. When she reached her room, Ruth lay on the bed and tried to call Dominic. There was no reply either from their home number or from his mobile, and so she ordered her meal, showered quickly and slept.

The meeting resumed early the next morning. The strain of the hours they had put in the previous day was visible on the faces of most people in the room, and even William Southern stumbled over his words from time to time. The only person who seemed unaffected was Malkin and again he drove the meeting forward relentlessly. When sandwiches were brought in at lunchtime, he refused to allow a break and they carried on talking whilst they ate.

As the negotiations continued Ruth noticed that Malkin began to glance at his watch from time to time. And then, towards the middle of the afternoon, he brought the discussions suddenly to a close. The next stage in the process would be for William Southern and his assistants to redraft the contracts based on what had been agreed, and this would take at least until morning. In the meantime, there was little for Ruth and Toby Malkin to do.

As the meeting broke up and the participants dispersed, Ruth was talking with one of the other lawyers. When she finished and turned round to collect her papers, she was surprised to see that Malkin had gone. Back in her room, she kicked her shoes off and eased herself out of her skirt. Then she climbed into bed and fell asleep.

When she woke, she tried to phone Dominic again, but his secretary said that he was with a client and she didn't know how long he would be. Ruth put on the television, climbed back onto the bed and flicked through the pages of a magazine.

Ten minutes later, she tossed the magazine on to the floor and reached for the telephone. She dialled Toby Malkin's mobile number. The call went straight through to voicemail.

"Toby, it's me. I assume we're going to relax a bit tonight and I really fancy getting out of this place for a while. I'm going for a swim now. If I don't hear from you I'll come and get you at seven? See you soon."

When Ruth came back from the pool, she showered and laid out her clothes for the evening, before drying her hair and applying her make-up. It was still well before seven and so she called Dominic again. This time she managed to get through on his mobile. It sounded as though he was in the car.

"Hello, sugar-bear," he said. "What's new?"

"Nothing much. Working hard, as always. Dom, I've tried you several times. Where have you been?"

"Oh, you know what it's like. Here, there and everywhere. Busy, busy, busy." He paused for a moment and she thought she heard another voice.

"Are you on your own?" she asked.

"Sure. But listen, can we speak later? I'm expecting another call."

She hesitated. "You can try, but I may be out. There's a dinner for everyone involved in the deal arranged for tonight."

"Maybe tomorrow then. You still think you won't be back before Friday?"

"It's not likely. Why in particular?"

"No reason. It's just that I may be away myself later in the week. Over the weekend as well, possibly."

"Where? Who with?"

"Sounds like you're checking up on me. I may be going to Paris. It's all rather tiresome, but you know how it is. Needs must. Anyway, have a good evening."

The line went dead. Ruth stared at the phone, before putting it down with restraint. She hated herself for lying about her plans for the evening, but she hated much more the evasive tone in Dominic's voice.

Her mind went back, as it had several times over the last two days, to what Malkin had said in the restaurant in London.

She pushed the phone away, and then put back in the wardrobe the trousers and top she had originally chosen to wear that evening. She threw a strapless black cocktail dress onto the bed in their place. Nodding in approval at her choice, she sat down at the dressing table and pinned her hair up on top of her head. It made her look elegant, but she knew the impact it would make if at any time during the evening she chose to unfasten the pins and shake the dark ringlets so that they tumbled down around her shoulders.

Satisfied with her hair, Ruth continued her preparations. From the bottom of her suitcase she pulled out a pair of sheer nylon hold-ups, which she pulled slowly over each of her legs in turn, smoothing them with her hands. She wondered for a moment whether her wantonness should extend to wearing nothing else beneath her dress, but finally pulled on a black thong.

Then she stepped into the dress. It was the first time she had worn it outside the shop, and she looked at herself critically in the mirror. She had to be sure it was right. She pulled the material down over her hips, and wriggled her upper body so that her breasts settled into place. She was pleased with what she saw. She completed the outfit with a pair of high-heeled shoes. Taking a moment to touch up her make-up, she threw one or two personal effects into a small clutch bag, and folded a jacket over her arm. At a couple of minutes after seven, she left.

She found Malkin's room and tapped on the door. Whilst she waited for him to answer, she ran her tongue round her teeth to wash away any rogue flecks of lipstick. Were the messages from her appearance too obvious, she wondered? No, they couldn't be, because not even she knew the true nature of her intentions.

She raised her hand to knock again. As she waited, someone came out of a room further down the corridor, and made Ruth feel a little self-conscious. It was then that she noticed that there was no light coming from underneath the door, and no sound from behind it. She knocked several times more, each time a little louder. Still no answer. Eventually, feeling bemused and a little deflated, she went back to her own room and tried calling first Malkin's internal number and then his mobile, both without success. She checked her own voicemail, and called reception to see if he had left her a message. He hadn't. Unable to think of anything else to do, she went back to Malkin's room, and knocked again and called out his name. Then she tried the door. It was locked.

Half an hour later, she went to the room a third time. But when this, and her slightly embarrassed calls to William Southern and Geoff Duval, yielded nothing, Ruth had little choice but to conclude that Malkin had disappeared.

SEVENTEEN

Tom Elliott had been away from work for a few days. Caroline's exams were over, and at last she had had some time to spend with him. Tom suggested they go away, but Caroline insisted they visit her parents at their house on the south coast. This wasn't ideal – they had to sleep in separate rooms and Caroline disappeared on a couple of major shopping trips with her mother. But Tom said he understood when Caroline told him he wasn't the only one with demands on her time.

On his first morning back in the office, Tom was busy from the moment he arrived. It wasn't until mid-morning that he saw an e-mail from Maria saying that she needed to speak to him. He went to see her, but as he approached her desk she caught his eye and gave a tiny shake of her head. Tom walked past without saying a word.

Back at his desk he found another e-mail:

Lunchtime – Coach House at 1.10.

It wasn't easy for him to get away, and when he arrived at the pub, Maria was already waiting for him. She beckoned him over.

"God, I've got so much to tell you," she said. "It feels like you've been away for weeks. Sit down – I've bought you a coke."

"You're looking very pleased with yourself," he said, drawing up a chair.

"That's because I am going to nail Toby Malkin."

"Said with confidence."

"Absolutely. It was quiet the other day, and so I went through his office from top to bottom. I pretended I was filing."

"And you found his mobile bills?"

"No. He must keep them at home."

"So why the big smile?"

All the time she had been talking, the palm of her right hand had been pressed flat to the table between them. Now she pushed it towards him and lifted it slowly, making a hinge of her little finger.

Tom looked first at what lay underneath, and then at Maria. She was like a young child who has brought a picture home from nursery school, willing him to express approval. He frowned.

"Maria, please don't tell me that you're thinking of breaking into Toby Malkin's house."

"It's not a house, it's a flat. And there won't be any need to *break* in, will there? Not now that I've got this."

"And how did you get hold of it?" Tom nodded at the single Yale key which lay on the table in front of him.

"He had a meeting on Monday that started around lunchtime. Just before he went into it, I told him that the car park attendant needed his keys because he was moving cars around – it happens sometimes – and then I popped into town to have it copied. It wasn't difficult. And now he's away in Dublin. It's perfect."

Still she tried to draw approval from him. Still his face remained gripped by concern.

"This is crazy, Maria. You can't really be serious?"

"Of course I'm serious. I can't believe you sometimes. Look, it won't take more than ten minutes. He'll never work out that we've been there."

"*What*? You don't really think I'm getting involved in this?"

"Of course I do. You said you would help."

He leaned back in his chair and held both hands up in front of him, pushing towards her slightly as if there were a need physically to restrain her.

"No way, Maria. Absolutely no way." He lowered his hands and placed them flat on the table. "This is going too far. Much too far. It's not worth it. I'm not doing it."

"But you've got to. You can't let me down now."

"I'm not letting you down. I never said I would do anything like this."

The effort Maria made to contain her feelings was almost tangible. "You do remember what this man's done? He's destroyed someone else's life. Have you ever stopped and thought for even a minute what Guy Leighton must have been through? Can you think of anything worse that could happen to someone like him? And what about his wife? It would be criminal to do nothing."

"So you say, Maria. I hate to disappoint you, but you're not being fair."

He glanced down, and at exactly the moment that he decided what he was going to do, she worked out that he was going to do it. They both grabbed for the key at the same time. It was nearer to Tom, and Maria had to reach across the table. She slammed her hand down hard, but

88

Tom was quicker and he snatched it away. Maria lunged at him again, trying to grab his wrist.

"Give it me," she hissed.

"Stop it, Maria," Tom said in a loud whisper, holding the key well out of her reach. "You're not having it back, because I'm not letting you go and do something so stupid. And I'm certainly not coming with you. It's just not worth it." She was staring at him through the narrowest of eyes. "What happens if you get found out? And there's no guarantee that you'd find anything – you're completely losing your perspective over all this."

"No I'm not. You can't spend your whole life thinking up reasons not to get involved."

"For Christ's sake, what's driving you, Maria? You really should…"

"Oh PISS OFF!" she shouted, standing up. "Thank you so much for your help and support. Have you any idea what you sound like?"

As she walked past him, she stopped and made one last effort to grab the key. When this failed, she muttered an obscenity under her breath and then, as she turned to leave, her eyes rested on his drink. Before he had chance to move she reached out and emptied the glass onto the table so that the sticky liquid flowed over the wooden surface and into his lap. By the time he had reacted to this, she was gone.

Later that afternoon, Tom overcame his annoyance at the stains on his trousers and tried to make peace. He sent Maria an e-mail, but she didn't respond. A little later he went over to her desk and tried to strike up a conversation. She cut him dead. At five o'clock she left without saying a word to him.

Tom was disappointed, but he was beginning to feel that this was all part of being friends with Maria. He hoped that her anger would abate soon, but he was also determined not to give in to her, and that evening he walked home from the office instead of catching the bus. His route took him across Trent Bridge, and when he was halfway over he stopped. The rush-hour traffic inched along behind him, and he looked downstream at the wide expanse of the river as it flowed past the dark cliffs of the football ground stands. He reached into his pocket for the key. Turning so that he was facing away from the oncoming headlights he held out his hand and let the shiny metal object drop. He watched as it fell spinning towards the oily black waters below.

As he walked on, he felt no regret. There was no doubt in his mind that it was for the best. He felt that he owed it to Maria to protect her from her own recklessness. But despite all this, he was slightly daunted by the prospect of explaining to her what he had done.

He needn't have worried, because he would never have to tell her. Maria's job required her to think ahead, to do the little things which meant that supposedly more important things didn't go wrong, and when she had borrowed Toby Malkin's key she had trusted her instinct and had two copies cut. One copy might now be lying in the mud at the bottom of the Trent. The other was hanging round Maria's neck, on a gold chain that also supported a locket with a picture of her mother.

EIGHTEEN

When Ruth Braebrook knocked on Toby Malkin's door, he was indeed sitting in a hotel room. But not a hotel room in Dublin. Immediately following the break-up of the meeting, he slipped out of the room, walked quickly across the hotel foyer and climbed into a taxi. The driver took him to the airport, and from there he caught a flight back to the East Midlands. By seven o'clock, he was sitting in a bedroom at one of the airport hotels, still immaculately dressed in the suit he had worn all day, waiting for a telephone call from reception. Whilst he waited he checked the items on a list on his laptop, and arranged on the desk beside him a number of papers and envelopes.

The phone rang. Malkin listened to what the receptionist had to say and then left the room. He made his way down the stairs which swept into the lobby. There he paused, looking round with affected exaggeration until he saw, sitting on the edge of an armchair by an open fire, the person he was looking for.

Malkin strode towards him, holding out his hand in welcome.

"Great to see you," he said in his most ingratiating tones. "How are you keeping?"

Eddie Tomlinson struggled to get to his feet and ended up shaking Malkin's hand from an awkward half-standing position.

"Shall we?" asked Malkin, gesturing towards the staircase.

He put his arm round Eddie's shoulder and guided him across the lobby. He continued to make small talk whilst they climbed the stairs and walked down the corridor.

"Sorry about the rather unusual arrangements," said Malkin as they entered his room. "But the thing is, I needed to speak to you rather urgently and I'm a little tied up with a deal that's going on in Ireland. And so, you see, there wasn't a lot of choice. But anyway, here we are."

He guided Eddie towards a chair. As he sat down, Eddie caught sight of one of the items on the desk. He stared at it with a look of total incomprehension.

"Something to drink?" asked Malkin. "There's the usual sort of things in the mini-bar, or we could phone down for something a bit more grand. A bottle of wine, perhaps. Or how about champagne? I've heard you've got a taste for the finer things in life."

91

Eddie caught the change of tone in this last remark, and looked round.

"Well?" said Malkin.

"Nothing to drink, thank you," said Eddie. He stumbled over his words.

"Are you sure? I think I'll just have some water then."

Malkin poured himself a glass of water and sat down. He beamed, and when he spoke the ingratiating tone had returned.

"Now then, Eddie. I really am indebted to you for coming here this evening. It must be rather an inconvenient time. For a family man."

"It's not a problem." Eddie was still staring at what he could see on the desk.

"But that intrigues me. Why should you agree to a meeting with me, at a time like this, in a hotel by an airport?"

"I assumed it must be something important."

"It is, Eddie. Very important. But you've not even asked me what it's all about. You just agreed to come. We hardly know each other."

"I know that you do legal work for Reverie Communications, and I thought that it probably had something to do with..."

"With what?"

"I don't know. With the review of our suppliers you were doing a few weeks ago, probably."

"I find this sort of thing fascinating. It really is amazing what a sense of guilt can make us do." Malkin dropped his gaze for an instant and glanced down at Eddie's wrist. "That's a Rolex you've got there, isn't it?"

"Yes."

"Very nice. And the car you now drive..." He leaned forward, picked up a photograph from the table and showed it to Eddie. "...is a shiny new Saab convertible. I bet that shifts."

Eddie looked as though he were going to reply, but Malkin picked something else up from the table.

"And why don't you tell me about the Tomlinson family holiday last year? Two-week trip for all five of you to Barbados at Christmas, wasn't it? Look – I've even got some copies of your holiday snaps. Don't your womenfolk look good in their bikinis?" He tossed the pictures onto the bed and snatched another document. "And you enjoy eating out, according to this credit card statement. Eddie, just how do you manage to make your salary stretch this far? You must be a financial genius."

"I'm very well paid."

Malkin laughed out loud. "Oh Eddie, come on! You don't earn enough to give you all this. To live like this you've had to … what's the right phrase? Supplement your income, I suppose. Granted, you've done it in a rather imaginative way. But, still, it is a little bit naughty, isn't it?"

Eddie's hands gripped the arms of the chair. He swallowed hard, and looked back at Malkin, avoiding his eyes. Then he glanced towards the door.

"Oh please," said Malkin. "Don't even think about it. There's nowhere you can run." He indicated with a movement of his hand the material on the table. "I've got more evidence here than even the most lenient of juries would require."

There was a long silence. Eddie stared at the floor, his eyes half-closed and his brows creased. Malkin sat still and watched him with an expression of mild enquiry. Finally, Eddie looked up, anguish drawn into every line on his face.

"You make it sound so sordid. It wasn't like that. I had a reason."

"Absolutely you did," said Malkin.

He picked up an envelope. From it he took two things – an enlargement of a photograph of Rachel Tomlinson, and, clipped to the top, a copy of a short article from a local newspaper. He passed them to Eddie. The photograph showed Rachel walking between buildings on her university campus, her long hair caught by the wind. The article described the circumstances of her accident.

"Where did you get all this?" Eddie asked.

Malkin didn't answer, but simply raised his eyebrows. Eddie put one hand across his face and rubbed the corners of his eyes.

"I can pay it all back, if you give me some time. With interest. Nobody needs to know."

Malkin looked at him long and impassively before shaking his head.

"No."

"Please. My family have been through enough. That's the only reason I did it – for them. I don't care what happens to me. But, can't you just…?"

Malkin shook his head again. Eddie's shoulders dropped and he slumped back in his chair.

"What's going to happen then?" he asked.

Malkin reached over to the desk again, this time lifting up his glass and taking a sip of water. He held the glass still in front of his face for a moment and then replaced it carefully.

"Nothing."

"Sorry?"

"Nothing's going to happen."

"What do you mean? I don't understand."

"Let me explain then. Contrary to what you seem to think, I have absolutely no intention of telling tales about you. If that was what I was going to do, I would simply have done it. And I certainly wouldn't have given up the opportunity to be doing what I could be doing in Dublin at this very moment."

Eddie's expression was now one of total confusion.

"No," continued Malkin. "What you've cooked up here is really rather good. And at the moment I am struggling to believe my good fortune in being the one to find out. I've been having a lot of luck lately, and I think it's important that one makes the most of everything that comes one's way, don't you?" He took another sip of water. "And what's going to come my way now, thanks to you, is more money than you could ever imagine. Let me explain."

Maria felt nervous and alone. Whilst Eddie sat listening to Malkin, she was sitting in the front room of her flat, dressed in dark trousers, ankle boots and leather jacket, ready to go out. On the table in front of her was the key to Malkin's flat, separated now from the chain around her neck.

Her plan had seemed so straightforward – and exciting as well– when she was blagging Jez Bradley's number and copying the key. Now she was frightened and she wished Tom were with her. She wished even more that she hadn't been so hard on him. She closed her eyes and winced with embarrassment as she remembered what had happened at lunchtime. It was the same old problem – mouth first, brain later. As full of imperfections herself as a factory shop sale, yet so unforgiving of the slightest flaw in others. Especially those she held dear. She thought about calling Tom now – telling him she was going through with it anyway, and asking him to meet her at the flat.

But she didn't. Instead she thought about Toby Malkin, and everything that had driven her this far. She couldn't give up now. She had to make him pay for what he had done. It just had to be, and doing it was more important to her than anything.

She sat still for a while longer, and she said a little prayer. She told herself there was no need to feel nervous. All she had to do was to let herself into an empty flat, and find a phone bill. The whole thing could be over in less than ten minutes.

She picked up the key from the table, put it into her pocket and left the room.

"You can't seriously expect to get away with that," said Eddie, looking at Malkin. "Surely it's just not possible?"

"Oh, it's very possible. And that's not for you to worry about. You just need to keep doing what you're doing already."

"And what if I don't agree to go along with it?"

"I don't understand." Malkin's face darkened. "It's not a question of agreeing. You have no choice."

"But you can't do it without me."

Malkin looked away and closed his eyes, working hard to exercise restraint.

"Tomlinson, I'm not sure you understand what I'm saying."

"I do understand, but you need me to…"

"Shut up!" Malkin snapped, pointing a finger at Eddie like a gun. "I do not negotiate with people who have nothing to bargain with. You will do exactly as I ask you, in every detail, or else all this…" He pointed at the material on the desk. "…sends you to jail. Think about that. Everything that's precious to you – everything – crumbles in your hands. You'll never work again, you'll lose your house, and your nice comfortable lifestyle will all just slip away."

Eddie looked as though he was going to speak, but Malkin stopped him.

"That's not all. What about your wife? Don't you think you've put her through enough already? She must be the long-suffering type, Eddie, because most women would have walked a long time ago." He leaned over and took a photograph of Julia from an envelope. "Do you know what? The person who took this photograph noticed what a good-looking woman your wife is. *I wouldn't mind giving her one were his exact words*, I believe. Who knows? With you in prison, not there to keep her honest, somebody might just get the chance."

He paused to make sure that his words were having their effect.

"Shall I go on? Perhaps talk about what might happen to the kids?"

"There's no need."

"Good. That makes me pleased. That makes me very pleased indeed."

There was nothing more to be said. Quarter of an hour after Eddie had gone, Malkin switched off his laptop and put his papers back in the case. Then he left the room and checked out of the hotel.

NINETEEN

She walked with her head bowed until she turned off the main road onto a footpath which ran along the riverbank. It was quieter here, and darker too, and she felt less conspicuous. She had decided to leave the car outside a pub, but the walk from there had taken longer than she had expected. As she passed narrowboats and pleasure cruisers, and then beneath the windows of the rooms for which she was heading, the rhythm of her pounding heart ran faster than the click of her boot-heels on the tarmac.

She left the path and made her way along one side of the building, then across the small car park in front of it. The cars here were shiny and expensive, with personalised number plates and tiny winking alarm lights. When they were behind her, she stopped and looked at the shadowy entrance hall in front of her. There was no one about, but she glanced around her anyway. Then she took a deep breath and walked towards the building, trying to look as casual as she could.

The key, which Maria gripped tightly in her pocket so that its serrations pressed into her flesh, opened both the door of the entrance hall and of the flat upstairs. The first lock was stiff, and it took a moment or two of careful easing backwards and forwards before it yielded. The door was heavy but tightly sprung, and it closed behind her with a quiet, final-sounding click. She paused again, before starting to climb the stairs.

When she reached the first landing, Maria could hear the sound of a television, very faintly, from behind one of the imposing-looking doors. The flats were not numbered, but she knew where she was going and she continued up the next flight, holding onto the wooden handrail and measuring her steps carefully. Halfway up, the stairs turned back on themselves. From there Maria started to climb towards the top landing and the door to Malkin's lair.

Suddenly she froze, one foot just about to make contact with the final stair. From below, she heard the sound of someone else inserting a key in the door of the entrance hall. Whoever it was did this far less timidly than she had. The door clicked shut. There was the sound of a mailbox being opened, and a moment later heavy footsteps moving across the wooden floor. Then there was silence again as the person reached the bottom of the carpeted stairs.

Maria had no idea what to do, and she stood transfixed, allowing vital seconds to slip away. She had played this scene through in her mind many times before, but had always started at the moment when she entered the flat. She couldn't risk being seen going in through the door, couldn't risk the possibility of awkward questions. She had nowhere to hide, and no further stairs to climb. So she did the only other thing possible. She turned round and started to head back down again.

As she rounded the first corner, she collided with a man coming the other way. He was dressed in a long dark coat, and looking at an envelope which he held in front of him.

"Sorry!" Maria exclaimed, her voice loud and high-pitched.

The man had her round the waist. For a moment she prepared to bite and kick and scratch. But then she realised that he was in fact being gentle, that he had caught hold of her to stop them both from falling. She saw that he was smiling.

"Steady," he said, laughing. "You don't often see women running away from Toby's flat. It's usually the other way round."

He held her for a moment longer, and laughed again. Then he let her go, and stooped to pick up his briefcase and the envelope.

"Are you alright?" he asked. "It looks like I frightened you."

Maria stared at him, unable to speak.

"I'm fine," she said at last. "I'm sorry – it was my fault. Not looking where I'm going, as normal."

She forced a smile and held her hands in front of her, indicating that she had recovered from the shock. Then she turned and headed down the stairs.

She walked slowly. When she heard the man's key turning in a lock upstairs, she darted back to the half-landing and peeped round the corner, making sure he had gone into the flat opposite Malkin's. Then she sank back against the wall.

What the hell am I doing? she thought. *This was supposed to be easy.*

A few minutes later, Maria let herself into Malkin's flat. The rectangle of light from the landing narrowed to nothing as she closed the door behind her, and she waited a moment before going on, allowing her eyes to become used to the darkness in the entrance lobby.

When she stepped through the door into the lounge, she was surprised. She had expected total darkness, but the room was in fact lit by a single lamp standing on an occasional table. *It must be on a timer*, she thought. *Or maybe he leaves it on all the time when he's away. Who knows?* She stood and looked at the room. It was years since she

97

had been here, but it had changed little – still the sparse furnishings with everything in its allotted place, still the appearance of a temple to the music which filled the walls. As she stood and took in the details of the room her eyes rested on the door which led to the flat's two bedrooms.

She shook her head as if trying to clear her mind. Then she walked slowly across the room, past the big sofa facing the music system, and into the alcove which Malkin used as his study. She was sure that he would keep his phone bills somewhere in here. It was just a question of finding where.

The office furniture which filled this space was made of hard, dark wood. Built into one of the corners was a desk on which stood a flat-screen computer monitor and another smaller music system. There were very few items on the desk. Everything was precisely arranged, fanatically tidy, and there was no sign of what Maria was looking for. But at the end of the desk, in the farthest corner, stood a glass-fronted cabinet. She could just pick it out in the half-light. This looked more promising.

Away from the entrance to the alcove, Maria crouched down by the cabinet and felt in her pocket for a small torch. She switched it on and pointed the beam through the glass doors in front of her. The light reflected back and dazzled her for a moment. As her eyes recovered and she peered more closely, she became sure this was the right place. She saw neatly ordered and labelled ring binders, storage boxes stacked on top of each other and a number of narrow drawers. Her heart was beating now with an excitement which displaced her anxiety. She was convinced that somewhere in here was a sheet of paper, and that on that paper was printed the particular combination of numbers which would allow her to visit upon Toby Malkin all that he deserved.

It was uncomfortable crouching, and so she eased herself down and sat on the floor. She was totally absorbed, and she wondered what other secrets the cabinet might contain. Now she was here, she was starting to feel good about herself. She had done this, all of this, on her own, and Tom and everyone else would be impressed. There was one file which particularly caught her eye. Such was her certainty about what she was about to find that she felt a desire to delay the moment of discovery, to savour every minute of the process. She put her torch on the floor and reached forward to slide back the door of the cabinet.

When Toby Malkin opened the door which separated the bedroom area from the lounge, it was so unexpected that it took Maria what seemed like an age to understand what was happening. She heard the noise first, and looked up in time to catch a glimpse of his reflection in the computer screen on the desk. She mouthed a silent obscenity and fumbled as she switched off the torch, her eyes wide with fear. How could he possibly be here?

As she strained to listen to the sounds of Malkin moving around – the opening and closing of doors in the kitchen, the faint humming beneath his breath – she collected her thoughts. He couldn't have noticed anything, or else he would have come in straightaway. The best thing was to stay where she was, wait until he went back to the bedroom. She eased herself silently to her feet and pressed herself into a small gap next to a bookcase in the darkest corner of the alcove, with her back to the wall.

For several long minutes nothing happened. Where was he? And what was he doing here in Nottingham? Maria tried to judge whether she would have time to get out if she could be sure he had gone back into the bedroom. Still she heard nothing. Should she risk looking out? Then the sound of a glass being placed on a wooden surface. He was in the lounge.

More sounds. Something being opened and shut, a brief whirring of something mechanical. Another moment of silence. And then, without warning, the almost deafening sound of an orchestra. Thundering chords, half-familiar. The music was dark and beautiful, and Maria now had no way of knowing where Malkin was. Suddenly she realised how frightened she was. She decided to run out now and take her chance with him where there was more room, rather than waiting here where she would be hopelessly cornered if he found her. But that was stupid. She had no choice. She had to wait and see what happened.

She tried to push herself even further into her little corner, and at the same time twisted her neck to see if she could see anything in the screen of the computer. The worst part of this was not knowing where he was. Something on the bookcase was digging into her, something sharp and metallic. She wanted to move away from it, but feared that she would knock it over. As she glanced down and tried to work out what it was, a shadow fell across the desk. Malkin had come into the alcove. When Maria saw him her face became contorted as if with physical pain and she wanted desperately to bury her head in her hands. It took all her self-control to make herself keep still, and she knew that this must be it. And that he would kill her. But somehow he hadn't seen her, and he sat down at the desk, no more than two feet from where Maria was squashed. She willed herself to become invisible, and prayed that he didn't turn round.

She watched as he switched on a small desk lamp, and then pressed a button on the computer. She was near enough to be able to make out each individual hair, still wet from being washed, on the back of his neck. She could smell his aftershave. But although she was this close, the thunderous music in the background also made her feel distant from him, as if she were watching him in a film. When the computer had booted up, he inserted a disk in the front, opened a document and scrolled down it, making an occasional adjustment and reading everything carefully.

Minutes passed. Malkin was engrossed in what he was doing and as he continued to work, Maria began, very slowly, to feel a little calmer. Over his shoulder, she could see every word on the screen, and to give herself something to think about she read the document, trying to pick out typing mistakes. But her eyes kept returning to the back of Malkin's head, and slowly her thinking shifted. Who was the one who was vulnerable here? By the light of the lamp she could now see that the thing on the bookcase which was digging into her was a heavy-looking metal statue of a musician. It would be the easiest thing in the world for her to pick it up. If she made any sound, the music would drown it out.

Feeling pleased with her cleverness, and moving with infinite care, Maria took a tissue from her pocket and covered her hand with it so there would be no fingerprints. Then she reached out and picked up the statue. It was solid and the heaviest part of it was the base. Now she looked at the back of the dark head in front of her and she imagined the damage the statue could do. She would have to hit him very hard, but she might get two or three blows in before he reacted and that would be enough. She raised the statue, forward and up. She stopped and then, like a sniper applying pressure to a trigger, and whilst the orchestra worked towards a climax, she lifted it slightly further still and picked out the spot on his head which she would hit.

The music stopped, and in the brief silence before the next movement began, there was the distant sound of a mobile phone. Malkin noticed it and stood up. He walked out of the alcove, and as he moved through the lounge he switched the hi-fi off. Maria suddenly felt ridiculous. She lowered the statue and put it down on the desk. She could just make out the low sound of Malkin talking. It came from a long way away. Maria screwed the tissue up and put it back in her pocket, and then stepped forward and risked peeping into the lounge. Malkin was in one of the bedrooms, and with all thoughts of violence against him now gone, she tiptoed to the door which led to the entrance hall.

Concentrating all the time on the sound of the voice, and taking every care to make no noise, she let herself out of this door and then that which led to the stairs.

Once she was out of the flat, she ran. She forgot any thought of not attracting attention to herself, and she ran. Down the stairs, out of the door at the bottom, across the car park and back along the path beside the river, her lungs screaming silently for air. She came to the road, and still she ran, never looking back, all the way to her car.

She struggled to open the door and collapsed inside, and then put her head down and beat the dashboard with relief and frustration. She had often felt alone, but never this alone. She had often regretted the things she had done, but never such profound regret at something quite so foolish. She hated herself for being so worthless. She wanted Tom, but she didn't know how she would ever face him again. Why had she ever thought she could do anything at all to hold back a man like Toby Malkin?

It was a good fifteen minutes before she felt composed enough to drive. Before she did she got out of the car, and to the amusement of a raucous group of young men coming out of the pub, she turned to face the bushes which surrounded the car park, and hurled the key to Malkin's flat into them. Then, to the sound of their teasing and their jeers, she drove off.

Early next morning, as Malkin gathered together what he needed before heading back to the airport, he went into his alcove office to collect some papers. Although he gave it a lot of thought, he never worked out why his statue was in the wrong place. It bugged him all the way back to Dublin.

TWENTY

In most negotiations there comes a point at which the two sides stop fighting and join in an unspoken alliance to slay the dragon that is the deal itself. The lawyers lose enthusiasm for scoring points. Preening themselves in public suddenly seems less important. Instead they start to concentrate on the more mundane work of actually getting the thing finished, the documents agreed.

This pivotal point was reached on Project Shamrock soon after Malkin's return to Dublin. He arrived back at the hotel as the last stragglers were finishing breakfast, well in time for the ten o'clock start he had arranged with William Southern. As he crossed the hotel reception he saw Ruth Braebrook talking to the woman behind the desk. Ruth had her back to him, and Malkin put his head down and quickened his step. But just as he reached the lifts, she finished her conversation and turned round.

"Toby," she called. "Toby. Where have you been?"

She was all eyes and smiles as she came across the lobby. Then she stood before him and smile turned to frown.

"I thought you'd disappeared. I couldn't find you anywhere last night." She pouted, little girl lost. "I thought we might go out and have some fun."

He looked her up and down, and then met her eyes.

"Don't worry. There'll be plenty of time for that."

"But where were you?"

She pushed her face slightly towards him, a measure of defiance now in her posture. The lift arrived and as Malkin stepped into it he winked.

"Oh, here and there. See you in a little while."

When the negotiation reconvened, this time in the offices of the Irish lawyers, Malkin's mind was fully engaged once more. Everyone around the table knew there was another long session ahead of them. But now the mood was different. There was a willingness to compromise on both sides, and some of the bit-part players in William Southern's troupe of performers drifted away, spending hours in corridors talking on mobiles.

This was where Ruth Braebrook and the junior lawyers on the other side really earned the relatively modest salaries their employers paid them. As each point of contention was resolved, they drafted clauses to capture the compromises. They ground through voluminous redrafts of documents. During breaks in the meeting, they sought opinions from colleagues in England. They ticked off items on checklists, and as the hours passed, they placed agreed versions of documents carefully on one side.

This time the meeting went right through the night. Some of the less devoted souls had suggested they break until morning, but the end was now in sight and they were over-ruled. And as always, there was a period towards the end, in the smallest, most difficult hours of the night, when some unforeseen problem threatened to derail the whole deal, and there were tense moments as exhausted people conducted side meetings, and absent decision-makers were roused from their beds by phone.

But as ever, the issue was resolved, and afterwards no one would remember why it had been so important. And then, as a dawn the intense orange of a child's ice lolly soaked across the Dublin sky, it was into the home straight. The rows of finalised documents grew longer, and the debris of the all-night session – the half-empty coffee cups and bottles of water, the plates of stale sandwiches and the chocolate wrappers – threatened to take over the room, until a bored accountant found a bin liner in a cleaning cupboard and cleared it all away.

Finally, around midday on the Friday, the deal was done. The chief executives arrived, and everyone gathered in the firm's boardroom for the completion ceremony. Suddenly the room was full of people – those who had done the hard work, and those whose contributions had been less obvious. Secretaries brought final versions of documents, printed on thick cream paper, and arranged them carefully at the end of the table. Catering staff came in with champagne. Public relations people fussed and jostled, and a surly photographer worried about the light.

When the fountain pens had been put away and the hands had been shaken, people lingered, putting their tiredness to one side and prolonging this moment of self-satisfaction. William Southern went into charm overdrive, showering Toby and Ruth with sincere-sounding compliments and making sure he spoke to everyone in the room. As the party finally began to break up, Ruth found herself trapped in a corner by the bored accountant. Emboldened by the Moet, he was clearly trying to hit on her. His efforts were tiresome, and she was

103

beginning to feel uncomfortable when Malkin came to her rescue. He dismissed the accountant with a withering smile and took Ruth's arm.

"Come on," he whispered. "It's time to go. We're going to have that fun you promised me."

They both knew exactly where the evening was leading. From the moment when Malkin walked towards Ruth from the lift, and with a simple gesture invited her to stand, there was only one outcome. He fixed her with a searching, appreciative stare. She returned it as she got to her feet, so that for a moment they looked like two flamenco dancers, not touching but locked together by their eyes.

But he wanted to savour every moment of the build-up, and she wanted to make him work for it, wanted to feel special. The conversation flowed easily. They talked about the deal, dwelling on their achievements, joking about the others involved. The bar where they went for drinks, and the restaurant where they ate, both seemed as sophisticated as they felt, and they pushed the boat out as far as it would go – *foie gras*, oysters, chateaubriand and lots of champagne. Malkin was attentive, Ruth alluring and the evening melted away like the rich chocolate mousse she chose for dessert dissolving on her tongue.

"Tell me the most wicked thing you've ever done," said Malkin, leaning forward at the end of the meal, a teasing glint in his eye.

"What do you mean, wicked?" she asked, giggling. "You mean like pulling my sister's hair or cheating on my expenses?"

"You know what I mean. Go on, tell me."

She drank slowly from her champagne flute, deep in thought whilst she considered his question, relishing the power she had over him as he waited.

"The most wicked thing I've ever done," she repeated. "OK. How about this? When I was a trainee I shared a flat with a friend. Young girls living in London. Acting like the whole place was our own private playground. For the first six months we're out most nights, and we get really close. Do everything together. And no, Mr Malkin, this isn't leading *there*. But then suddenly she meets this guy, and everything changes. She won't stop telling me how wonderful he is. *Absolute dreamboat*, she said. The big He – all that sort of thing. I'm really not sure I should be telling you this."

"Keep going," he insisted. He reached out and covered her hand with his.

She smiled and looked down before continuing. "Well, she'd been seeing him for about three weeks, and I hadn't met him. I was getting tired of her going on about him all the time, to tell the truth. But I just had a feeling about him – you know the way you do sometimes, without knowing why. I'd spoken to him once on the telephone I think, and there was something about the sound of his voice. Anyway, one evening he was meant to be picking her up from the flat, but she was out. She phoned to tell me that she'd been held up and would I mind looking after him for an hour until she got back. *Just keep your hands off him, girl*, she told me. She was joking, but I could tell she meant it. Anyway he turned up, and I opened the door and it was just one of those Wow moments. I'm not kidding, he was gorgeous – tall with blue eyes, gorgeous. I'm standing there just gawping at him and wishing I'd brushed my hair."

"And then?"

"Eventually I remember to stop staring and invite him in, and I think I offer him a drink, and we stand in the kitchen talking about nothing. And I'm feeling like I'm in a dream, because before I know what I'm doing I walk over to him. I stand in front of him and he sort of carries on talking, and then I just kiss him. I can't believe it. I've met him no more than five minutes ago and I just walk up and kiss him. And just in case he hasn't got the message..." Ruth leaned forward even closer to Malkin, and lowered her voice. "...I undo my top, one button at a time. For a moment he hesitates, but then suddenly he's all over me, and he actually picks me up and carries me across the room. Two minutes later we're at it like knives on the sofa. And on the floor. And in the chair. And Toby, it's truly *wonderful*. Mind-blowing. I'm still not sure whether it was him or just the situation – I've never done anything like it before or since – but it was fantastic."

As Ruth related this, she felt Malkin's fingers caressing her knees.

"And then what happened?" he said hoarsely.

As she continued his fingers moved higher.

"I can't really remember every detail. We kept going for what seemed like for ever, and then we stopped for a while. We didn't say anything. Just lay there. I was beginning to think that maybe we should get dressed, but then he started again. This time he was tender and slow, and it's even better than before. And then all I remember is that I'm lying back on the sofa, and the phone rings, and I nearly don't bother to answer it. But something makes me, and it's my flatmate. She's walking along the road from the tube station, about four hundred yards away, and she's just phoning to make sure he's turned up. We have a manic two minutes as we get dressed and tidy up and..."

He gripped her hand. "Don't tell me any more," he said. "Let's go. Now."

He pulled her to her feet and waved for the bill. She laughed and tried to take a final mouthful of champagne. He thrust a credit card at the waiter, and while they waited his sense of arousal was palpable. She stood on tiptoed feet and whispered in his ear.

"Did you like my story, Toby? Do you think it's really true?"

In the cab that took them back to the hotel, Ruth had to push Malkin away. Such was his insistence that she wondered if it would actually happen there and then. At the hotel, they more or less ran to the lift, and on the short journey to her floor he kissed her hard and pushed the skirt of her dress up to her waist.

All the time she laughed and feigned prudishness. But once they reached her room she became as intense and demanding as him, tearing at his clothes and pulling him onto the bed. She gasped when he entered her and nearly screamed when she came.

"My God," she said afterwards, lying beside him staring at the ceiling. "You know how to keep a girl waiting. I've been expecting this for weeks."

"I know," he replied, propping himself up on one elbow. "But don't you think there's almost as much pleasure in the waiting as in the doing?"

"Speak for yourself, Toby. There was plenty enough in the doing for me."

They stayed in the room for much of the next two days. On the few occasions they did leave – to swim or to eat or just to walk the streets – they struggled to keep their hands off each other and hurried back as soon as they could. And although there was lots and lots of sex, they also talked and they laughed and they drank. It was the longest Toby Malkin could ever remember having spent without doing anything related to work. He also ignored a number of increasingly irritated phone messages from Patricia Andrew.

"What's it like being Head of Department?" Ruth asked him on the Sunday morning, as they lay in bed reading the papers. "That was a stroke of luck for you, wasn't it, old pervy Leighton getting found out? He could have been in your way for another ten years. There can't be many people your age who've made it into the inner circle of a firm like Yates and Wood."

"The job itself isn't quite as exciting as I thought it might be, if I'm honest with you. But in other ways it's fantastic because of what it brings." He turned over and took Ruth's head in his hands. "Because sometimes I feel that I can have absolutely anything I want."

He kissed her – a full, deep kiss – and eased himself nearer to her. She was totally different from Patricia Andrew. Where Patricia wanted perfectly executed textbook sex – technique, refinement, control – Ruth craved contact. She was all energy and unashamed enthusiasm, and with Ruth it was simply a whole lot of fun. More than once during the weekend she stopped him as he started on some sophisticated foreplay technique of Patricia's, and pulled him onto her. More than once when he was inside her, she told him to do it harder or faster.

But the last time they made love – on the Sunday afternoon before they left for the airport and the journey home – there was real tenderness from both of them, and they clung to each other for each other and not just for the sex. And afterwards she wept, and he stroked her hair and held her to him.

"What the hell did you marry Dominic for?" he whispered as he kissed away the saltiness of her tears. "What the hell did you marry anyone for?"

"Don't, Toby," she said. "Let's not go there. Please."

That afternoon Malkin left it until the last possible minute before he called a cab. When they arrived back at the East Midlands Airport and collected their luggage, Ruth asked him to leave her there. She told him she wanted to travel back home on her own, needed some time to collect her thoughts. He tried to talk her out of this, but for once he didn't get his way. When he left her she was standing in the middle of the airport concourse, searching in her bag for her phone. She looked troubled.

TWENTY-ONE

Alec Shaker sat in his office, with its tired paintwork and its draughty windows, and fought hard to stop himself from jumping on his desk and dancing in delight. He knew it was foolish to feel this excited so soon, but he couldn't help himself. He had waited so long – so very long – for something like this. To give release to his enthusiasm he phoned his wife, Samantha, and told her his news.

Like Toby Malkin, Alec Shaker was a lawyer in Nottingham. But the similarities ended there. Alec was a rangy, slightly awkward man with a schoolboy haircut and a permanently eager expression, and he worked at a firm called Dobson White. With its old-fashioned, unimposing offices overlooking a garden with beautifully tended lawns and flowerbeds, and its clientele of Legal Aid claimants and families who had used the firm for generations, Dobson White inhabited a different world from Yates and Wood.

Alec reread his scribbled notes to check that he hadn't imagined what had happened. Could this be the break Samantha had always said would come his way one day? His role at Dobson White was to look after the firm's handful of corporate clients, and although he did it well, his practice had never quite developed in the way that he had told the partners it would. He tried to convince himself, more often than he cared to admit, that this didn't matter – that your quality of life was more important than what you earned. But every morning, his drive to work took him past the beautifully restored edifice that housed Yates and Wood's highly paid specialists, and if his day was disappointing or dull he struggled to suppress a feeling of what-might-have-been as he passed it again on his return.

Today would be anything other than disappointing or dull. Alec's secretary had put the call through first thing that morning. The man on the other end of the line checked carefully that he was indeed talking to Alec Shaker.

"My name is Ritchie Ripley," he said. "I'm the general manager of a company called Monte Cristo Software. I'm calling to see if you would be interested in acting for us in connection with a dispute."

Down near the canal, Toby Malkin sat in a meeting of the partners of Yates and Wood. This was the third of these gatherings that he had

108

attended, and to his mind they should have been a forum for succinct discussion and focused thinking. He reflected on how sadly very different the reality seemed to be. Whilst the disappointing drivel droned on around him, he dreamed.

"What do you think, Toby?"

He realised that the face of every other person in the room had turned to look at him. He paused for a moment and furrowed his brows, deliberately for effect.

"Oh, I agree," he said. "We should definitely go ahead."

The faces turned away and resumed their discussion. Two minutes later, Malkin made an excuse and slipped out of the room. He wondered if he would ever know what piddling administrative change he had just agreed to. He hoped that he would never care.

In the corridor outside, he tried Ruth Braebrook's number. Ever since their return from Dublin she had been on secondment with a client in Birmingham. She would be there for some weeks yet. Her secretary was a little hesitant and said that Ruth was in a meeting. Malkin cursed – they seemed hardly to have spoken since they parted at the airport – and then made another call.

It was pointless asking any lawyer – even one with Alec's integrity – if he would be interested in doing something which involved earning fees. There could only ever be one answer.

"Certainly," he said in response to Ritchie Ripley's enquiry. "Can you tell me a little bit more about it?"

Ripley explained that the other party in Monte Cristo's dispute was Reverie Communications. He was hopeful that it would be sorted out without the need to involve lawyers, but was making this call as a precaution.

"Let me give you some contact details," he said. "It's normally easiest to catch me on my mobile." He read out the number.

"And are you based locally?" asked Alec.

"No. Quite the reverse. Monte Cristo operates out of the South of France – Cannes, to be precise. We do a lot of business outside the UK, so I'm often travelling. If we do fall out with RevCom we thought it would be sensible for our lawyers to be local – that's why we've come to you. They've already mentioned the person they use – a lawyer called Malkin from a firm called Bates and Wood, I believe."

"Yates and Wood," said Alec, correcting him.

The company operates out of the South of France. We do a lot of business outside the UK. To Alec Shaker, these words fell like

109

diamond rain-drops. He could already hear himself dropping them into conversations with colleagues and friends, and imagining his own embellishments. *They're not your average East Midlands outfit, you know. Don't you find it's very important to have an international angle to your practice these days?*

"I'll call you again next week to let you know what's happening," said Ritchie Ripley, bringing Alec back to the present.

"Sure." He tried to think if there was anything else he should ask. "I'd better give you my mobile number as well. You know what it's like when you're in and out of meetings all day."

The call came to an end. Alec clasped his hands together. He then spent the next twenty minutes dictating a perfectly composed file note of his conversation with Ripley.

TWENTY-TWO

Maria shut the front door of the house behind her. Her hair was still wet from the shower, and her stomach was empty. Every evening she vowed that breakfast would be fresh fruit or yoghurt. Every morning the reality was either no breakfast at all or, if she felt she needed a treat, a bacon cob oozing brown sauce bought from one of the sandwich shops she passed on her way across the city centre.

She glanced up at the sky, and wondered whether she should go back upstairs for her umbrella. But she told herself she didn't have time, and so she set off, her bag strapped to her back like a knapsack, her flouncy skirt bouncing above her knees. As she walked, she tied her hair back using a clasp in the shape of a pink and white clematis. This was one of her favourite things, its tacky prettiness so often making up for the lack of time in her morning routine to do anything with her hair.

When she had crossed the little park near to her flat, Maria turned onto the road that led into the city. She quickened her step. On the corner she saw a woman she had once worked with heading in the opposite direction, and further on somebody else she often passed, an old man shuffling along with an overweight dog on a lead. Both times Maria smiled her broad smile and waved. She enjoyed mornings, despite the rush. Mornings were for optimism. Mornings were when nothing had had time to go wrong.

These were times to cherish, for there was now a point in every day when an incoming tide of cares and concerns first touched the sandcastles of her dreams, and after that the day was different. Over the last two weeks the tide had been running strong, and Maria had to screw her eyes up tight and try her very hardest to get as far as half past ten before corrosive thoughts about Malkin, or heavy, painful thoughts of Tom, swamped her fragile early morning happiness.

She hurried along the canal to Yates and Wood's offices. When she reached her desk she noticed Malkin look up at her from his office and then down at his watch. In a little act of defiance Maria looked at her watch as well. It was about two minutes to nine. It was close, but she had made it.

At lunchtime Maria left the office and walked up into the city centre. She had planned to look for a new blouse, but couldn't be bothered now, and so she bought some lunch and walked across the concrete

111

thoroughfare of Maid Marian Way, then up a cobbled street to the grounds of Nottingham Castle. There were very few people around – one or two other lunchtime wanderers, and a handful of tourists trying to reconcile the glamorous Hollywood scenes of Robin Hood's medieval escapades with the ornate nineteenth-century mansion that now stood at the top of the mound.

Maria found a bench in an avenue of plane trees and sat down to eat. This was a cherished place – once the haunt of kings, now a little oasis of tranquillity that seemed so underused. It was a place where in the past she had brought lovers and friends, a place where there was little chance of seeing anyone else you knew. At the end of the avenue was a cast-iron statue which celebrated the workers from the city's industrial past – four proud and upright figures, two men, two women. Maria sat with her back to them.

She hated to admit it, but she felt broken. The perception of being useless which had come to her after the escape from Malkin's flat still lingered, together with frequent and distressing visions of what would have happened if she had been discovered. She felt weighed down by her own stupidity. And then one afternoon the previous week, it had all become worse when Malkin had called her into his office without any warning. This was the first time Maria had had anything other than passing contact with him since that night in the flat and for one awful moment she thought that somehow he had found out. Instead, Malkin passed her a piece of paper. On the paper were four dates – dates which went back weeks – and next to each date was a time between 9.00 and 9.10 a.m. Without looking her in the eye, Malkin told her that these were occasions on which she had arrived at work later than her contracted time, and that he was therefore giving her a written warning. If she received another she would be treading a path to dismissal.

Maria muttered something about how in any week she worked far more than her official hours, but Malkin interrupted her.

"That's irrelevant," he said. "You're supposed to be here at nine o'clock and that's when I expect to see you. There's nothing else to discuss. Please go now. I have work to do."

Just for a second, Maria's body had stiffened and she had stayed where she was. Every instinct within her was pushing her towards resistance. She wanted to stand up and scream at her smirking tormentor, to fly at his cruel eyes with her nails. But this didn't happen. The mundane, monetary truth was that she was powerless before Malkin. Just another office girl who couldn't afford to lose her job.

Maria threw away her half-eaten sandwich and hurried back to work.

Later that afternoon, she had to visit the Deed Room to return a pile of documents. It was deserted. Maria sat down at the computer, and began searching the database. In the semi-darkness of the underground vault, she had to strain her eyes to see what she was doing.

A few minutes later, she became aware of somebody standing at the top of the stairs looking down at her. It was Tom.

"Hello, Maria," he said.

"Hi. How are you doing?"

"Fine, I guess." He started to walk down the stairs. "How are you?"

They had seen very little of each other since their row about the key to Malkin's flat. In the meantime Tom had moved departments, and now worked on a different floor.

He reached the bottom of the stairs. Maria made as if to leave. Tom glanced back over his shoulder.

"Don't go," he said, turning to face her again.

Maria stopped, then slumped back into the chair.

"Well?" she asked.

He stepped towards her, so that when he spoke he could do so quietly, but looked at her for a long time before he said anything.

"Do you know that I've bought so much chocolate in the last two weeks I can't get any more in the drawers of my desk."

"What are you talking about?"

"And I've got so many documents from this place on top of the desk that I've hardly any room to work."

"And I need to know this because…?"

"Because…" He leaned forward, speaking in little more than a whisper. "…I go to the sweets machine and I come here because there's a chance I may bump into you. Not much of a chance, I admit. But there doesn't seem to be any other way of seeing you. Why are you behaving like this?"

"Behaving like what?"

"You know."

"I've no idea what you're talking about."

"It's because I wouldn't come to Malkin's flat with you, isn't it?"

"No, it isn't."

"It must be."

"Maybe it was. Anything could have happened to me."

"What are you talking about?"

Maria realised her mistake. "Just forget it," she said, and again she prepared to leave.

"OK, then," said Tom, blocking her way. "I'll come with you. Get another copy of the key – I'm sure you'll find a way – and then we'll go. If it means so much we'll do it."

"No. There's no point now. It's not important."

"What do you mean?"

"I mean there's no point now. And it's not important. Which bit don't you understand?"

"The bit where you're refusing to talk to me for days on end because I won't come and do something which you then say doesn't matter when I offer to do it."

"Tom, I can't cope with this." Maria closed her eyes and made an exaggerated effort to calm herself down. "Maybe we've been kidding ourselves – believing in something which doesn't exist."

"Sorry? Have I missed something? Is this a national Secretaries Talking Nonsense Day that nobody's told me about?"

Maria wasn't listening. She was looking over Tom's shoulder. Somebody else was coming down the stairs into the Deed Room.

"Not disturbing anything am I?"

Tom turned round and saw another secretary from the Corporate Department.

"No," said Maria. "Of course you're not."

The woman smiled as she eased past Tom and stood where she could see them both.

"How are you getting on in Litigation, Tom?" she asked in a loud voice.

"It's fine, thanks."

"And I hear you're getting engaged."

Maria's head made a sharp little movement. Tom said nothing but the woman's face demanded a reply.

"Yes, that's right," he mumbled.

"That's wonderful news. I hear she's a really lovely girl. Really classy." She turned to look at Maria as she said this. "Congratulations!"

"Thank you."

The woman disappeared into the racks at the back of the room. With her lips pursed and her eyes down, Maria flicked her hair out of her face, and pushed past Tom on her way out.

TWENTY-THREE

Waiting for Ritchie Ripley to call back was purgatory for Alec Shaker. He tried to think about other things, but found himself drawn several times each day to the basic information on Monte Cristo Software's website, or to books on the law relating to computers. In his lowest moments a shadow of doubt began to dapple the sunshine of his enthusiasm.

But the wait was worth it. His new client called back late one afternoon.

"Al, things have moved on quickly. We need to meet ASAP. How are you fixed early next week?"

Trying to disguise his eagerness, Alec said that he could clear his diary to suit Ritchie.

"That's great. Tuesday would work best for me. The thing is, and I know this is a lot to ask, but I'm travelling all over the place for the next two weeks, and I have meetings in Rome on Monday and Wednesday. I wouldn't normally ask anybody to do this, but is there any chance at all that you could fly out and meet me there? Say no, if it's not convenient. Monte Cristo will pay for the flights and the hotel."

In his mind's eye, Alec had already boarded the plane. Every time he spoke to his new client, he liked this case more.

The night before his trip he slept badly. Several times during the early hours he stirred, worrying that he would miss his flight and that Monte Cristo would realise the mistake they had made in instructing him. They would find somebody else. Some big-shot lawyer from a well-known firm who did this sort of thing all the time. When the alarm sounded, it woke Alec from the only decent sleep he'd had all night.

From the send-off his family gave him, you would have thought he was leaving for a month, not a day and a half. Sam insisted on getting up with him and making breakfast, and whilst she did this, he showered and climbed into the specially purchased smart-casual attire he had decided would be most appropriate and which she had laid out for him. At their request, she woke the two eldest children, and as he made his way to the car the three of them gathered by the dining-room window and waved.

A few hours later he, Alec Shaker from the backwater of Dobson White, was in Rome, the eternal city, riding in a taxi amongst gorgeous youths on scooters and the relics of a glorious civilisation. When he walked into the hotel off the Via Veneto where Ritchie Ripley had said they should meet, he was precisely on time, his Oxford shirt and chinos a little creased from the journey, but still looking good. He stopped for a moment to take in his surroundings – the marble, the spectacular display of flowers in the middle of the lobby, the furniture upholstered in rich red and gold. He couldn't believe that this was actually happening. In a little alcove to his right he spotted a dark-haired man dressed almost identically to him sitting on a sofa. He had a briefcase open by his side, a number of papers spread out on a low table in front of him. Alec walked over.

The man became aware of Alec's presence and looked up. He smiled.

"Hi there. You must be Al. I'm Ritchie."

He stood up and the two men shook hands.

"It's great to see you," said Ripley, continuing to grip Alec's hand. "I feel so guilty, making you come all this way. But when something's important I think you need to have a face-to-face."

At that moment his mobile phone rang. He answered it using a hands-free headset whilst waving at an empty chair opposite the sofa.

"Can you give me a minute, Al?" he said and moved away towards the reception desk.

Whilst he was gone, Alec made himself comfortable and took a hard-backed notebook from his case. As he waited, he glanced at the documents on the table, and reflected on one decision he had already taken. When he met new clients in the future, he would tell them that they could call him Al. He'd always thought Alec sounded lawyerly. But Al was better. Al was the way forward.

Ritchie came back and ordered coffee, and for a while the two men chatted about Italy. Alec congratulated himself that his preparation for the meeting had included reading a couple of travel books.

"Right, to business," said Ritchie.

"You said you have a dispute with Reverie Communications," said Alec, opening his notebook.

"That's correct. It's a pain to be honest. But shall I tell you a little bit about Monte Cristo first?"

"Fire away."

Ritchie Ripley leaned back in his chair.

"OK. It's quite a low-profile outfit really. It was started a few years ago by some guys who wrote some very clever software. Streets ahead of anything else in the marketplace. They've deliberately kept the organisation small and they run it from the South of France."

"Cannes, I think you said."

"That's right. They're Brits, but one of the guys is married to a Frenchwoman."

"A nice place to be."

"It's great. I can't deny that, although I don't spend that much time there myself. I'm usually on the move."

"I see. And what is your role exactly?"

Ritchie paused, and it looked as though this question caused him difficulty. He eased himself forward and lowered his voice.

"To answer that, Al, I have to be totally open with you. But I guess we need to trust each other. Between you and me, Monte Cristo is struggling. It's not doing as well as it should. There's no doubt about the product they sell – that's world class. But the guys running the show don't really understand money. I've been brought in by one of their backers to sort out the financial problems."

"That's a shame. That they're struggling, I mean."

"It happens all too often. But hey, let's not give up hope just yet. We're good for a few months at least. And you may be able to help us."

"I certainly hope so. Anyway, what does this software do?" asked Alec.

"To be honest with you, Al, it's highly technical stuff. Not easy for a simple mind like me. Basically it's all about data. You put the software onto a large computer system and it allows you to combine data from various sources into a single picture, of a person, a company, whatever."

Ritchie spent the next few minutes drawing diagrams of databases, computers and the connections between them, and talking Alec through a number of examples.

"I must admit," he said, looking up from his final illustration, "I don't fully understand it myself – I'm just a businessman. I just know it's very, very clever. How much more do you need to know?"

"That's plenty for now. Shall we talk about the dispute?"

"OK. Monte Cristo's natural customers are big organisations – banks, insurance companies, government bodies. And we sell the software under licence arrangements where the customer pays according to the size of their computer network. The bigger the network, the more they pay."

"I'm with you," said Alec. "And presumably there are some issues with Reverie Communications?"

"That's right. I think they're paying less than they should."

"How much are they paying?"

"At the moment it's three grand a month. But that's the smallest amount we charge – it only really buys you a licence to try the product out. We think Reverie are doing far more than just trying it out, and that they should be paying us a lot more money."

"Any idea how much more?"

Ritchie paused before answering. "It's difficult to be exact. It depends on a number of things, but I think they could be underpaying by something like fifteen k a month. Maybe more."

"And how long's this been going on for?"

"About eighteen months."

Alec made a quick calculation.

"So you're looking at a basic shortfall of something north of two hundred and fifty grand."

"That sounds right. I know it's not a king's ransom, but it's a lot to us."

Alec smiled, but inside he felt a first tinge of disappointment. Two hundred and fifty thousand was a reasonable figure, but he had secretly hoped – expected, even – that the number would be a lot bigger. The glamour of this situation in contrast to his normal working life demanded that it should be.

He put these feelings to one side and spent the next forty-five minutes poring over a contract between Reverie Communications and Monte Cristo Software which Ritchie produced from his briefcase. Alec asked a lot more questions. Then the two men looked at some correspondence.

"OK," said Alec, after Ritchie had finished dealing with another call on his mobile. "How do you know that Reverie have been misusing the software?"

"A stroke of luck really. We were contacted by an ex-employee of theirs. Somebody senior who knew what they were doing and who seemed to be after blowing the whistle. He wasn't that specific, but he told us enough."

"Do you know his name?"

"Lesley King."

118

"OK. And have you put this to RevCom? Have they admitted that they're in the wrong?"

"Yes and no, in that order. We've had conversations with them – I deal with a guy called Eddie Tomlinson – but although he's pleasant enough, they're just stonewalling. I've laid on as much charm as I can, but I'm not getting anywhere. Look."

He reached into his briefcase and handed Alec some papers on which were printed a number of e-mails.

"I see what you mean," said Alec after he had read them through. "He's not answering your questions at all."

"To be fair to him, I think it's coming from higher up. Tomlinson reports to somebody called Cooper. But you're right. They're not taking us seriously."

For a while there was silence as Alec read the e-mails again and turned things over in his mind.

"Look, Al," said Ritchie, "unless you need anything more from me at the moment, I have a couple of calls to make." He picked up his mobile and looked at it. "Sometimes I feel like I'm married to this thing. Would it be helpful if I left you alone for a while so that you can have another look at the documents? I know you guys like to have time to reflect, but I do need to get an initial view from you today if I can. Is that OK?"

"That's fine. It would be quite useful, actually."

"Grand. I'll see you in half an hour or so."

When Ripley had gone, Alec reread the notes he had made so far, filling in gaps, and amending the odd point here and there. Then he went through the contract again. Once or twice he stopped and screwed up his eyes as he thought a difficult point through.

On one of these occasions Alec's train of thought was derailed by the sight of a woman who had come into the hotel lobby. Tall with long honey-coloured hair and legs which went on for ever, she stood chewing the end of her sunglasses as if she were looking for somebody, and for a moment she glanced at Alec. Then she disappeared from view. Alec went back to his deliberations.

"So, Al," said Ritchie when he returned, "what do you think?"

If legal cases were won by enthusiasm alone, Alec would have triumphed there and then. Leaning forward in his chair and doing his best to avoid technicalities, he explained how in theory Reverie Communications had committed various infringements ("we would probably focus on the copyright angle"), that in theory Monte Cristo had a very good claim ("the contract really is quite clear"), and how in

119

theory damages would be payable ("you would at least be entitled to the licence fees that should have been paid"). He seasoned his explanation with thoughts about the disgraceful ways in which large companies treated small ones – faceless snakes squeezing the life out of enterprise, in his view – and he tried to sound as though he handled this sort of dispute all the time.

As he finished talking, Alec saw that somebody was approaching them. It was the woman he had spotted a few minutes earlier. Despite his very best efforts, he was helpless to stop the swinging of her hips – emphasised by a thick leather belt with a large buckle – from monopolising his attention. Ritchie noticed his distraction and turned round.

"*Principessa!*" he said beaming and standing up to greet the woman. "Thanks for coming."

He leaned forward and kissed her on each cheek. She received his attentions gracefully and smiled at Alec over his shoulder.

"Alec, can I introduce you to Claudia." He pronounced it *cloudier,* not *clawdier.* "She does some translation work for us here." Ritchie took a large envelope from her as he spoke. "Claudia, this is Alec Shaker, our legal counsel from the UK."

Alec was flattered in equal measure by this description and by Claudia's attentive eyes as they talked about his journey. After a few minutes she looked at her watch and said she had to go. Ritchie thanked her for bringing the envelope and kissed her again. She stood as if waiting for Alec to kiss her as well. He offered his hand. She laughed and shook it, and left.

"Where were we, Al? Oh that's right, you were telling me about how you're going to get us some money. I knew you were the guy to make things happen for us."

Alec held up his hand to indicate caution.

"It's not quite that straightforward, I'm afraid. There's a practical side to these things as well. If you have got a claim, you've got to be able to *prove* it. You need evidence. If you don't have evidence it's like trying to catch an elephant with a butterfly net. It gives RevCom and their fancy lawyers every excuse to ignore you."

"So what do we need to do?" asked Ritchie.

"I'd like to follow up on this chap Lesley King. He could be the key to it all. If we could find him and persuade him to give us a statement, we'd put ourselves in the box seat. Do you think you can track him down?"

"We can try. Leave it with me."

The two men then spent another half an hour going over much of what they had already covered. When they had finished, Alec dealt with the formalities of his terms of engagement. To his surprise and pleasure Ritchie gave him a cheque on account of his fees, saying that he wouldn't want Alec to be put off by what he had said about Monte Cristo's financial position. Then they collected their papers and belongings together, and walked upstairs to the roof garden. The two men sat in the warmth of the late afternoon sun, looking down at the chaotic traffic in the street below. They talked about Alec's family, and Italian football, and they drank a couple of beers.

"Right," said Ritchie, looking at his watch. "I think even Monte Cristo can afford to treat us to a bit of an evening out, don't you? How about I meet you in the bar of your hotel at eight and we'll find ourselves a nice restaurant?"

"If you're sure. But there's really no need."

"Of course I'm sure. And I'll tell you what, I'll give Claudia a call as well – see if she's free to join us."

He winked and drained his glass. A few minutes later, at the front of the hotel, Ritchie shook Alec's hand warmly and watched as he hailed a cab. Waiting until Alec was well out of sight, he made a little fist-clenching gesture of celebration. He smiled and walked back into the hotel.

TWENTY-FOUR

Alec picked up the message twenty minutes before they were due to meet in the bar.

"Al, it's Ritchie. Something's come up and I have to catch a flight out of here tonight. I won't be able to join you. But Claudia's already on her way over – she must have her phone switched off. I can't get hold of her. You two go out anyway. Charge it to Monte Cristo and have a good time. I'll catch up with you in a day or two."

Before he went downstairs to meet Claudia, Alec phoned Samantha. He enthused about his day, and was rather vague about his evening, and although his wife was pleased for him and said so, she seemed to detect that he wasn't relaxed. She asked him several times if he was OK.

"I'm fine, darling," he said, looking at his watch and making a tiny adjustment to his hair in the mirror. "Honestly. I'm fine. I have to go now."

When Alec walked into the bar, Claudia was sitting on a stool at the far end of the room, smoking. She seemed totally unfazed being a woman on her own in these surroundings. Her clothes – dark trousers and a silk blouse – fitted her so well they looked as though they had been made especially for her. Alec went up and greeted her ("call me Al") and bought her a drink. They sat at a table and chatted. He complimented her on her English. She told him the story of how her grandfather's village had been liberated during the war, and how she and all her siblings and cousins had been brought up to think of the English as friends.

They walked outside and took a cab across the darkening city to the restaurant, an intimate establishment in the Trastevere area. The shelves on its wood-panelled walls were stacked high with wine bottles, and there was an all-pervading aroma of steak cooked on charcoal. Alec sometimes worried that he struggled with small talk – that clients and colleagues might find him hard work – but there was none of this with the doe-eyed Claudia. They seemed to move effortlessly from one subject to another, and she was serious, alert, interested in everything he had to say. She made him feel good. It was easy to forgive the cigarettes between courses and the occasional glances at other men in the restaurant. When a peddler came to the table offering flowers, he bought her a rose, and she laughed.

He drank more than he meant to, but told himself he was still in control. As they waited for their desserts she excused herself and went to the Ladies' room. Alec let the waiter top up his glass, and smiled. He was still struggling to believe that he was here in this wonderful city doing this. He was resolved to do everything he could to help Monte Cristo Software, determined that he would make a difference. And right now he wanted this evening to last for ever. A little bit of him wanted to be ten years younger, handsome and Italian. He wondered what Sam would say if she could see him. He hoped that she would see the funny side. He had a sense that Claudia was only humouring him, just being polite, but she did it so wonderfully well. Why shouldn't he enjoy it? He began to think about what he would say and do when they parted. Maybe, if he were bold, he might take her hand and kiss her cheek, and be left with a fleeting sense of her perfume.

But when Claudia returned to the table, she seemed different. She looked at him and then raised her hand to her eye.

"What is it?" he asked, leaning forward. "What's the matter?"

"It's nothing." She forced a smile.

"But you've been crying. Is it something I've said?"

"Of course not. That's silly. I'm OK."

"You can tell me. Really, I don't mind. You mustn't cry."

She looked at him, the candlelight from the tables around them picking up the moistness in her eyes.

"I can't tell you," she said. "I just don't want to go home tonight, that's all. I'm frightened. It's my boyfriend."

"Why? What's happened?"

"I'm so sorry. I can't tell you." She reached into her bag and took out a tiny mobile phone. "Forgive me, I need to try to find somewhere to stay."

Alec's concern was fuelled by the wine and it was unbearable to him that she should be distressed. He reached out and stopped her from switching on the phone.

"This is dreadful. There must be something I can do. Why don't you stay at my hotel? Come back with me. I'm sure they'll have a room."

"It's no good. I have no money. He won't let me..."

"I'll pay. It's not a problem."

He didn't think he had ever seen a lovelier smile.

"You can't do that for me," she said. "I can't – what is the word? – *impose* like that. You don't need my sadness. I'm so sorry. I didn't want you to see I was crying. We must enjoy the rest of our evening."

"Please. You don't have to tell me anything. I won't ask. But you must let me help you."

She reached out and stroked his arm with a lazy, feather-like touch, and then withdrew her hand.

"If I could, it would be such a help. Tomorrow I can call my sister. You really don't mind?"

"I really, really don't mind. It's the least I can do."

She sighed. "Al, you don't know what this means to me. It's like my grandfather told me. All Englishmen are gentlemen."

One of the waiters held the door open for them as they left the restaurant and he gave Alec a look that was both knowing and approving. In the cab on the way to the hotel Claudia reached out her hand and Alec took it in both of his. When they arrived he suggested that she sit down whilst he sorted out a room.

"I don't want to sit here like this," she said, pouting. "Everybody will stare. Can we go to your room until I feel better?"

He would have agreed to anything she asked. He felt awkward in the lift, and he worried about the untidiness of his room. But when they reached it, Claudia seemed not to notice anything. She sat on the end of the bed, and declined his offer of a drink. He took off his jacket and sat in a chair until she turned the full force of her eyes on him, when he moved so that he was next to her.

"I know I said I wouldn't ask," he said, "but whatever it is that's troubling you, if there's anything, anything at all, that I can do to make it better, then please tell me."

Again there were tears. She shook her head.

Then she leaned towards him and he took her in his arms, pressing her head into his shoulder.

"You poor, poor thing."

He held her for several minutes. Then Claudia pushed him away gently and stood up in front of him. She smiled, and suddenly the tears were gone. He sat transfixed whilst she raised her hand to her throat and started, very slowly, to unbutton her blouse. He couldn't stop himself from watching. One by one the buttons were released, and as her hand moved lower it became clear that there was nothing beneath the shimmering material. She leaned back and shook her hair. Her breasts were small and round, and Alec looked at them with a longing that hurt.

But then he stopped her.

"Claudia, no. It isn't necessary. I don't want you to do this."

124

"Yes you do," she whispered. She stepped forward and put her knee on his. With her left hand she held the back of his head and with the other she cradled one of her breasts, pushing it gently towards him. "Kiss me. Kiss me there."

For a moment his desire threatened to overcome him, but he fought it and resisted it. He moved her away from him, saying nothing. Her expression was first one of confusion and then one of offence.

"What's the matter?" she asked, pushing her shoulders back and her chest out. "Don't you like them?"

He stood up and pulled the two sides of her blouse together as if he were drawing curtains.

"Claudia, I love them. They're as wonderful as the rest of you. But you don't understand. This isn't what I want."

She shrugged and suddenly seemed very distant. He kissed her lightly on the forehead, then took her hand and guided her back to the edge of the bed.

"Listen, I need to go to the bathroom. When I come back I'm going to phone reception and find a room for you. You need to sleep. We can talk more in the morning."

He was away for no more than two minutes. When he came back she was gone, and although he rushed to the lift and ran to the entrance of the hotel, and then walked up the stairs, he couldn't find her. He went back downstairs again and spoke to the night-porter, but he couldn't make himself understood. He even went outside and walked the streets, imagining that he might find her doing the same. But he didn't. In the end, he returned to his room and not knowing what else to do he drank all the whisky from the mini-bar. He stood at his window looking out over the lights of the city, wondering where the girl had gone and why, regretting her departure but worrying for her more. Eventually, feeling helpless and more than a little sad, he went to bed.

Alec overslept. When he woke the next morning he realised he was short of time. As he dressed and stuffed his belongings into his overnight bag, he discovered that it wasn't only Claudia who had disappeared the night before. His wallet had gone as well. He turned the room upside down, and phoned reception, but to no avail. He couldn't find it. Fraught, hungry and tired, and without money or plastic his last hours in Italy were difficult as he dealt with the hotel staff and the police, and somehow made his flight with minutes to spare.

Somebody else who experienced a Roman morning was Toby Malkin. But his morning was serene and relaxed. He ate a breakfast of warm rolls and coffee on the roof garden of the hotel where Alec's meeting had taken place the day before, laughing several times during a long conversation on his mobile phone. Then he checked out, left his luggage to be collected later and headed for the designer boutiques around the Spanish Steps. There he wandered from name to famous name – Louis Vuitton, Laura Biagiotti, Giorgio Armani – imagining that with his wrap-around shades and dark complexion, people might take him to be a local. He examined jewellery, clothes and accessories, sometimes deep in thought, sometimes taking advice from assistants all of whom he thought could have been models or film stars.

After a leisurely break at a small café, where he ordered espresso and a pastry, he returned to one of the first shops he had visited and bought a dress. It was a risk, he knew, because he couldn't be sure of the size, but it was a risk worth taking. The dress was wonderful – black chiffon, exquisitely cut, glamorous yet refined. It reminded him of the one Ruth had worn in Dublin.

He watched in rapt attention, his eyes lingering on every movement as the assistant folded the diaphanous material, wrapped it in tissue paper and placed it in a box tied with ribbon. Then he paid. He enjoyed paying. The amount he spent was by many people's standards obscene. But he intended that this would be an investment. He intended that by giving this gift, he would receive so much more in return.

TWENTY-FIVE

Alec Shaker stood by the window of his office and reread the letter for about the tenth time that morning. He wasn't sure about it. He was worried that it would turn out to be a mistake. But Ritchie Ripley had been in touch several times since the meeting in Rome, and Ritchie Ripley had other ideas.

Alec scanned the letter again. There wasn't anything wrong with the wording. In fact, he was rather pleased with what he had written. The letter announced to Reverie Communications that Monte Cristo existed and that Monte Cristo had a problem. But its tone was measured and reasonable. Nothing too aggressive – a gentle request that RevCom should pay what was owed, not a battle cry. It was just right.

What troubled him was the timing. Was it really wise for Monte Cristo Software to cross swords with Reverie Communications just yet? Shouldn't they first do all they could to track down Lesley King, their potential star witness, the man who had blown the whistle? Alec thought so. Despite the loss of his wallet, and the questioning he had faced from Samantha, he was still enthused by the prospect of acting for Monte Cristo. There was little doubt that they had a case, and it was a case Alec was sure he could win. But if they sent the letter now and it disappeared into Reverie Communications only to be ignored, what were his options? Very few – he would have nowhere to go, no leverage.

He looked out over the tranquil beauty of the garden outside. Spring was his favourite time of year, and on any other day he would have stopped and looked to see which of the plants were showing signs of renewed growth. Today he sighed and turned away. Whatever his judgement might tell him, he knew he had no choice. Ritchie Ripley had been very clear and Ritchie was the client. Alec made a couple of minor changes to the text of the letter and then told his secretary to send it.

The letter in fact found its way quickly from the desk of Eddie Tomlinson to that of Lewis Cooper, and then, less than forty-eight hours after Alec had sent it, on to Toby Malkin.

Malkin read it sitting at his desk, then looked up through the glass front of his office at the lawyers and secretaries outside going about their normal daily business. He felt a sudden and dramatic crescendo of panic.

He forced himself to calm down. *Nobody knows. Nobody could possibly know. Don't give anyone any reason to suspect.*

He picked up his dictating machine and started to speak.

"New file." He switched off the machine and cleared his throat before carrying on. "Reverie Communications – Software Dispute. Then a note on that file. TM speaking to Lewis Cooper regarding a new matter. Potential dispute with a supplier. LC saying it was probably just an irritation. Requesting that I speak to Eddie Tomlinson (who is closest to the detail), look at a letter from the supplier's lawyers and advise."

Two days later, Malkin phoned Lewis Cooper.

"Lewis, it's Toby. Have you got a few minutes to talk about this Monte Cristo business?"

"Monte Cristo?"

"Yes. The letter you asked me to look at. The complaint from the little software supplier."

"Oh that. Won't take long, will it? I'm about to go into a board meeting."

"I won't keep you more than five minutes, but we do need to go through it."

"OK. Fire away."

"I hope you'll forgive the formality," said Malkin, "but before we look at the detail I would recommend that you keep this confidential. Don't involve anyone at your end unless you really have to."

"That sounds serious."

"I don't think so, Lewis. I'm hopeful we'll be able to keep it under control, although I suppose you may end up having to pay these people something to go away."

"So how should we respond to this letter?"

"I suggest that I write back on your behalf, without getting into any detail. I'll say that you don't believe there's any substance to what they are saying. In the meantime Eddie Tomlinson can complete his investigation, and if they carry on pushing it, we'll have another think."

There was a long silence on the other end of the line. Malkin had to use all his self-control to stop himself from filling it.

"OK, Toby. You're the expert. I'm sure we've all got better things to do with our time than sorting out Lesley King's cock-ups."

"Exactly."

The two men spoke briefly about other matters, and then Cooper was called into his board meeting.

"Thanks, Toby. I'll speak to you shortly."

The line went dead. Malkin replaced the receiver with exaggerated care.

When Alec received Toby Malkin's dismissive letter the next morning he put his head in his hands. This was what he had feared – it was very difficult to argue with someone who refused to engage, especially if you were the little guy. He knew that Ritchie Ripley would want to hear about the response as soon as possible, but he delayed calling him until the end of the day. The two men spent some time on the phone discussing their next steps. Ritchie had heard nothing further from Lesley King.

The next morning Alec spent an hour working in his office with the door shut, preparing himself for the call which he thought could be the pivot on which this whole case was balanced. Whatever it took, he had to avoid being fobbed off.

He caught Toby Malkin on his car-phone.

"I'm going to have to be quick," Malkin said when he answered. "I'm on my way to see a client. What can I do for you?"

"I wanted to talk to you about your letter on the Monte Cristo matter."

"What about it?"

"I suppose I found it a little surprising. You seem to be suggesting that your clients have nothing to answer for."

"Well do they?"

"My instructions are that they have an awful lot to answer for."

"Oh really?"

"Really. We have evidence – good evidence – to suggest that your clients have done things with Monte Cristo's software that no responsible company should do."

"What sort of evidence?"

"It's not something I want to discuss on the phone."

"Well when are we going to discuss it?"

"That's the reason for the call. As I said in my letter, my clients will resort to legal action if they have to, but they would much prefer to sort this out by sensible discussion."

"And?"

"And," said Shaker, speaking slowly, "to that end, they have suggested that there should be a meeting, as soon as possible, involving

Lewis Cooper, and presumably yourself, together with me and Ritchie Ripley of Monte Cristo Software."

There was silence. While he waited for Malkin to reply, Alec looked down his list of points to make when this request was refused. The list suddenly looked very short.

"I suppose that's a possibility," said Malkin. "Do you think that would help?"

"Sorry?"

"I said, do you think that would help? Will it allow us to sort this out quickly?"

"Yes ... well I suppose so ... I wouldn't be asking otherwise."

"I have to warn you that Reverie Communications have no intention of giving into speculative threats from little software companies – even those with fancy foreign addresses. But if it makes this easier – if it needs a meeting to make your clients see sense – then I will put it to Lewis Cooper. I'll call you back."

"Thank you."

Malkin brought the call to an end. Alec sat at his desk looking surprised. Maybe he had got Toby Malkin wrong – maybe he wasn't the bully everyone said he was. Or perhaps it was him. Samantha was often telling him to believe in himself more. She could be right. Perhaps Toby Malkin had realised that Alec wasn't a lawyer to be messed with.

That afternoon, Malkin called Lewis Cooper.

"Lewis," he said after they had exchanged pleasantries, "I'm a little embarrassed about this. You remember Monte Cristo Software, the little company who say they have a claim against you? We spoke the other day. They're based in Cannes. I'm afraid they're not going away as I hoped they would. I've spoken to their lawyer several times. He's like a dog with a bone. Very persistent. Very confident about his own position. I've tried everything I know, everything, but it's not having any effect. We just end up in a slanging match every time. No, I don't think it's any more serious. It's probably just the lawyer. He's got a reputation for playing hardball. I wouldn't normally want to trouble you with this sort of thing, but I wonder if a meeting may be the quickest way to get rid of this. Make them see that we won't be intimidated. Can we get the secretaries to find a time when we can see them for half an hour? Thanks, I'm sure we both want to get this one off our desks."

TWENTY-SIX

It is one of those evenings when office workers start to notice that the days are getting longer. They emerge at six o'clock expecting dusk, but then see that, for the first time since autumn, the light has offered meaningful resistance to the night. Ink-smudge clouds are gathered along horizons, and in the west can be glimpsed, like the first sign of a smile after tears, the promise of a promise of summer.

But with the clear skies comes the cold, and as the employees of Yates and Wood leave the building they pull their coats around them and hurry on. Many of them head for a nearby pub, because this evening there is to be a leaving do for a middle-ranking lawyer. The firm expects a regular turnover of staff at this level. If for whatever reason you don't make it to partnership – because you don't bill enough, or introduce sufficient new clients, or if your face just doesn't fit – there is an understanding that you will do the decent thing and seek another furrow to plough.

Maria arrived early for this shindig with a couple of girlfriends. They established themselves near to the middle of the bar. The pub filled up rapidly, and soon the place was heaving. Maria smiled and chatted, and made mischievous eyes at any man the right side of ordinary.

She noticed Tom the moment he came in, and watched him struggle to the bar. But her attention was diverted when out of the crowd in front of her appeared the lawyer Tom had seen her kissing at Christmas.

"Maria Cracolicci, my favourite runaway," he shouted above the noise around them. "I'm buying. Can I interest you in anything, if you know what I mean?"

She held up an almost full glass and smiled a tolerating smile. "Not at the moment, thanks."

They talked for a few minutes, and as they did the lawyer pushed himself nearer to her all the time, so that his face was almost touching hers. Eventually he placed his hands on her hips and started to move her body suggestively.

"This time, I'm not letting you go," he said, shifting his hands round and squeezing her bottom beneath the thin cotton of her dress. He leaned forward and started to nuzzle her ear. "And certainly not for some prick-squeak of a trainee. You know how it works, Maria – I'm six years qualified. I get first refusal."

Imagining in his drunkenness that he was being as subtle as it was possible to be, he tried to place her hand against his groin.

"Did you hear something?" asked Maria, taking her hand away and laughing.

"No. What do you mean?"

"I'm sure I heard a mobile phone ringing. I thought that maybe it was your wife calling so that you could say goodnight to the kids."

He squeezed her bottom again. "Leave it out, Maria. I know you're as up for it as me. I'll see you later."

His eyes challenged hers, and then he turned away and stumbled off through the crowd. Maria began chatting to her friends once more, but a few moments later found her eyes resting on Tom again. He noticed her and made his way across to the bar.

"Can I have a word?" he asked.

"It depends what it is."

"I just wanted to explain why I didn't tell you about me and Caroline."

"There's no need," she said. "You don't have to say anything." She smiled, and for a moment all the old warmth was there. "And by the way, I'm sorry."

"Sorry for what?"

"For the way I've been. For the way I've treated you. You don't deserve it."

He studied her face before replying. "It's not a problem. I guess I let you down over the key thing."

"Careful what you're saying in here. But it wasn't only that. Just ignore me, Tom. Everyone else does. I've got some news as well, by the way."

"What's that?"

She stood up on tiptoe so that she could speak into his ear without anybody else hearing. Her hair brushed against the side of his face.

"Nobody else knows yet, but I'm leaving. It's so exciting – I'm going to Australia. Maybe for good."

His eyes widened. "Is that definite?"

"More or less. I've got a friend who lives in Sydney. She says that I can go and stop with her for a while. If it all works out I may stay." She put her hand on his shoulder to steady herself as a group of people pushed past.

They looked at each other for a moment, their eyes making an uneasy contact.

Eventually Tom offered a simple: "I can't believe it. I'll miss you, you know."

"Don't say any more," said Maria, forcing a smile.

Then her head bobbed forward and she kissed him on the cheek. Before he realised what had happened she had disappeared back into the throng around them.

Half a mile across the city, the light in Alec Shaker's office was now the only light left on at Dobson White. The garden lay in darkness, as did every other window in the neat low-lying building. From time to time the wind moved the frame of the door which, in more clement conditions, opened from Alec's office onto the immaculate lawn. Inside, Alec was working, his head close to the desk. Papers and files were strewn around him, as if somebody had thrown them up in the air and let them land where they would. In one corner of the room, against the wall, lay a number of carrier bags from the city's leading department store.

It had been a remarkable day. The day on which the slow-burning fire of the Monte Cristo case had found the oxygen it needed to turn it into an all-consuming conflagration. That morning, Alec had sat down to think about the meeting with Reverie Communications which his client had so confidently insisted he arrange. It was due to take place the next day, and Alec was worried. Worried that he and Ritchie Ripley would turn up able to do nothing other than repeat the general allegations he had made in his letter. For all Ripley's bluster and enthusiasm, they still had no supporting evidence, and without evidence he feared that Toby Malkin would make them look foolish. If he did, then that would be that. All Alec would have to show from his encounter with Monte Cristo Software would be a modest fee, the embarrassment of his lost wallet and a familiar nearly-but-not-quite feeling.

But then, shortly after ten o'clock, he had taken a call from his client and everything had changed.

"The bad news, Al, is that I can't make the meeting tomorrow. I've got to fly out to the States. You'll have to tackle our friends at RevCom by yourself."

Alec closed his eyes and cursed silently. The thought of being on his own appalled him.

"But the good news is that we've found him. We've found Lesley King."

"Really?" asked Alec, his mood suddenly improving. "How?"

"We called in a lot of favours. Used our contacts. It turns out he's working in South Africa. And it gets better – he's written everything down. Al, you will never, ever believe the things he's told us. It's incredible. I so wish I could come with you tomorrow. You'll wipe the floor with them."

A few minutes later, a copy of Lesley King's statement arrived on the fax, sent from an airport hotel in Manchester, and from then on the day had disappeared. Alec read and reread the statement. He checked and rechecked points of law. With every passing hour the size of Monte Cristo's claim grew, and by mid-afternoon it was by far the biggest thing Alec had ever worked on. He even started to feel good about his client not being with him the next day. Here was a chance for him to shine.

By the end of the afternoon, he was ready to start preparing what he would say tomorrow. But he needed a break and, acting on an impulse, he left his office and set off to do something he had thought about doing when he first heard from Monte Cristo.

On his way into the city centre he looked at his watch. It was twenty to five – he had about an hour. The shops were quiet. He went first to the glassware section of a department store, and bought presents for his parents – a set of crystal goblets for his wine-loving father, a beautifully crafted paperweight for his mother. They would chide him for the expense, no doubt, but he would tell them he was doing well at work, and they would be delighted both by the gifts and by this news. Whilst he was there, he added a vase for his secretary.

Next he went to the toy department where he bought for each of his children something which he was sure would delight them – for the eldest a Gameboy Advance, for his daughter the in-line skates she had coveted for months, and for his youngest son a Hornby train set.

Then he left the department store and hurried to a jewellers. He arrived just as they were shutting, but he knew exactly what he wanted, because the first time he had seen the ring in the shop window a few weeks earlier he had known it was the one. It had taken him some time to get used to the idea of the price, and he had tried to talk himself out of it. But every time he walked past the shop it seemed to reach out and draw him to it, and he imagined himself a humble version of something from Wagner or Tolkien. It was simple and unfussy, with a large single diamond in the middle – in every way the perfect engagement ring. When the assistant removed it from the display cabinet and let him handle it, he knew that he wouldn't leave the shop without it. He made a mild and unsuccessful attempt to haggle on the price, and then handed over his credit card. He had the ring gift-wrapped and left the shop.

Alec had intended to make one last purchase – the digital camera that had been on his own wish list for months. But he realised that now he was short of time, and decided that in any case he had spent enough. He would wait until the litigation with Reverie Communications was over before he treated himself.

He went back to the office and immersed himself once more in his work. He thought another three hours would be about right – he wanted to be as well prepared for tomorrow as he could be, without making himself too tired. He worked hard, but from time to time, as he needed to think something through, he was unable to resist standing up, walking to the pile of presents and fingering the box which contained the ring. Despite the expense he knew that Samantha would adore it. At the time of their engagement he had been a struggling articled clerk, able to afford nothing more than the cheapest ring from a catalogue, and although his wife had always worn it with a defiant pride, she deserved more. At long last he was able to provide it.

Each time he returned quickly to his desk and carried on with his preparation. Despite the mess around him, he worked with method and with diligence. Alec Shaker was a good lawyer and he was on top of things, handling the matter professionally, making out the best possible case for his client.

He would carry on working hard. He would carry on doing things well. But he never would buy that camera.

TWENTY-SEVEN

Alec was not the only lawyer in Nottingham working late that evening. At Yates and Wood several people sat at several desks. One of them, inevitably, was Toby Malkin.

The phone in front of him rang. He picked up the receiver and his face broke into a rare grin when he heard the voice on the other end of the line.

"Ruth Braebrook," he said. "What a privilege. I thought you'd forgotten all about me."

"Don't, Toby. I want to talk to you. It's about … us, I suppose. It's all your e-mails and messages. I want to…"

"Where are you?"

"I'm in the car. On my way back from Birmingham. About forty minutes away. Is there somewhere quiet we can meet?"

"Sure – why don't you come to the flat? I've got something for you. You'll adore it." He paused. "And perhaps you can tell me some more stories about the wicked things you've done."

"I'm not sure that's a very good idea."

"We'll see about that. Bye for now."

Malkin had only just had time to shower and change, and open a bottle of wine, when the doorbell sounded.

He pressed the button on the intercom and simply said, "Come up," before releasing the lock.

Soon afterwards there was a light tap at the door to the flat. Still straightening cushions and adjusting the level of the lighting, he went to let his visitor in.

"Hello," she said, smiling and fluttering her eyelashes with deliberate exaggeration.

She walked in, stopping to kiss him on the cheek and to sigh with appreciation at the smell of his aftershave. He closed the door and scurried after her.

"Oh how sweet," she said. She was standing in the middle of the room, looking back at him over her shoulder with provocative eyes. "Wine, two glasses, your best aftershave. And is that a present? You must have been expecting me, darling. Do you think it's something telepathic?"

She tossed her coat onto the sofa and walked towards him.

"But let's just go straight to bed," she whispered as she placed her head against his chest. "You can skip the romance. It's really not my style."

With great restraint he pushed her away and took hold of her wrist. He started to lead her towards the door.

"You have to leave," he said. "I want you to go."

She stopped, and for an instant he continued to try to pull her along with him, but she resisted. He relaxed his grip, but kept hold of her wrist.

"You can't ask me to leave, Mr Solicitor," she said. "It's been more than three weeks. You've been ignoring my calls. That's against the rules."

"There are no rules, Patricia. You know that. You have to leave."

He let go of her and walked to the sofa. Picking up her coat he strode back in the direction of the door. She reached out a hand to stop him, and he hit out at it, as if he were swatting away a wasp.

"You bastard," she hissed. "How dare you raise your hand to me?"

"Oh fuck off, Patricia." He hurled her coat across the room towards the door and turned to face her. "I dare because this is my flat. I dare because I didn't ask you here tonight. And I dare because you have absolutely no hold over me. Now get out before I throw you out." His face was taut with constrained rage. The veins on his neck stood out like steel cables.

"Well listen to you! You big-talking barrow boy! Come on then, who is she?" She flicked her hair disdainfully in the direction of the bottle and the glasses. "Some giggling secretary who's fooled by the veneer? Or is it some helpless schoolgirl from the tennis club, perhaps?"

She turned away and walked back into the lounge.

He stood still for a moment and then strode after her. By the time he reached her, she had picked up the wine, and was looking at the label as if she were wondering what to serve with the fish at a dinner party.

"What did you say?" Malkin asked, his words precise and threatening.

She ignored the question and poured a small amount of wine into one of the glasses.

"Mmm, not at all bad." She breathed in the bouquet and took a sip. "Bit of class, is she? Worth spending a few quid on?"

"What did you say, Patricia?"

137

She continued to study the wine glass for a moment longer, then looked up.

"Tennis club, Toby. Young girls." She paused to study his reaction. "You don't suppose that your hand in all that Guy Leighton ugliness isn't as transparent as the day is long? You didn't really think that nobody would realise?"

"I don't know what you're talking about."

"Oh my God, you did." She put her hand over her mouth in a gesture of melodramatic surprise. "I don't believe it. You actually thought you were going to get away with it."

He stepped towards her. She remained unfazed, and took another sip of wine.

"Don't worry, lover. Your secret's safe with me." She raised her eyebrows and winked. "You scratch my back, as they say…"

He lunged towards her, his hands reaching out for her neck. She was too quick, and managed to step backwards, out of his grasp. His arm caught hers, knocking the glass out of her hand. It hit the coffee table and smashed. In trying to grab hold of her, Malkin lost his balance, and as he stumbled forward Patricia reached out with a surprising nimbleness, grabbed handfuls of his hair and pushed him down. They fell to the floor together, landing heavily. She straddled him, keeping hold of his hair with one hand, and pressing the long, manicured nails of the other into the flesh on the side of his face.

"Listen to me. Do you want me to slash that pretty face of yours? Gouge those gorgeous eyes? Because I will if you make me."

His body went limp, and he eased his head round so that he could see her. He stared at her before he spoke.

"OK. I shouldn't have done that. I'm sorry."

"How sorry?"

"Let me make one call and I'll show you how sorry."

"Now that's more like it."

The pressure on his cheek eased, and Patricia started to move. At that moment he roared, and pushed upwards, forcing her off him. He hit out in an uncontrolled volley of blows, catching the side of her head with one of them. As he rolled on top of her and pressed her down to the floor he narrowly avoided the broken glass on the carpet. He manoeuvred himself so that he was restraining her with his knee. She tried to bite him, but he placed one hand over her mouth, so that all he could see of her face was the blazing hatred of her eyes.

They lay like that until he felt her resistance begin to ebb away and fear take over. He smiled, felt for his handkerchief and stuffed it into her mouth. Then he reached out and picked up the jagged angry stem of the glass.

"Patricia Andrew," he said, holding the glass so that it was millimetres from her eyes, "if you fight with me, you will lose. I will hurt you, Patricia. I will hurt you very badly."

He shifted the position of his body so that he was looking towards her feet. In their struggle, her skirt had ridden up and now he tugged it up further, exposing the whiteness of her thighs. He leaned forward and with a surgeon's precision started to draw the glass up and down the inside of her legs, so that it was just making contact with her skin. He felt her body stiffen.

"Just think how much damage I could do down here," he murmured.

He pressed harder with the glass so that it punctured the skin and drew blood. She tried to twist her body away.

"Careful, Patricia. If I slip, it could be really nasty." He dragged the glass lazily back over the inside of her other thigh. "I wonder how you would explain that to your husband. If he ever bothers to look down here, that is."

He leaned forward and licked the trickles of blood away with the tip of his tongue. Then he forced her legs further apart, and prodded a razor-sharp tip of broken glass against the thin white cotton of her underwear, and the vulnerability beneath.

"It's just such a shame that we don't have more time. We really could have a lot of fun."

He pushed the glass against her again, and felt her body go rigid with terror. Then he sighed and placed the glass carefully on the carpet. He lifted himself off her and, making sure that she couldn't strike out at him or kick, he pulled her up and walked her across the room. Stopping to pick up her coat from where it lay on the floor, and to remove the handkerchief from her mouth, he opened the door, checked that nobody was on the stairs, and then marched her quickly down to the ground floor.

When they reached the door at the bottom, he pushed her arm up her back so that she winced in pain. Smiling, he put his mouth next to her ear.

"If you think that what happened to Guy Leighton was impressive, it's nothing compared to what I'll do to you if you start messing up my plans. Now, fuck off. You were right about one thing, she is a bit of class. Real class, Patricia."

He pushed her out of the door and into the night.

Sitting in her convertible on the edge of the car park, Ruth Braebrook wasn't quite sure what she had just seen. She watched as this woman she didn't know turned and stopped, as if she were considering going back into the building after the retreating figure of Toby Malkin. But then she strode to her car, and as she passed beneath a security light, Ruth caught a glimpse of the woman's face. She looked furious. She threw her coat onto the passenger seat and then pulled out of the car park at speed, forgetting to switch the headlights on until another car flashed her as she raced up the road.

Ruth sat and watched Malkin pass in front of a window upstairs. She pushed herself back in her seat. When he disappeared from sight, she turned on the engine and pulled away. Half a mile up the road she stopped and called Malkin's work number, leaving a brief and garbled message about her car having broken down. Then she switched her mobile off and drove home.

TWENTY-EIGHT

The pub was still full of Yates and Wood employees, and Tom Elliott was looking the worse for wear. His hair was dishevelled, the knot of his tie now halfway down his chest.

"Steady on, mate," said one of his colleagues as Tom insisted on buying another round. "It's not a race."

"It's up to you. But I'm getting one in anyway."

Whilst he waited for the barmaid, he looked round for Maria. When he spotted her at the back of the room, he screwed up his eyes in irritation. She wasn't actually kissing the guy, or at least she wasn't when he looked, but they were embracing and his hands were everywhere, and from the way she was laughing it seemed she was quite at ease with this.

Tom left the bar and pushed his way through the crowded pub until he was standing next to her. He reached out and put his hand on her arm.

"We need to talk."

Maria smiled when she saw it was him, but looked confused.

"Are you alright?" she said.

"I'm fine. I just want a word. In private."

"Get lost, Elliott." Maria's companion reached out and placed his hand against Tom's chest. "She doesn't want to talk to you."

Still pushing against Tom, he moved his head forward and tried to kiss Maria.

Tom snapped. "How do you know what she wants?"

He pushed the man's wrist away, and grabbed at him, trying to catch hold of his lapels. In the same moment Maria gripped his arm and spun him round to face her.

"Don't be so stupid," she said. Then turning to the other man, "Can you just give us a minute?"

She led Tom by the hand to the door of the pub and stopped when they reached a small lobby which housed the cigarette machines.

"What's the matter with you?" she said. "I think you should go home. You're making a complete fool of yourself."

"Me? What about you? Do you know what you look like?"

"And it's got anything to do with you?"

Realising his foolishness through the haze of the drink, he bowed his head and leaned forward against the wall. The door which led back into the pub opened and a group of people from Yates and Wood came out. Maria smiled and let them past, then turned back to Tom.

"You're in a right state. How much have you had?"

"I can take it."

"It looks like it." She reached out and moved his face so that she could see his eyes. "I don't know why I'm bothering, I really don't. Come on – let's find you a taxi."

Out on the street, Tom steadied himself. Maria began to walk away from the pub.

"You don't have to do this," he said to her back. "I wouldn't want to keep you from lover boy."

She ignored this and continued walking. He followed.

"Why do you do it, Maria?" he shouted. "Why do you give yourself away?"

She stopped, and waited for him to catch up, but with her back towards him still.

"Will you not say these things, please," she said when they were side by side.

"But can't you see? He's not interested in you."

Maria took a deep breath, and walked on a few steps.

"He only wants a shag."

Maria stopped and turned again. "Do you really think I don't know that?"

"So why do you do it? You just look so cheap. You're better than that."

She screwed her face up and folded her arms across her chest.

"I really, really do not need this. It's easy for you. So easy – you've got everything. A family to support you, somebody who loves you. A future. You really don't understand, do you?"

He didn't move. "You've got somebody who loves you. I do."

She looked at him and met his eyes for a moment. Then she shook her head.

"Don't be silly. You don't mean that."

"Yes I do."

"No."

"You can think what you like. But I know one thing – I respect you, Maria. Unlike that twat back there. He doesn't care for you. Do you know what you look like behaving like the office tramp?"

She moved closer to him and pressed her forehead against his.

"Don't keep saying that," she whispered. "Please."

"I'd care for you, Maria," he said. "I really would."

She closed her eyes. Breathed deep. Then shook her head almost imperceptibly.

"That's so sweet, and I wish it were true. But it's not."

"How do you know?"

"I just do. You'd only end up hurting me."

"But I don't want to hurt you."

"I know you don't, but you would. You think you mean all these things, but you're not going to leave Caroline, are you? That's not what you're saying."

He didn't answer.

"You see?" said Maria. She took his head in both hands and kissed him tenderly on the lips. "Something to remember me by. Now can we go, please? I'm getting cold."

A little later they found themselves on the Market Square. A young girl huddled in a shop doorway with a dirty blanket asked them for change. Tom reached into his pocket and pressed all the money he had – notes and coins – into her hand.

"Now how are you going to get home?" Maria asked.

"I'll walk. I'm used to it."

They moved on. Maria pulled her jacket round her and rubbed her hands together.

"You've gone all quiet," she said. "What's the matter?"

He stopped and turned to face her. "I want to kiss you again. I want to come home with you tonight."

"No."

"Don't say that. I want to be with you so much."

"*No.*"

"Why not? Please, Maria."

"It's because… No, it doesn't matter."

"Tell me why."

She reached out and hugged him, but then she moved away from him and took his hands in hers.

"Tom, I think you're fantastic. I really, really do. We've had some great times together. The best I've ever had. But the thing is – and please don't take this wrong way… No, forget it. We really shouldn't be here saying these things."

"Tell me."

She took a deep breath. "Tom, I just don't feel anything for you...like that. I don't *fancy* you. I can't put it any other way."

He looked dismayed. "And there's supposed to be a right way of taking something like that?"

"I'm sorry. You made me say it. Please don't be upset. You're a wonderful person."

"Obviously not wonderful enough."

"Don't, Tom. When you wake up tomorrow, you'll see things differently. You've got so much going for you. You've got Caroline."

She smiled at him and squeezed his hands, then she turned and walked away. He watched her as she crossed the Market Square. Her pace quickened and she started to run, chasing after a bus and catching up with it seconds before it pulled away. He didn't realise until it was too late that she wasn't going to stop and turn back.

TWENTY-NINE

Alec Shaker took a moment to allow his heartbeat to slow, looking first at Toby Malkin and then at Lewis Cooper. The two men were positioned so that he couldn't see them both at the same time. It was deliberate. Cooper looked solid and serious, small eyes peering out from beneath dark brows in a massive head that reminded Alec of a medicine ball. Malkin had affected a supercilious boredom. *Take your time*, Alec told himself. *You've got all the aces. Use them wisely and the next hour could be the hour that defines you.*

They waited whilst Lewis Cooper's PA served coffee. She seemed to sense the tension – eyes down, whispered questions, the chink of teaspoon on china. If ever a room was designed to crush spirits this was it, and everything in it seemed to speak hushed words to Alec. Imposing, perfect furniture in dark, hard wood said *power*. Intense, original oil paintings of rural English scenes said *money*. Grave groups of golfers in photograph frames, crystal keepsakes from career-advancing deals, ornaments in unison chanting *success*.

Malkin turned to face Alec.

"Well? It's your meeting."

As he had followed Cooper's PA through the building from reception – up several floors in a silent lift made entirely of glass, across vast spaces filled with people sitting before computer screens in endless individual corrals, through security doors, then along a wide corridor with capacious offices in which important-looking executives worked – Alec had thought hard about how to start this meeting.

"I just need to be sure," he said, looking at each man in turn and opening his palms towards them in a gesture he imagined was slightly theatrical. "You've told me on the phone, and in writing as well, that you have nothing to answer for. As far as your use of my client's software is concerned."

"That's right," said Malkin.

"You've looked into the issue, then?"

"Yes."

"Good. So, nothing to hide?"

"Look, Shaker, if you've got something to say, then say it. I don't know about you, but we both have better things to do with our time."

"I asked you a question. Nothing to hide?"

145

Malkin sighed and rolled his eyes. "This is tiresome. We have looked into the very general allegations which you have made in your very generally worded letter – allegations which I would remind you are unsupported by any evidence – and we have found nothing to suggest that they have any foundation."

"So your position remains that you have done nothing wrong with my client's software?"

"Correct. Nothing wrong."

Alec opened a file which lay on the desk in front of him. From it he removed a single document.

"That's interesting," he said. "I wonder, then, what you will make of this."

He cleared his throat and started to read.

12/04/2001
Cape Town

My name is Lesley King. Until March 1997 I was IT controller of Reverie Communications' operation in Nottingham. I have over twenty years' experience in the computer industry. I am making this statement because something which I did when I worked for Reverie Communications has weighed on my mind ever since. It was shameful and unforgivable, and I know that through this statement I may incriminate myself. But however misguided my actions may have been, they were the result of having been put under pressure which I can only describe as intolerable.

To understand the enormity of what I did one needs to understand the importance of data. Data about individuals is one of the most valuable commodities in the modern world. Data is to businesses today what wool and coal were to Britain in the nineteenth century. Any modern company which knows who its customers are, where they live, how much money they earn, what they spend it on, how they pay their bills and many other things besides, but more importantly is able to use all that information intelligently, will be very well placed to succeed.

A few years ago, Reverie Communications was an unbelievable place to work. The Internet was really starting to open up and the business was riding a wave. We were taking on new customers in unprecedented numbers, showing the rest of the industry the way to go. We seemed to be moving into bigger premises every few months and our personnel department did nothing but interview new staff all day every day. Those of us who had been there from the outset had a ball.

146

The company showered us with salary raises, share options, bonuses and cars. We worked hard for it, but we played hard as well. Too hard, in both cases. It is a matter of the greatest regret to me that the pressures of working in an environment such as this led eventually to the break-up of my marriage.

"Greatest regret?" interrupted Malkin. "What a joke! You do realise that Lesley King was an incompetent drunkard who thought that the only reason he had a desk in his office was so that he had something to bend his latest girl from the call centre over?"

"Why don't you listen to the rest of this before you start making comments?" said Alec.

Malkin shaped as if to come back at him, but Alec noticed with a sense of quiet satisfaction a restraining gesture from Lewis Cooper. He continued.

There was another, less appealing side to Reverie. Whilst you continued to succeed you were treated well. But if you slipped up – and whether it was your fault or not – the recriminations were swift and unpleasant. More than once I turned up for work to find that a colleague had been marched out of the building the evening before. But at that time I was doing well and this was not a concern for me.

My job gave me overall responsibility for the company's computer systems. It took me most of my time just to keep up with the rate of expansion, making sure that networks and systems kept running. It was a case of constant firefighting.

But although there was little time to consider strategy, the way in which the company gathered and used its data troubled me. It was all happening too quickly. We had vast seams of information about customers, but it was being collected in an unsystematic way, scattered across the organisation on different computers, managed by different people. It was a problem that was only going to get worse, a real weakness for the future. We needed to address it.

This line of thinking led me to a company called Monte Cristo Software. They were very small, not known in the industry, and they were naive. But they had a world-class product, ideally suited to our needs. Technically it was brilliant. It allowed data from various sources to be combined and integrated without the need to rewrite systems. It could give a complete and intelligently presented picture of everything we knew about any individual or business. I was convinced that this software could save us huge amounts of time and money.

I was very excited about what I had discovered and wanted to install the product as quickly as possible. But Reverie Communications had many other priorities. I knew that in order to persuade the board to release the funds I wanted to invest, I would have to demonstrate the product's worth. So I came to an arrangement with Monte Cristo. This allowed me to take the software on a pilot basis. I would pay a relatively modest fee and have an option to expand our use later. They were in fact so desperate to land a large customer that in return for a slightly higher monthly amount (£3,000), they allowed us the first year without paying anything at all. They also gave me the source code – the valuable underlying code which shows how the software is compiled – so that I could test its compatibility with our systems. Like I said, they were naive.

As ever, events within Reverie Communications overtook me and I never found time to start the pilot scheme. And then everything changed. Reverie had a bad year – for the first time ever it failed to meet its target. The reaction from head office was extreme and Neanderthal. There were redundancies and cost cuttings. Suddenly Reverie Communications was not such a pleasant place to be.

Matters for me came to a head when the company suddenly woke up to the data problems I had foreseen. Despite having no time, no resource and no budget, I was asked to produce a solution to these problems. Our competitors had all got ahead of us. These were very difficult times. My marriage was in trouble and I feared for my job. It was made clear to me that I was drinking in last chance saloon. And so I did something that I will always regret. I stayed in the office late one night and I dug out my copy of the Monte Cristo software. I removed all references to the rightful owners. I dressed it up to make it look as though it was something we'd written ourselves. And the next day I handed it to a team of outside contractors and told them to use it to produce a solution for the whole of Reverie Communications' UK business. Within weeks every one of its seven thousand computers was running software that I had stolen from Monte Cristo and then butchered.

The product worked well and it was easy for somebody in my position to cover my tracks. I told myself that when things improved within Reverie Communications I would go to Monte Cristo and do a deal which would give them a fair return. But I never had this opportunity. In fact things got worse. One of the American businesses in the group needed a similar data solution in a hurry, and they asked the UK to help. I had no choice – I couldn't admit what I had done. And so the *package based on the stolen Monte Cristo software was shipped to the US and installed there.*

Despite the success of these projects, my fate at Reverie Communications appeared to have been sealed. There had already begun what I can only describe as a whispering campaign against me, and a new senior figure seemed to want me out. Before long, the company to which I had given so much pushed me aside.

I am aware that I have acted in a way which is totally unacceptable for somebody with the responsibilities that I enjoyed. I understand that what I did was unlawful, and that it has deprived Monte Cristo Software of substantial revenues. I began my own career in a small boutique company, and I know how hard it can be to get a business like that up and running. Producing this statement has been a difficult experience for me, but I hope that it will assist Monte Cristo in recovering what is rightfully theirs.

There was a long silence. Alec looked first at Lewis Cooper and then at Malkin. He knew how important silence could be at moments like this. He sat back, folded his arms and waited for someone else to speak.

"So, Lesley King's a crook," said Cooper eventually. "Tell me something I don't already know."

"I don't understand your point," said Alec, hamming up the furrowed brow a little.

"Let's just suppose everything you've read out is true. What's it got to do with me?"

"Everything. As Toby will undoubtedly advise you, Reverie Communications will take the legal responsibility for everything that Lesley King did. The liability will be yours. And don't forget we're talking about liability for things which happened in the US as well. I understand they take their liability very seriously over there."

Cooper and Malkin looked at each other.

"We need to talk to Eddie Tomlinson," said Cooper. "Let's take ten minutes."

THIRTY

It wasn't so much what they had taken – they had obviously been looking for cash and jewellery and Maria had little of either. It was all the other things about break-ins which cause distress – the mess, the violation of privacy, the fear. When Maria had arrived home, already drained by the emotions of the evening, she found that her front door had been forced. She had not known what to do. Although she thought it unlikely that anyone would still be in the flat, she hadn't dared to go upstairs.

For a while she sat on a wall on the other side of the road. She thought about going to Tom, but it seemed irresponsible just to leave the scene, and she couldn't cope with any more heaviness tonight. She thought that it might be hours before the police arrived, and so she felt no urgency to report the crime. In the end she roused a woman she knew from a few doors up the street, and persuaded her husband to come with her and check the flat over.

Despite the mess – and they really had trashed the front room – she had gone straight to bed. She had slept for a few hours only and had woken feeling lost and afraid. Finding any enthusiasm to start putting everything back together had been hard, and she kidded herself into thinking that it would be better to leave it until the police had been. Now, whilst Malkin watched Alec Shaker across Lewis Cooper's polished table a few miles outside the city, Maria sat on her sofa talking to a policeman.

"I just get sick of these things happening to me."

"Well I hope you're not expecting us to catch them," said the policeman, sniffing and shaking his head. "But things might improve if you put some better locks on the doors."

"It's going to take a bit more than a few locks to improve things for me."

"Feeling a bit sorry for ourselves are we?"

"Too right we are. If you knew the half of it you'd feel sorry for me too."

They talked for a little longer and the policeman took a statement, and she noticed his comments edging towards the personal. She had no energy for flirting and so she sent him away.

150

Then she began to tidy the flat. As she picked up books and cassettes and sorted through her clothes it occurred to her that it wouldn't be long before she did this again, in preparation for Australia. *Australia –* she said the word out loud and still it didn't seem quite real. She knew she was running away. She had never thought of herself as a loser, it just wasn't the right word for somebody with her energy and ability to enjoy. But that was how she felt. *Although it consumes me, I can't make Toby Malkin pay for what he's done, because he's just too clever for me. Too strong. I would lose. And Tom. I must have hurt him so much.*

And this is where it all started. She picked up a photograph which was lying face down on the carpet. The glass in the frame had smashed when it fell to the floor in a pillaging search for something of more liquid value. Staring out from behind the cracks was an image of her mother – smiling but not at ease. A snapshot from a rare family outing. Sunburnt shoulders and a melting ice cream. *I think I understand why you left Dad, even though I wish so much that you hadn't. But what did I do wrong? How can it ever have been so bad that you never wanted to hear from me again?*

THIRTY-ONE

They took much more than ten minutes. Alec caught glimpses of them through gaps in the blind which covered the glass partition separating Lewis Cooper's office from his conference room. The large man sat at the desk, and from time to time walked round the room. Malkin looked serious and pored over a copy of Lesley King's statement. They both huddled over the speakerphone, presumably talking to Eddie Tomlinson.

Alec tried not to watch too much of this. He helped himself to coffee from a pot on a side table. He was buzzing, delighted at how it had gone so far. But the hardest part was still to come. He sat down, reviewed his notes and waited.

In due course, Malkin and Cooper returned. They positioned themselves in different chairs, so that now they were both directly opposite Alec. Malkin studied Alec carefully before he started to speak.

"We are making no comment on what you've said. At the moment we have no idea whether there's any truth in King's statement."

"Every word of it is true," said Alec. "And Lesley King is prepared to stand up in court and say it all again."

Malkin ignored this. "We will conduct our own investigations. But let's try to be pragmatic about this. Neither of us wants this to be more difficult than it has to be. Leaving aside all the rights and wrongs, leaving aside what may or may not have happened to this software, let's talk sensibly. You would only be here if you were looking for money. You must have some sort of financial settlement in mind. It would help us if you could give us some indication of what that figure is."

Alec took a controlled breath and looked at each man in turn. How best to manage the expectation?

"Before I answer that," he said, "I want you to understand just how my clients feel. You need to be clear that this isn't some speculative punt. This is for real. Monte Cristo are very, very upset, and their case is very, very strong."

"What's the figure?" asked Lewis Cooper.

"I'm not finished yet. I want to remind you of one thing that Lesley King said. This is about data, and that data could be a gold mine to you."

"What's the figure?"

Look them in the eye as you say it, Ritchie Ripley had told him.

"Five million pounds. And you remove all the software."

Cooper looked genuinely shocked. Malkin was a little slower to react, but first to speak.

"You can't be serious."

"We're deadly serious."

Lewis Cooper laughed a hollow, bellowing laugh. "I can't have a discussion around that sort of figure. The software itself can't be worth anything like that."

"The figure," said Alec, his voice taut with emotion, "is five million pounds."

"Get real, man!" roared Cooper. He made a backhanded swipe at the papers in front of him, scattering them across the desk. "You can't justify that. I thought…" He glanced at Malkin. "…this was a dispute about a few hundred thousand at most."

Alec sat statue-like, steeling himself to tough this out.

"Well you were wrong. And you want to know how I justify a figure like that? Easy. I justify it because this software represents a lifetime's work to the people who created it. They risked everything – livelihoods, homes, everything. I justify it because Reverie Communications in its gleaming offices makes millions of pounds in profits *every day*. I am not going to let you sit here making even more on the back of somebody else's effort. And I justify it because by anybody's standards what Reverie Communications has done is an outrage. Misuse of software is one thing – it happens all the time. But to take something knowingly and to do what Lesley King did is on another level. Reverie Communications forced him into that position, Reverie Communications didn't have the systems to stop him, and Reverie Communications should pay."

"Don't give me that bullshit! You're dreaming. I don't have to listen to this."

"Yes you do! You may not listen today. You may not listen tomorrow. But one day you will have to listen." He turned and looked at Malkin. "And, Toby, you know that. You can sit there now looking smug, but you know exactly where this is all going to end."

Alec looked back at Cooper. He was shaking, and looked as if he were about to start shouting again. Malkin reached out and put his hand on his arm.

"Alec," said Malkin, with one eye on his client, "can we step back from this for a moment? Can we try to bring this discussion into the real world? You don't need me to tell you what a struggling little company like Monte Cristo would have to do to get that sort of money out of an organisation the size of Reverie Communications. Even if you had the best case in the world. We would have no choice – we would have to fight you every step of the way, make it as difficult for you as possible, drag it on for years and years. For every expert you field to support your case, we can field three. For every barrister you hire, we can hire two. Your clients can't afford the fees and they can't afford the time. You know any litigation is a lottery. Why don't you make a sensible suggestion?"

"I have made a sensible suggestion. You can interpret it as you like. We are deadly serious. Not only will we take you to the highest court in the land, we will have your name splashed all over the press, we will contact all your other suppliers, we will involve the police if need be. If you want to fight dirty, Toby, we are more than ready."

Lewis Cooper sat seething, and looked to his lawyer for a response. But for once there was no withering comment, no acerbic put-down. Alec decided it was time to be gone.

It was more than two hours before Toby Malkin left Lewis Cooper's office. He left in the company of Eddie Tomlinson, who had been hauled in to take part in the discussion that had followed Alec's departure. The two men walked in silence. Eddie's face was pale – he looked distant and in shock. Malkin seemed much less concerned. They travelled down in the lift to the reception and stopped, ready to go their separate ways.

"Well that was pretty spectacular," said Malkin in a low voice. "The famous Cooper temper. He's vicious, isn't he? When he really gets going."

"*Five million pounds?*" said Eddie "It's crazy. Total madness."

"Keep your voice down, Tomlinson." Malkin spoke through clenched teeth. "It's important to aim high."

"I can't go on with it. I just can't."

Malkin took Eddie by the arm and guided him through the reception area, smiling at the security guard as he did.

154

"Pull yourself together," he muttered when they were outside the building. "I'm sure you don't want me to remind you what your alternatives are. Anyway, that's the difficult bit done. For you, at least."

THIRTY-TWO

From: Ritchie Ripley (Ritchie@montecristo.com)
To: Alec Shaker (ashaker@dwsolicitors.co.uk)
Re: Meeting with RevCom.
Thanks for the report, Al. It really sounds like you did great. I've just got a feeling (but I can't tell you why) that these guys <u>will</u> pay us something.

Let me know as soon as you hear more. I have to be honest with you, we need cash fast. I'm out here in the US trying to persuade our American backers to keep investing. I haven't told them too much about the situation with RevCom, and if you can pull a rabbit out of a hat for us here it could mean so much. It really could be the difference between survival and going under.

Keep going, Al. We're depending on you!

R

From: Toby Malkin (toby.malkin@yateswood.co.uk)
To: Lewis Cooper (Lewis.Cooper@RevCom.com)
Monte Cristo
Lewis,

You will have seen Eddie Tomlinson's report. As we suspected, it confirms that what Shaker said the other day is largely true.

We really don't have much to play with here. Monte Cristo's case is more or less watertight and I think they will sue – you saw how fired up Shaker was. If they do, we lose control of the process. That would be bad news. We have to avoid that happening. We need to start talking to them. Bluffing would be dangerous.

My instinct tells me they will settle, and for a lot less than £5 million. I've also thought that we might come at this from another angle. Instead of treating it as a <u>dispute</u>, we could position it as an <u>investment</u>. If we try to buy the rights to do what Lesley King has done, and the right to do the same in the future, this could look like a far-sighted step to secure a vital asset. It would preserve RevCom's reputation. There would be no need for people to know exactly how much trouble Lesley King had created. It would be a thoroughly sensible business decision.

Let me know what you think.

I should stress again the need to keep this confidential – involve your people on a need-to-know basis only.

Toby

From: Lewis Cooper (Lewis.Cooper@RevCom.com)
To: Toby Malkin (toby.malkin@yateswood.co.uk)
Re: Monte Cristo

Like I said on the phone, I'm still finding this difficult. But I guess the investment idea's a good one – it probably means I don't need to have it cleared at global level.

Talk to the guy. See what sort of deal he's prepared to do. The last thing I want is any disruption to the business.

LC

From: Toby Malkin (toby.malkin@yateswood.co.uk)
To: Ruth Braebrook (ruth.braebrook@yateswood.co.uk)
Dublin

We really <u>must</u> get together for a proper debriefing on what happened in Dublin. Such a shame that you didn't make it the other night. I'm looking forward to us being able to work together again soon. You performed so well when we were in Ireland, I think it's only right you should get the chance to do it all again as soon as possible. Lots of lawyers talk about it, but there are only a few who really can keep going all night like you did!!!

I think an off-site meeting would be best. Let me know when would be convenient.

TM

From: Alec Shaker (ashaker@dwsolicitors.co.uk)
To: Ritchie Ripley (Ritchie@montecristo.com)
Reverie Communications

The good news. Toby Malkin asked me for a meeting and came along as humble as you like and offered to settle. No posturing, no rudeness. RevCom want to be creative about it and buy a backdated licence of the software (the legal equivalent of a total absolution of their sins). It's a neat idea.

The bad news. They're offering £750,000 and a vague promise to buy more from you in future.

I said the figure was too low. Let's see what they come back with.

Regards,

Alec

From: Toby Malkin (toby.malkin@yateswood.co.uk)
To: Alec Shaker (ashaker@dwsolicitors.co.uk)
Monte Cristo
Without prejudice or admission of liability

Alec,

My clients are disappointed that you were not able to accept the offer put to you this morning. Nevertheless, Reverie Communications is eager that this should be resolved quickly, provided the figure is sensible. We are therefore prepared to increase the offer to £1.2 million.

I look forward to hearing from you.

Toby Malkin

From: Ritchie Ripley (Ritchie@montecristo.com)
To: Alec Shaker (ashaker@dwsolicitors.co.uk)
Re: Settlement Discussions

How's the weather over there? It's lousy here. The worst April in California for fifty years, apparently. Just my luck.

The increased offer is great but this will go to 2 mil. If I think back to where we were when we met in Rome, I can't believe I'm saying that now. But, Al, we need to resolve this quickly. The people here are saying that we have another month or so to convince them not to pull the plug. How quickly we get the money is almost as important as the final amount. I'm happy for you to negotiate whatever you can – it's going to be difficult to track me down over the next couple of days.

If this all works out, I want to arrange for you to go away somewhere nice. Rome again, perhaps. Take the family if you like (unless you want to catch up with the lovely Claudia!). No expense spared for the man who saved Monte Cristo.

R

From: Alec Shaker (ashaker@dwsolicitors.co.uk)
To: Toby Malkin (toby.malkin@yateswood.co.uk
Re: Monte Cristo
Without prejudice.

Toby,

My advice to my clients remains that they should seek recovery of the full £5 million. However, they are reasonable people. In order to avoid the inconvenience of court action, they would be prepared to accept settlement on the basis of a licence fee of £3.75 million.

Alec Shaker

From: Toby Malkin (toby.malkin@yateswood.co.uk)
To: Alec Shaker (ashaker@dwsolicitors.co.uk)
Re: Monte Cristo
<u>Without prejudice</u>
Alec,

Your offer is a step in the right direction. But RevCom have had their auditors look at this and they value the licence at no more than £1.5 million. They will add a further £300,000 as a gesture of goodwill. That makes a total of £1.8 million.

We think this is generous and would urge you to consider it very carefully.

Toby

From: Alec Shaker (ashaker@dwsolicitors.co.uk)
To: Toby Malkin (toby.malkin@yateswood.co.uk
Re: Monte Cristo
<u>Without prejudice.</u>
Valuation of these things is an imprecise science. We couldn't possibly accept less than £3 million.

Alec

From: Toby Malkin (toby.malkin@yateswood.co.uk)
To: Alec Shaker (ashaker@dwsolicitors.co.uk)
Re: Monte Cristo
<u>Without prejudice or admission of liability</u>
Alec,

With great reluctance, my clients have agreed to increase their offer to £2,100,000. It's around this figure that they start wondering if they may as well take their chance in court.

Toby

From: Alec Shaker (ashaker@dwsolicitors.co.uk)
To: Toby Malkin (toby.malkin@yateswood.co.uk)
Re: Monte Cristo
<u>Without prejudice.</u>
Your clients have no chance in court. But if this can be done in the next 7 days we will take £2.7m.

Alec

From: Toby Malkin (toby.malkin@yateswood.co.uk)
To: Ruth Braebrook (ruth.braebrook@yateswood.co.uk)
Dublin (2)
Ruth,
I need to hear from you on my previous e-mail as a matter of urgency.
Speak to me soonest.
T

From: Toby Malkin (toby.malkin@yateswood.co.uk)
To: Alec Shaker (ashake@dwsolicitors.co.uk)
Re: Monte Cristo
Without prejudice or admission of liability
Alec,
We'll split the difference. £2.4 million, paid within 7 days. Final
offer.
Toby

From: Alec Shaker (ashaker@dwsolicitors.co.uk)
To: Toby Malkin (toby.malkin@yateswood.co.uk)
Re: Monte Cristo
Without prejudice.
Done.
Alec Shaker

From: Becky Hardcastle (Becky.Hardcastle@RevCom.com)
To: Toby Malkin (toby.malkin@yateswood.co.uk)
Cannes
Dear Mr Malkin,
Lewis says that the transfer of the money has had all the necessary
internal approvals.

He has also received a last-minute invitation to a conference in Nice
next week. He has a spare afternoon on Wednesday, and would like to
go to Cannes to visit Monte Cristo Software and shake hands on the
new deal. Could you please let me have their address and a contact
name? Also, would you be available to join Lewis?
Many thanks,
Becky Hardcastle
PA to Lewis Cooper

From: Toby Malkin (toby.malkin@yateswood.co.uk)
To:BeckyHardcastle(Becky.Hardcastle@RevCom.com)
Re: Cannes

Becky,

There seems to have been a bit of a crossed wire – probably my mistake. Monte Cristo Software are actually based in Caen in Normandy, not Cannes. I would be grateful if you would let Lewis know. But I will have a word with Alec Shaker and suggest that a meeting some time in the future could be a good idea.

Thanks,

Toby

THIRTY-THREE

It took Malkin and Alec Shaker three or four days to sort out the legal documentation which would govern the deal they had struck. In other circumstances it could have taken weeks, but Alec was in no mood now for confrontation or unnecessary difficulty, and he found that Malkin apparently felt the same. He kept in touch with Ritchie Ripley, although his client seemed to lose interest once the numbers had been agreed.

"I'll leave all the heretos and aforesaids to you, Al. I've got to visit a client in Germany."

When the contracts were finalised, Alec e-mailed them to Ritchie and shortly afterwards received signed pages back by fax, sent from a hotel in Frankfurt. He called Malkin, who confirmed that Reverie Communications had signed as well. The two lawyers exchanged their various pages, again by fax, and then Malkin authorised the electronic transfer from Yates and Wood's account to Dobson White's of the two million four hundred thousand pounds which had come in from Reverie Communications the day before. In accordance with Ritchie Ripley's careful instructions, Alec then deducted the very modest amount which represented the balance of his fees and sent the rest of the money on to a Monte Cristo account. The bulk of the money was in Alec's hands for less than an hour.

And that was it. Deal done. Sitting in his office, with its chairs in need of re-upholstering and the cases of law books which were stored there because Dobson White had no room for a proper library, Alec regretted that technology made the conclusion of so many deals these days such an anticlimax. It was a shame, because Alec's delight was intense. It was for moments like this that he had come into the law – moments when it was clear that he was succeeding in his ambition always to be a better lawyer. Moments like this were much dreamed about but infrequently experienced. He wanted people to shake his hand and ask him how he had pulled off such a stunning victory against all the odds. He wanted to overhear people whispering that he was indeed the man who had saved Monte Cristo Software.

But there was none of this. It was as if the world had already forgotten what he had done, and moved on. Alec couldn't relax today, couldn't concentrate on any other work. In the end, he put on his jacket and walked down the road to a bakery where he bought himself and his secretary each a cream bun.

On the other side of the city, Toby Malkin also sat reflecting on the outcome of the deal. Not for him were there thoughts about signing ceremonies or pressing flesh. The lawyer in him struggled briefly against a resentment at being on the losing side. But it didn't matter. On the failure of Reverie Communications to resist the Monte Cristo claim was built a much greater personal success.

The planning and the execution had been perfect. *You've done well, Toby. Very well.* A good mother loves each of her children differently, but with equal strength. She will understand and allow for their individual needs. Malkin had applied the same attention to all those he had manipulated, finding exactly the right way to make each one do his bidding.

He was proud of what he had done. He hoped that one day he would be able to tell at least one person the whole story. And he knew exactly who that person was. A dark-haired woman sitting in an office in Birmingham who seemed to be avoiding him now. After the displacement of Guy Leighton, after the fortune he had just made, she was the only thing left that he still needed.

Malkin put these thoughts to one side – but only for now – and with a sense of ironic satisfaction he went to his computer. He pressed a button, typed in some details and instructed the system to draw up a bill for the time he had spent losing the battle with Monte Cristo Software.

THIRTY-FOUR

They were such little things. Things of no importance. Not considered, not pondered. And yet, if one – just one – had been otherwise…

If Alec Shaker had parked his car somewhere else; if the family had chosen to see another film at another time; if the waiter had been a little quicker or slower to serve them; if one of them had chosen something which took longer to prepare; if Samantha hadn't insisted that the children all visit the toilet whilst Alec paid the bill; if the rain had drifted in from the west a little sooner and sent them scurrying on with their heads bowed; if Alec's daughter hadn't asked that they go past the Robin Hood statue on their way back to the car; if the streets had been busier so that they had kept the children by their sides.

If … if … if. *If only.* If any one of these things, or a hundred others like them, had been very slightly different, it might have been as effective in averting what was to follow as the clued-up, tooled-up superhero in the film they had just seen.

As the Shaker family crossed Maid Marian Way, Alec put his arm round Samantha. The children ran on ahead, up a narrow street from which traffic was banned, pretending to be characters from the film. Located on this street was a restaurant – one of the city's best – in a building with a small courtyard in front of it, and in order to escape her chasing brothers, Alec's daughter turned off the street and ran across the courtyard. Her elder brother stopped and looked back at his parents, seeking with his expression permission to proceed. But the youngest child followed his sister regardless, and there in front of the restaurant a fight broke out.

"Pipe down, you two," said Alec as he jogged up the street. He turned into the courtyard and walked towards them. "People don't want to hear your squabbling."

"But he pushed me."

"No I didn't!"

"Yes you did!"

"Come on," said Alec, his voice persuading rather than rebuking. "Let's not spoil a lovely evening."

The two children were standing beneath a large window. Alec knew that this was one of the restaurant's private rooms. He crouched down and put an arm round each child. At exactly the same time, a waiter started to draw heavy curtains across the window. He did it with one decisive action. The movement caught Alec's eye, and he looked up. In the moment before the two pieces of material were brought together, he caught a glimpse of the scene inside the room. He checked himself and looked again. But then the curtains met and what he had seen was gone.

"What's the matter, Daddy?" his daughter asked.

He didn't answer, but took each child by the hand and walked away. As the three of them reached the entrance to the courtyard, Alec turned and looked back. He stared at the now dark window as if by sheer willpower he could see through the curtains and into the room. What he had just seen was beyond all understanding. He considered going into the restaurant to check that it was not some unbelievable trick of the light, but a vague, English desire not to make a fuss held him back.

He turned away and rejoined his wife. The little group made its way towards the car. As they walked, the first spots of rain began to fall.

Forty miles north-west of Nottingham, in the Derbyshire hills, it was already raining, and had been for hours. Swept across open moors in almost horizontal sheets, the water penetrated every inch of the landscape, dripping from rocks, soaking into bogs, washing through gullies and ditches. Little hilltop trickles which in drier times flowed unseen amongst pebbles and grasses swelled, and tumbled their contents into a thousand thirsty brooks. Pulled ever downwards, with the inevitability of death, the water flowed from the hills into the rivers of the valleys below, giving them anger and strength.

Over the coming days the rain would continue and the rivers would run with relentless, increasing power, pushing at their banks like caged animals testing the bars of their confinement. The rain would turn roads into waterways. The dark hills would visit upon the lower ground the unwanted gift of floods. And the Trent – the unremarkable, prosaic Trent – would be stirred from its normal muddy torpor and transformed into something different, something murderous and mighty.

THIRTY-FIVE

Toby Malkin discovered – by snooping in her online diary and asking subtle questions of her colleagues – that Ruth Braebrook liked to visit the gym early on Sundays. He knew where she went, and he knew what time she went there. Not long after daybreak on this wettest of mornings, the brand-new Jaguar, which was one of the accessories of his elevation, was parked a discreet distance from the junction at the end of her road.

He sat pretending to read a paper, and listening to some appropriately sacred music, before he saw her red convertible appear. She glanced in each direction and then turned. Waiting until she was almost out of sight, he started his car and followed.

He drove with care, keeping Ruth always in view, but never directly in front of him. She didn't seem to be aware that he was following. They crossed the city centre and made their way into a smart suburb on the other side of the river. As Ruth turned into the entrance of her health club, Malkin's Jaguar came quietly to a halt on a side street nearby. He watched her climb out of the car, and raised his eyebrows with lascivious interest as she reached back in to take out a sports bag. Like a security camera recording every detail, he tracked her with impassive eyes as she crossed the car park and headed up the steps into the building.

It would take her about ten minutes to change and start exercising, he imagined. To be safe, he waited twenty before he started his engine again and moved the car slowly forward and into the car park. He found a space at the bottom of the steps, and reversed in to it.

Persuading the staff on the reception desk to let him through was easy. He told them he was thinking of becoming a member and wanted to look round, and he went through the motions of a cursory tour of the premises, before finding a seat in the lounge from which, unseen by her, he could watch Ruth whilst she exercised.

When she emerged from the changing rooms dressed in boot-cut jeans with her hair wet and her bag slung over her shoulder, Malkin ducked his head and let her go past. Then he stood up and followed. He needed there to be other people about and he was lucky. As he caught up with Ruth just outside the building, a family group with children and tennis racquets was disembarking from a people carrier at the bottom of the steps. Malkin quickened his pace, then reached out and took hold of Ruth's arm.

"Darling!" he said in a loud voice. "You've taken for ever. Come on – we're going to be late."

She turned to look at him. Disorientated, she allowed herself to be guided down the steps. He moved her to one side to allow the family to pass, smiling and rolling his eyes at one of the adults.

"Busy, busy, busy," he said. "You know what it's like."

He hurried Ruth down to the car, gripping her arm tightly now. Before she had chance to resist he had manoeuvred her into the passenger seat and was climbing in beside her. He started the engine and pulled off at speed.

"What the hell are you doing?" asked Ruth, rubbing her arm.

"I'm sorry," he said as he powered the car round a corner. "You don't give me any choice."

"Where are we going?"

"Somewhere quiet."

He drove back across the city centre and began to weave his way through the deserted roads of an industrial estate not far from the racecourse, until he turned into the forecourt of a large factory – a run-down, shabby-looking place – and parked the car at the back next to a loading bay which couldn't be seen from the main road. Then he turned off the engine and moved round to look at Ruth.

"Toby, I really don't like this. Please tell me why we're here."

He studied her without saying anything, then lifted his hand and touched the side of her face. He leaned forward to kiss her.

"No. Please don't." She turned her head away.

He caressed her cheek, then her hair, with a lingering touch before taking his hand away.

"Sorry about the abduction, but it's fantastic to see you," he said. "I've got something for you."

Keeping his eyes fixed on her, Malkin reached into the back of the car. On the parcel shelf behind lay the coloured box from the shop in Rome, with its extravagant pink ribbon. He picked it up and handed it to Ruth.

"This is hardly the setting I imagined," he said, glancing at the back of the factory. "But I wanted you to have something to know how much what happened in Dublin meant to me. It seems so long ago now. We've got a lot of catching up to do."

He placed the box in her lap.

She looked at it and shook her head slowly. "No. I can't. I'm very touched, but I can't."

"Open it, Ruth."

"It wouldn't be right. I wanted to…"

"Open it."

The words were spoken robotically. She paused, as if weighing up the relative risks of compliance and resistance. Then slowly she began to pull at the ribbon, her hands shaking slightly, her lips pursed. When the knot was undone she looked sideways at Malkin, then quickly away again. She lifted the lid from the box, and peeled back the rustling tissue paper to reveal the dress. She stared at it, and touched the material with her fingers. Then, making an effort to take control of her breathing, she placed the lid back on the box.

"It's beautiful – very beautiful – and I know it's going to make you angry, but I can't accept it."

"Yes you can. You'll look fantastic in it."

"No."

This time there was nothing caressing about his hand on her face. He gripped the line of her jaw with finger and thumb as if it were a paper cup that he could crush, and pulled her round so that she had to look at him. Her eyes were wide.

"Stop it, Toby. You're making me scared."

He gripped her face more tightly still.

"You cannot treat me like this," he said, his nostrils flaring. "The last time you spoke to me with any decency we were making love. Doesn't that count for anything? You've done nothing but ignore me ever since. You didn't even come to the flat when you said you would."

"Let go," she said, her voice little more than a whimper. "I can explain."

He held her head still for a moment, then dropped his hand.

"Go on."

Ruth touched the place where his grip had been strongest. She turned and stared ahead at the misted-up windscreen with the rivulets of rain running down it. When she spoke, her face was expressionless.

"I'm not going to pretend that I didn't enjoy what we did in Dublin. You made me feel very special. But it was wrong. It's not an excuse, and I hate myself for it, but I thought that Dominic was having an affair. That's why I let it happen between us. But the thing is, I think you encouraged me to believe that."

"No I didn't. And how do you know that he wasn't, anyway?"

"Because we've spoken about it."

"You've told him about us?"

She hesitated.

"I'll take that as a no, then."

"Toby, I have spoken to Dominic about what I thought. He was behaving strangely, but he's explained why. There are other problems. Work problems. And I have decided that we are going to make something of our marriage. I will have to find a way of living with what I've done, and that will be very, very hard. But this is the right decision to make."

"So I'm just some sort of sorry mistake?"

"You're making this very difficult for me."

"Oh please forgive me," he said. "Why didn't you say anything to me sooner? You've led me on."

"That's unfair. I never made any promises. You must have been to bed with lots of women."

"Not anybody like you."

"There's nothing special about me. We're both adults. We make decisions – some right, some wrong. You and I don't owe each other anything."

He gripped the steering wheel with both hands, his knuckles standing out like white stones.

"I don't accept this," he said.

"What do you mean?"

"I'm not accepting your decision."

"Toby, it's not a question of *accepting* it. You don't get to choose. I'm sorry – we both have to put it behind us." She put her hands in her lap and nodded as if she believed that the discussion was over. "Now will you take me back to my car? Please."

"Look at all this!" he shouted, indicating with a sudden and angry gesture the scene outside. "This crappy weather in this crappy city with all its crappy people. Like your crappy fucking husband. How can you possibly want to stay here with him? He's a loser, Ruth. You should be with somebody like me. That's the *right* decision to make. We can go away together. Somewhere warm – we can drink champagne every lunchtime and make love every afternoon. I've got the money – more money than we could ever need. We can go now."

"No, Toby. It isn't going to happen."

"It has to," he said through gritted teeth. "I have to leave. Very soon. You have to come with me."

"I don't know what you're talking about."

"OK." The effort he was making to restrain himself was visible. "I know that I haven't been very attentive since we got back from Dublin. You probably feel neglected. But you've not been around and I've been very busy. I've got time now – all the time in the world. I can make it all up to you."

"There's nothing *to* make up. What I'm saying, what you don't seem to understand, is that you and I are something that happened, not something that's carrying on. I want you to take me back now."

Malkin had stopped listening. He was very still and his eyes were closed. He looked to be in a trance. But then, like the birth of a wave in the depths of the ocean, something started to stir and swell within him. Something consuming, something powerful. His face contorted and he breathed the deepest of breaths, drawing on everything inside himself to fight a battle with himself. It was a battle of and for control. Then he snapped.

"NO!" he bellowed, his clenched and quivering fists beating at the air. "NO, NO, NO!"

With violent movements he started the car and put it into gear. The engine spat and roared as he revved it hard, the tyres screeching as he pulled forward. He turned the car on the tightest of circles and then accelerated across the concrete apron of the factory, heading straight towards a wall on the other side. With the spray and the rain it was difficult for Ruth to see what was happening, but she was sure that they would hit the wall. She screamed. At the last moment Malkin threw his weight at the brakes and turned the car, bringing it to a halt. But then they were off again, back in the direction they had come from, heading for the factory this time. Again the car swerved and stopped, again it accelerated away, repeating the process time and again.

"Stop it!" screamed Ruth. "You're going to kill us."

Then Malkin took the car out onto the main road. He drove like a madman, like a man possessed, back across the river, swerving inside and outside other drivers, slowing only when his bumper was inches from a car in front. Ruth put her head in her hands and begged him to stop, but it had no effect. He drove across red lights, took corners on two wheels. When he pulled into the car park of the health club he missed another vehicle by no more than a coat of paint.

He drew up by Ruth's car. When she realised it was over, Ruth looked at him in horror.

"You're crazy," she said.

"When I want something, Ruth, I get it. I've got everything else I need now. Everything apart from you. You may not realise it, but

there is no way, no way at all, you are staying with Dominic. I will not
let it happen."

THIRTY-SIX

By mid-afternoon the reception was in full swing. The speeches were made and the cake had been cut and now it was time for the dancing.

"There's a great atmosphere in here," Maria said to Tom. "The families obviously get on."

They were sitting by themselves at a long table with a heavy white cloth, on which there were crumbs and wine glass stains. The cutlery and crockery had all been cleared away. The flowers which decorated the tables had been left.

"I love weddings," said Tom. "It's the best sort of party."

"It will be you and Caroline soon. And she certainly seems to be having a ball."

They looked over to the crowd of people jigging and jiving in front of the band on the stage. The wedding and the reception had been held in an old stone building in the grounds of a country manor house, and they were now in a large airy room decked out in yellow and white. Caroline was dancing with one of the partners from the department where the bride worked. He was slightly overweight with very little hair, and they both danced with stilted movements. They were having fun.

"She seems to feel comfortable with men like that," said Tom. "You know, dignified and successful. Even if they are ugly."

"Like you one day – apart from the ugly bit."

"Thanks very much."

"You will be."

"You were the one who said I wasn't enough of a bastard to make it as a lawyer. So what's changed?"

"I say a lot of things I don't really mean."

Tom swirled the ice round in the bottom of his glass and then drained it. Maria bobbed her head to the beat of the music.

"I'm glad you were here today," said Tom. "And I'm glad we managed to make up. I would have hated for you to go away just remembering what happened that time on the Market Square. I wasn't as upset as you thought."

Underneath the table Maria reached out and squeezed his hand.

"I'll remember lots more about you than that," she said. "But please, nothing heavy today – it never does us any good. We don't need too much *talkin'* and *thinkin'*." She spoke in the mock Karen Carpenter accent and withdrew her hand.

"So when are you actually *travellin'*?" Tom asked, laughing.

"Next Saturday. Just think, one more week of Yates and Wood, one more week of Toby bloody Malkin, and it's sunny Sydney here I come."

"I was *wonderin'*, have you thought about what happened to Guy Leighton any more?"

She pulled a face. "Not really. I thought perhaps I should write a letter or something – you know, to Hugo Sanderson, just telling him what I suspect. But you're right. When you sit down and think about it, we never really had any evidence. And I wouldn't want to drag you into anything. You've still got your career to think about. We all need to move on."

"You seem to have lost all your anger about what Malkin did."

"No, I haven't. I've just learned to hide it better."

"I wish we'd never fallen out about that. It was my fault."

"No regrets, Tom. Let's remember the good things."

She smiled and squeezed his arm, above the table this time.

"Are you still looking forward to going?" he asked.

She stiffened slightly. "What? Like anybody wouldn't be? It's going to be brilliant, really brilliant – I just know it. Why do you ask?"

"No reason."

Tom leaned forward and placed his glass on the table. He started to play with the flower arrangement in front of him, teasing a single primrose out from the green oasis, taking care to make sure that each of its petals remained in tact. Whilst Maria carried on bobbing to the music he tore from the base of the arrangement a small sheet of tin foil and wrapped it tight around the stalk of the flower. He took a strip of tinsel from a spent party popper, tied it round the foil and laid his creation down on the white tablecloth.

"What are you doing?" asked Maria.

"It's for Caroline. Primroses are her favourite flower."

Maria looked at him and shook her head.

"What?" he said.

"You are just so unbelievably sweet sometimes."

The band reached the end of a number and everybody clapped. The clarinettist nodded a beat to the drummer and they were off again, a louder, foot-tapping tune this time. The movements of the dancers became more frenetic. Tom clasped his hands between his knees and leaned forward over the table, huddled as if he was cold.

173

"Look," he said, "I know you didn't want anything heavy. But I just wanted to say thank you."

"Thank you? What for?"

"For not letting anything happen between us. I think it could have done, even if you never, you know, really felt that way about me. But you've helped me see how important what I've got with Caroline is. We're going to have a nice life together. I'm sure of it."

He stared at Maria as if he longed to say something else, but she made a tiny, complicit nod to indicate something behind him. He looked round and saw Caroline walking towards them. She was with her dancing partner, laughing and looking up at him. The two of them stood and talked for a few minutes, whilst Tom and Maria sat in their chairs like children told to be seen but not heard. Then Caroline looked over her shoulder at Tom. She made a small beckoning gesture with her fingers.

"We're going," she said. Then she narrowed her eyes at Maria and forced a smile. "I don't suppose I'll see you again. Enjoy the Antipodes."

She picked her handbag up from the chair next to Tom and strode off. He shrugged and stood up. He looked at the retreating figure of his fiancée, as purposeful in making this little exit as in everything else she did. He picked up the primrose from the table and rotated it between his fingers.

"I would offer you a lift," he said. "But…"

"I understand."

Tom shrugged again and made as if to follow Caroline. Then he stopped. He turned and gave the flower to Maria.

174

What Alec Shaker had seen the night before caused him to be awake very early that Sunday morning. He tried to lie still whilst he turned it over in his mind, but at around dawn his restlessness disturbed Samantha.

"What is it?" she demanded, pulling the duvet up around her. "Why are you awake?"

"It's nothing. I can't sleep, that's all. I'm going downstairs."

"Try not to wake the kids."

In the kitchen, he made tea and sat watching the faltering daybreak. Here he could be a little more rational, and although he could think of no convincing explanation for the scene he had glimpsed in the restaurant the night before, he tried to persuade himself that there must *be* an explanation. But before he could put his thoughts in any sort of order, the first of the children came downstairs and amid the amiable chaos of a morning in the Shaker household he became distracted from his worrying.

After the family had been to church and eaten lunch together, Alec sent Sam to lie down whilst he cleared away from the meal. The children were all playing happily. There was a little tradition between Alec and his wife that when he had finished washing up on a Sunday he would go upstairs to join her on the bed. They would kiss and cuddle. If he was tired, they might doze. Just occasionally, if the children were engrossed in a video or a game, they would lock the bedroom door and, feeling thrilled by their daring, Alec and Sam would make furtive, giggling love.

Today Alec went upstairs as normal, and as he leaned over Sam, she reached up to pull him into a sleepy embrace. He resisted, not allowing himself to be drawn towards her. Instead he kissed her lightly on the forehead.

"Sweetheart, I'm sorry about this, but I have to go to the office. There's something I have to do before tomorrow. It shouldn't take long."

He left the room before she woke sufficiently to protest.

When he arrived at Dobson White's offices, the little car park was of course deserted. Cursing the incessant rain as he fumbled with the keys, he unlocked the heavy front door and let himself in. The building

175

felt cold and a little damp, and before he began doing what he had come to do, he fetched an electric fan-heater from the room where his secretary worked. Whilst his office began to warm up, he cleared his desk of everything, moving all the papers he had left there on Friday evening to the floor. Then he sat down and placed in front of him the Monte Cristo Software file.

He had decided that he would go through everything from beginning to end, and that as he did he would write a summary of what had happened. He read and reread every letter, file note and e-mail, filling in the gaps from his own memories, taking care to add details to his summary only if he was absolutely sure that his recollections were accurate. Whilst he worked he tried to keep his mind free of fear or suspicion. He wanted to be scientific, to see if the facts themselves would speak to him.

He worked for more than two hours. By the time he had finished, he had several pages of scribbled notes. A premature darkness was beginning to invade the room. He stood up and walked to the window, pulling the threadbare curtains back as far as they would go. For a minute or two he lingered by the window and looked out at the garden, green and beautiful even in this dreadful weather.

Then he returned to his chair and switched on the desk lamp. He picked up his summary and read it out loud, stopping only to make a slight correction here, an embellishment there. He could see that Monte Cristo Software was an unusual client – for him, at least – but he knew that already. And there was nothing wrong with being unusual. The case itself was fairly straightforward. Monte Cristo had turned out to have compelling, well-supported arguments. Reverie Communications had behaved as you would expect, resisting the claim until he, Alec, had made it very clear that it was serious and would be pursued. Once they had accepted that they were going to have to pay, they had negotiated. And when the settlement came, it was linked to a creative solution of the sort you would look to a lawyer like Toby Malkin to provide.

One thing that did stand out was his evening with Claudia in Italy. A sorry tale, certainly. But anything more? He couldn't see how. No one else knew what had happened, or indeed not happened. Nothing had come of it. It was conceivable that the girl had been offered to him in a language he didn't understand as some sort of corporate gift, and he wondered if such things were more common than he imagined. But that was all.

He tossed the summary onto the desk and leaned back in his chair. What was he missing? What couldn't he see? Everything seemed to be as it should. But he knew there must be something wrong. How else could you explain three things which had happened in the fortnight since the dispute had been resolved?

The first was a frustrated, angry e-mail from Ritchie Ripley, thanking him for this efforts, but telling him that it had all come to nothing. The money Alec had helped win had been pocketed gleefully by Monte Cristo's backers, who had then cut their links with the company, leaving it to go to the wall. Ritchie was owed three months' salary and was bailing out now before things got worse.

The second was a slightly garbled voice message he had received from Eddie Tomlinson of Reverie Communications a few days later, saying that he had heard some terrible news on the industry grapevine. Ritchie Ripley was dead – meeting his end in a drunken smash late at night on a Californian freeway. Alec had a clear picture in his mind of him immersing his sorrows in some lonely bar before setting off on this last journey.

But the third – the strangest thing of all, the reason for him being here in this dark and lonely office on a Sunday afternoon – was what he had seen through the restaurant window the night before. When he looked up from attending his children, Alec had caught a fleeting but undeniable glimpse of the man he knew as Ritchie Ripley, not dead, but very much alive. And in celebratory mood as well, a bottle of champagne gripped tightly in one hand, a large cigar between the fingers of the other. He was walking into the room sharing a joke with a man on one side of him, whilst a woman on his arm with shocking pink lipstick and a low-cut dress looked on.

He wondered if he might have been mistaken, but although the clarity of the image was fading, the certainty he had felt at that moment would just not go away. There was no mistake. It was Ritchie Ripley he had seen.

Alec wished now that he had gone into the restaurant and challenged him. He wondered if Ripley had perhaps seen him. And now there were too many questions. Had Eddie Tomlinson's agitation been a sign that he was lying, or had somebody else given him false information that he was only passing on? In any case, why should Eddie bother to tell Alec at all? The two men barely knew each other. And what was Ripley doing here in Nottingham? Alec was sure he had never been aware before of any link the man had with the city.

Alec looked at his watch, took his glasses off and rubbed his eyes. It was dark outside now, and the warmth from the heater was making him drowsy. He switched it off. He felt frustrated. He had come here today expecting that thinking things through would give him an answer, that somewhere in all this lay an innocent explanation. All he had uncovered was confusion, more questions and a number of fingers pointing vaguely in the direction of Eddie Tomlinson. He had a half-formed idea that somebody was trying to sever his links with Monte Cristo Software. He was certain that he was not meant to be probing in the way that he was. And he had a suspicion that he was playing with something very dangerous.

THIRTY-EIGHT

Maria held the phone away from her at arm's length and pulled a face. She rolled her eyes and returned the handset to her ear.

"Mr Shaker, I can assure you that I have left messages for Toby." She hesitated slightly whilst she selected the right secretarial fib. "I spoke to him briefly and told him that you've been calling. Unfortunately his meeting has gone on a lot longer than expected. I'll let him know you've called again."

She made another expression of frustration when this failed to bring the conversation to an end.

"There is one other possibility. I'm not sure, but I think there may be somebody else who has worked on that file. If you can leave it with me for half an hour, I'll have a word and see if he can help. Yes, I do have your number. And your mobile. Yes, I will make sure somebody calls you back. Goodbye."

"Moaning git," she said to nobody in particular, timing the comment so that it was delivered the precise instant that the phone receiver hit its cradle. "It's my last week – I don't need this."

She left her workstation and walked to Toby Malkin's empty office. From the bottom drawer of one of the filing cabinets she took out his Monte Cristo file. Then she perched on the end of the desk, picked up the phone and dialled Tom's extension number.

"Hiya, it's only me... Yes, I left soon after you... And thanks for the flower, by the way. It was lovely... Look, I'm sorry to disturb you, but you couldn't be a real poppet and do me a favour? It's this Monte Cristo Software file – didn't you have something to do with that when you were working up here?... I thought you did."

She frowned whilst she listened to his reply, then pouted.

"You couldn't help me anyway, could you? This guy Alec Shaker's really hassling me. He's the lawyer on the other side. He's called three times for Malkin today, and he's in a real state about something. I don't know where Malkin is; he's disappeared again. You wouldn't come and have a quick look at the file and see if you can sort it out? I bet it's all a fuss about nothing." Her face relaxed as she heard Tom's answer. "You're a sweetheart. I've put the file on his desk."

A couple of minutes later, Tom appeared next to her.

"I really shouldn't be doing this, you know," he said quietly. "I don't work in this department any more. It's only because it's you."

Maria smiled and led him through to Malkin's office. Tom sat down in Malkin's chair and started to flick through the file. Maria sat opposite him, her legs crossed, her elbows resting on the desk, cradling her chin in her hands.

"You said that Malkin's disappeared *again*," said Tom. "What do you mean?"

"I mean he spends most of his time out of the office at the moment."

"He's working on a deal then?"

"No idea. If he is, it's a deal without documents, because he's not giving me any typing."

"That's odd. Anyway, this file looks pretty straightforward. What's the problem?"

"I don't know. Can you just give Alec Shaker a call? Make him leave me alone."

"It's not really for me to do that."

"Pleeeeease."

He gave her a look of exasperation. "You'll have to back me up if he says anything."

Maria stood up and left the room. She went back to her desk and sorted through some filing. From time to time she glanced at Tom through the glass front of Malkin's office. He studied the file for a while longer. When she next looked, he was on the phone – his face was serious and he was making notes.

A few minutes later, her own phone rang. She answered it and heard Tom's voice. She watched him through the glass as they spoke.

"Come through," he said. "Something's not right here."

Moments later she was sitting in front of Malkin's desk again.

"What do you know about Monte Cristo Software?" Tom asked, his eyes shifting between her face and the scene outside the office.

"Not a lot. It's a little matter Malkin handled for RevCom. Some sort of dispute, I think."

"Hardly little. RevCom ended up paying out two point four million."

Maria shrugged. "It's just a deal. They're all just deals. Anyway, there's no point asking me. I only typed a few letters."

"You're right about one thing, though. I did do a little bit of work on this. Just some research – I'd forgotten about it, but I remember now that I thought there was something odd at the time. I couldn't find very much out about the company. I thought Malkin would be annoyed, but he seemed OK about it."

"What's the problem now?" asked Maria. "What did Alec Shaker want?"

"He wouldn't be specific – he was desperate to speak to Malkin. Absolutely desperate. All he said was that he thought there were some irregularities."

Whilst he spoke, a memory began to flicker inside Maria's head. Nothing definite as yet.

"So?" she said.

"I don't know. Something's bugging me about this. Are you sure you don't know anything else?"

Then Maria remembered, and she blushed.

"No, nothing at all," she lied. She glanced over her shoulder. "Look, you'd better go. People will wonder what we're doing here. Thanks for making the call."

Being dishonest with Tom rested uneasily with Maria. For the rest of the day she pretended to be busy with things which didn't need doing and avoided talking to him.

But later that afternoon, just before she left work, something occurred to her. She made her way out of the Corporate Department and down the stairs to the Deed Room. From a shelf high up on one of the racks in the lower room, she retrieved two thick packets, wrapped and sealed inside blue plastic envelopes. They were heavy and she had to take care as she lifted them down, placing one on the floor before reaching up for the second. She wiped away the dust from the shiny surface of the top one, and strained her eyes against the dim light to check that these were the right papers. Satisfied that they were, she picked them up, signed them out and went back upstairs.

The files made a thud as she dropped them on Tom's desk.

"What are these?" he asked looking up from his work.

One or two other people looked round.

"That matter you helped me with this morning." She spoke slowly and implored him with her eyes to understand. "The software company." She mouthed, "I'll call you," and left.

Two minutes later, Tom's phone rang.

"I'm sorry," Maria said in a low voice. "I didn't want to say anything with people listening. I'd forgotten – those files are some other papers to do with that Monte Cristo company. Malkin had me put them there some time last week. He seemed to think they were quite important." And then as an afterthought, "Oh, and when you put them back, they're not filed under M for Monte Cristo. He wanted them to go under 'Reverie Communications, Supplier Dispute'. I'll see you."

Tom put the phone down and looked at the files. He blew away a little dust which still clung to the top one.

"Working late again tonight?" asked the paralegal who sat at the desk opposite him.

"I hope not. I've just got one or two things to look at before I go."

He carried on chatting to his colleague as he removed the tape which had been used to seal the first of the packets, and then tore back the plastic. Inside he could see that there was a thin wallet file, but that the bulkiness of the packet was caused by two solid parcels wrapped neatly in white paper, each the size of a telephone directory. Whilst the woman across the desk told him about a car she was thinking of buying, Tom lifted one of these out of the envelope and placed it in front of him. He opened it.

"I don't really know much about cars," said Tom.

Time seemed to stop as he realised what he was looking at when he folded back the paper. Fortunately his colleague was going through the process of tidying her desk and she didn't see the look on his face. Acting by instinct, he covered what was in front of him with a notebook, and looked around. Although there were plenty of people about, they all seemed preoccupied. He was sure nobody had seen.

"Well?" asked the paralegal.

"Sorry, I was miles away. What did you say?"

"It doesn't matter. It wasn't important. I'll see you tomorrow."

Tom waited until the woman had gone. Trying to appear relaxed, he pushed the parcel back into its plastic wrapping and then placed some law books on top. For five long minutes he stared at some papers in front of him whilst he tried to work out what to do. He called Maria, but she didn't answer.

Making an effort not to appear hurried, he left his desk a few moments later and went into one of the offices nearby. It belonged to a senior solicitor and Tom knew that this person kept a large pilot case in a corner of his room. He picked it up and returned to his desk.

Looking round all the time, and acting as quickly as he could, Tom shoved the files into the case. It was a tight fit, and the top wouldn't shut properly. That didn't matter – the files were inside and couldn't be seen. He went through his normal routine of putting the things on his desk in order. Telling himself that he mustn't display any outward signs of what he was feeling, he picked up the case and left the building.

THIRTY-NINE

When Tom's knocking brought no answer, he banged hard on Maria's door and shouted up at the window of her flat.

"What are you doing here?" she asked when finally she came to the door. She was ready for bed, dressed only in a tee shirt. "What's going on?"

"Are you going to let me in? I'm getting wet."

She opened the door a little wider and Tom stepped through into the hallway. He was carrying the pilot case.

"What's that?"

"Something I need to show you. Come on."

Upstairs, Tom went into the front room whilst Maria found a pair of jeans. When she came back, he was standing at the large bay window that overlooked the street, making sure that there was no gap between the curtains.

"Nobody can see in," said Maria. "Why are you so nervous?"

Tom didn't reply. Instead he took the two files out of the case and placed them on the floor.

"OK," he said, crouching over them. "The Monte Cristo papers. Supposedly. These are the packages Malkin asked you to put away in the Deed Room?"

"Yes."

"You're sure? There couldn't be any mistake?"

"No. That's my writing on the label."

"And he told you to file them under a name which makes no reference to the Monte Cristo company itself?"

"Yes. What's the big mystery?"

He leaned forward and started to undo the first of the files, taking care not to damage the wrapping. He took out the parcel inside, removed its contents and laid them out neatly in a row on the floor. Then he repeated the process with the other file, folding the packaging when he had finished, and putting it back in the case. He turned to Maria.

"Wow!" she said, her eyes wide with disbelief. "How much is there?"

"Two hundred and fifty thousand pounds. Half of it in sterling, the rest split between euros and US dollars."

"My God! What's it doing there?"

He shrugged. "I don't know. What do you think?"

"Don't ask me. I had no idea. The packages were already bound up when he gave them to me."

On the floor next to the wads of banknotes lay a thin wallet file. Tom opened it and removed a floppy disk.

"Do you know anything about this? There are some documents on it. I can't read them on my PC at home – I don't have the software that we run in the office."

"He didn't say anything to me about a disk."

Tom picked up one of the wads from the floor and ran his thumb against the ends of the notes, as if this would coax their secrets from them. Maria folded her arms across her chest.

"But … there is one other thing I know," she said.

"What?"

"I don't want to tell you. You'll think I'm mad."

"I think that already. So you may as well tell me."

"Oh, bloody hell."

Looking a little embarrassed, and with a lot of hesitation at first, she proceeded to tell Tom the story of what had happened on the evening when she let herself into Malkin's flat, and how when she was trapped in the alcove she had looked over his shoulder and watched him working on a document. To take her mind off her fear, she had concentrated on what was on the screen. Although she couldn't remember exactly what it said, it was certainly something to do with Monte Cristo Software.

"It was some sort of timetable – there were dates and descriptions. You know, meetings with lawyers, letters to Reverie Communications, that sort of thing."

Tom was sitting on the floor next to the banknotes.

"You are mad, by the way. Absolutely crazy. But what possible reason could there be for putting this amount of money somewhere like this?"

"I don't know," said Maria. "We need to find out."

"Do we?"

"Of course we do."

"Why?"

"There must be something dodgy going on. And Toby Malkin's involved. This could be a chance to get even with him."

"What do you mean, *get even with him*?"

She hesitated before she replied. "I mean we can get even for Guy Leighton."

"Yesterday you said that you had to put all that behind you."

"But that was before we found this." She pointed at the money on the floor. "I'm meant to be leaving the country in five days, remember. No way am I going to spend the rest of my life wondering if this was the chance to nail Toby Malkin. Do you understand that? No way. It's more important to me than anything else."

"Well you'll be doing it on your own."

"Oh, for God's sake! Don't talk to me about what I said yesterday. You said you were sorry we fell out. But every single time we find something out, every single time there's a chance to do something about Toby Malkin, you go all prissy on me."

She had adopted the same hands-on-hips posture that he had seen when he first saw her arguing with Malkin about Guy Leighton. He met her wild-eyed defiance with a much more understated, but equally effective, version of his own.

"I'm not going to help you, Maria, because even though we've come this far, you still haven't told me everything. You're hiding things. You accuse everybody else of doing that, but you're just as bad. I know – I know for certain – that there was something between you and Malkin in the past. You've had some sort of relationship. I want to hear the truth. I want to know what drives you to do something as stupid as stealing his key and breaking into his flat when he's there. Do you know how dangerous that was?"

"I didn't know he was there."

"That's irrelevant. I want to know why this is more important to you than anything else. I want the truth."

"There's nothing."

"Stop lying to me, Maria."

She stared at the wall on the other side of the room, her eyes glassy and expressionless.

"Look, you really do not want to know. Believe me. I can't tell you."

"You must do."

"No."

There was a finality in this word, and it hung in the air like the last word of a song. Eventually Tom held his palms upwards in a gesture which said "What more can I do?" and began slowly to place the money back into the case.

"Please don't do this," said Maria.

"I have to. I can't go on being told half the story."

She sat with the same impassive face whilst he finished putting the money away. The locks on the top of the case sounded like little gunshots as he snapped them shut. He stood up, met Maria's gaze, then turned and walked into the hall.

"I'll see you tomorrow."

She made no reply, and looked away. He reached out and undid the latch on the door which led to the stairs.

"He raped me."

The words were said in the smallest of voices. Tom stopped and turned back. Maria was bent forward, huddled over herself, rubbing her arms in agitation.

"Oh no."

"He raped me. I've never told anybody. And right now I really could do with you coming over here and holding me, please."

He put down the case and went to her. Her body was rigid, not yielding to his comforting in any way. Her eyes were screwed up in pain, as memories long buried invaded her consciousness.

"Maria, I'm so sorry. I had no idea it was anything like that."

There was no sound in the room, just the occasional noise of the rain outside being blown against the window. They sat together in their awkward half-embrace like teenagers in a first unknowing clinch. After a long time a little of the tension in Maria's limbs eased and she opened her eyes.

"I'd like to tell you the whole story."

"There's no need."

"I want to."

Speaking very slowly, Maria began to explain. The incident happened soon after she had joined Yates and Wood. In those days, she said, Malkin used to join in more, and on the evening in question a big group of people from the office went out drinking, then back to the flat into which Malkin had just moved. He wanted everyone to see it.

"He was talking to me all evening and I was so flattered, and he kept giving me more to drink. And when we got to his flat there was music and we were dancing, and suddenly I was in a bedroom with him. That was OK. It was fun and he was saying kind things – it all felt good. It was nice."

She stopped and steeled herself for what was to come. She was holding the end of Tom's jumper between her forefinger and thumb, working it like a child with a comfort blanket.

"But just as we were about to, you know, he started laughing and saying something about making a profit on the night. I didn't understand – I asked him what he meant and he laughed again and said didn't I know that there'd been a bet? Some of the lawyers had put twenty pounds in each, and the first one to have me won it all. It was terrible. He said he wasn't interested in me or the money – he just liked winning. I felt so cheap and I tried to stop him. I said I wanted to leave, but he told me I couldn't and then he got angry. I tried to shout out, but he put his hand over my mouth and said that nobody could hear me anyway because of the music. And then..." Maria was swallowing hard between words, struggling with the memories. "...he just forced me. It was awful.

"When he'd ... finished, he got dressed. I just lay there curled up in a ball, wishing it had never happened, praying for him to go away. He did, but then he came back. I tried to ignore him, but he pulled me over so that I was looking at him. There was such hatred in his eyes, I thought he was going to do it all again. But he sneered and told me that I'd enjoyed every minute of it, and he said that there were all these witnesses who would say that I was willing. And then the dirty, evil bastard gave me the money – he'd been to collect it and he held out his hand and let these screwed up notes fall into my face."

Tom moved her closer to him. Still her body was unyielding, still her expression distant.

"Maria, I just don't know what to say."

"There's nothing to say."

"But you've had to see him every day since then. That must be awful."

"At first I thought I would have to leave Yates and Wood. But then I thought, why should I? Why should *I* make it easier for *him*? And so I told myself that every time he saw me he would be reminded of what he had done, and that somewhere deep, deep down he would know that it was wrong."

"You're very brave," said Tom.

"Maybe. But even Toby Malkin has to sleep at night – when there's nobody else to answer to but himself. Lies you tell yourself are never totally convincing."

For the first time she allowed something mutual into the embrace, putting her arms round his chest and pulling him tight.

"Guy Leighton helped as well," she said. "He looked after me. He didn't know anything about what I've just told you, but he seemed to sense that I needed somebody to watch out for me."

187

"That's why you feel so strongly about him now, I suppose."

"Yes."

Tom stroked Maria's hair and kissed her forehead. Then he let go of her, and knelt on the floor in front of her. He took hold of her hands.

"I feel terrible. I've let you down so badly."

"Don't be silly. You've been far nicer to me than anybody else ever has. I don't deserve it."

"Yes you do. And I *have* let you down – if I'd had any idea about this I would have helped more, or I would at least have tried. It makes me so unbelievably angry that he did what he did. It was evil, and what he did to Guy Leighton was evil, and he just seems to get away with everything. But I'll make you a promise now. Whatever the reason for this money being here may be, we're going to find it out. And if it's anything wrong or illegal we're going to ruin him; we're going to use it to make him pay for everything he's done."

"My hero."

"Please don't, Maria. I'm serious. But I want you to promise me something. I need to do it at my pace. Finding out half the picture isn't good enough. Having some vague suspicion isn't good enough – we have to know everything and we have to be sure. Will you promise me?"

"I promise."

"Good. Now get your coat. We're starting now."

FORTY

There may have been some truth in Maria's belief that there would be times when Toby Malkin would reflect on the morality of what he had done to her. This evening was not one of those times. This evening he was at a business function, with something very different on his mind. It was a regular gathering of local professionals, a carefully orchestrated event with all the dignity of a school disco, the sole purpose of which was to bring people together in the hope that they would make deal-brokering, career-developing contacts. The day afterwards, junior lawyers and accountants would be asked to report on their success by revealing the number of business cards they had managed to collect as they made their fledgling efforts to work a room.

Malkin didn't often bother with these events. He had progressed far beyond them years ago. If he did attend, it was usually because he had nothing else to do. But tonight he was there for a reason. As he stood cradling a glass of wine and talking to a banker, his eyes flicked from group to networking group. Whilst managing to maintain some sort of meaningful conversation he kept a watchful eye on the door.

The banker droned on, and Malkin drank, refilling his glass every time a waiter passed. When he had nothing more to say to this person, he made an excuse and drifted away. He edged towards a group of lawyers from Loxleys, and interrupted their conversation to ask if they knew whether Dominic Braebrook was coming. They said they were sure that he was.

Malkin moved on, stopping at the bar, switching to whisky from wine, and always, always watching. He stood with a group of surveyors and lent a bored ear to a conversation about planning permission. He was buttonholed by a tax advisor anxiously seeking a favour. Then, at last, he saw Dominic. His old rival made what Malkin felt was a meek entrance and then hovered on the fringes of the crowd. Malkin began to disengage from the people he was with and to plan his route across the room. But then the senior lawyer who was chairing the event asked that everybody move into an adjoining lecture theatre where there was to be a presentation about the region's fastest-growing businesses.

Malkin avoided Dominic as everybody crowded through the door, and he chose a seat at the back. He could see Dominic a few rows in front of him, and for minutes at a time he stared at the back of his head, fixing his gaze on the closely cropped blonde hair above his neck. Halfway through the talk, Malkin slipped out and took a drink at the bar on his own. Then he went back in.

At the end of the presentation everybody filed out for more contrived networking. Although the alcohol was starting to dull his senses a little, Malkin knew he should wait for the right moment. Dominic was looking more confident now – he was standing in a large group of people, engrossed in an animated conversation with some other guy in a suit. Malkin stood statuesque, staring at Dominic until the other man noticed him and gave a puzzled half-smile of recognition.

Malkin nodded in response and started to make his way across the room. He moved clumsily, knocking into people but not apologising.

"Dominic," he said expansively. "Great to see you."

"Good evening, Toby. How are you?"

Malkin placed himself in front of Dominic, isolating him from the circle of people.

"I'm fine. Never better. I'm just surprised we haven't bumped into each other sooner. It must be nearly a year since you came back from the big city."

"Something like that."

"But maybe our paths haven't crossed because you don't have any clients, Dominic. Maybe you've found it just a little bit harder to get in on the serious deals than you thought you would. We provincial lawyers are a little more streetwise than you're used to, perhaps?"

Malkin's face was pressed up close to the other man's, with his arm round his shoulder to stop him from stepping back.

"I've got something to tell you," he said, lowering his voice and looking around conspiratorially. "Something I think you should know. I thought you might want to chew it over, and so do you know what I've done? I've written it all down for you."

He reached inside his jacket and took out a single sheet of A4 paper, folded three times. He pushed it into Dominic's top pocket. Then he moved even closer.

"And I'm sorry if I'm spoiling the surprise, but just so you know – on that piece of paper I've given you the details of what it was like every time I fucked your wife. The time of day, the positions we tried, all that sort of thing."

He looked into Dominic's eyes and winked. Dominic was slow to understand, and he cocked his head in puzzlement.

"You don't expect me to believe that, do you?"

190

"Well you could try asking the good lady herself. She seemed to have formed the idea that you were having some sort of fling yourself. Can't imagine how she got that impression. I do hope it's not true – she's a little minx, but she deserves so much better than that. She deserves so much better than you, you loser."

Dominic lurched forward, but Malkin gripped his wrist.

"Don't make a scene, Braebrook," he hissed. "You can't afford to. You need to hang on to what little reputation you've still got in front of all these very important people."

Malkin gave an enquiring look to somebody nearby who had noticed the little exchange. Keeping his arm round his rival, he led him over to this person and made a great show of introducing them to each other. Then, as Dominic tried to absorb what had happened, Malkin left.

It was later that evening that Samantha Shaker became a widow, her children part of a one-parent family. Alec was killed on the steps of his office, in the shadows on the edge of the garden he so loved. At the time when her husband's life was being taken, Sam sat cosy and warm in front of the television, her only anxiety whether the floods predicted by the local news would extend as far as the children's school.

The killer would tell himself afterwards that he hadn't gone there to hurt Alec – far from it. He would tell himself that there had been a misunderstanding, that he couldn't be held responsible for Shaker's stupidity. He would tell himself that it was wet, that he had slipped, that the struggle on the steps could so easily have been avoided.

But in his heart he would know that, when he grabbed Alec by the lapels and beat him about the head before pushing him backwards, he meant to do him harm – real harm – and that in the eyes of the law that was enough to make it murder.

The cause of death was the impact of Alec's head on a concrete pillar at the bottom of the steps. Alec flayed with his arms as he stumbled, trying to break the fall, but it made no difference. There was a sickening thud as his skull crashed into the unyielding structure. He fell motionless to the ground. His killer stood equally unmoving, and then he began to comprehend what he had done.

He looked round to check that nobody had seen, then he walked down the steps and put a tentative hand to Alec's neck, feeling for a pulse which wasn't there. He moved the body further into the shadows and then flung it into a flower bed. An upright bamboo stick supporting a growing plant ripped through the flesh on the side of the face and punctured an eye.

191

The killer stopped to catch his breath. He looked round again to check that nobody was watching. Then he dragged Alec's lifeless form to the end of the garden and hurled it, like so much rubbish, down a short flight of stairs which led to a little building where tools were stored. As an afterthought he returned to the body and searched for a wallet. He removed cards and money, then tossed the wallet aside. He straightened his clothes and walked away.

At home, Samantha yawned and stretched, and flicked from one channel to another. She looked forward to her husband's return. She wanted him there with her, out of the violence of the storm.

FORTY-ONE

Maria parked on a street not far from Yates and Wood's offices. The passenger door of her car stuck as it usually did, and she had to walk round and let Tom out. They huddled together beneath a flimsy umbrella and made a complete circuit of the building, looking for lights. The offices were in total darkness, even the cleaners now gone. Agreeing that there couldn't be anybody still inside, they let themselves in.

They decided to use Tom's PC. As they moved up through the building the automatic lighting flickered on, leaving behind them a trail as clear as footprints in wet concrete. Tom put the pilot case with the money in it on the floor beneath his desk and took out the floppy disk. They waited impatiently for the computer to boot up. As soon as it was ready, they loaded the disk and looked at what it contained.

A long list of documents appeared on the screen, but the titles, a mixture of letters and numbers, meant nothing. They looked at each other, and then Maria moved the mouse and selected one at random. Tom swore when a pop-up box told them that it was password-protected, but Maria reached forward and hammered a sequence of letters into the keyboard. The document opened.

"What did you type?" he asked.

"His password. E-R-O-I-C-A. He doesn't know I know – something to do with a girl called Erica, I suppose."

Tom frowned and leaned forward to read what was on the screen. It was a letter to Alec Shaker. Tom skimmed it and then tried another document. The password worked again, and this time brought up a history of Monte Cristo Software. He tried another, and then another, and each time they typed in the password a different document appeared – another letter, a note of a conversation, a contract, a list of meaningless words, numbers and acronyms.

"Does he normally do this – download everything to disk at the end of a transaction?"

"No, I don't think so," said Maria.

"There's so much here. I need time to look through it all."

"Well we can stay all night if we have to."

"No way. I want to be out of here as soon as we can. Let's print it all off and take it home."

They worked methodically. Tom printed each document and saved it to his hard drive. Maria stood by the printer, a stapler in her hand, taking papers as they emerged, fastening them together and placing them to one side in a neatly ordered pile.

"I need that correspondence file from Malkin's room as well," said Tom, when they neared the end of the list of documents. "I'll fetch it whilst you finish off here."

There were three ways to reach the Corporate Department on the top floor – by the lift, the main stairs, or a fire escape at the back of the building. Tom chose the main stairs, again leaving a trail of illumination behind him. In Malkin's office, he retrieved the file from the cabinet and started to leaf through it, unable to stop himself from looking for answers to some of the questions which were starting to take shape in his mind. This absorbed him until he heard the sound of the lift working. He presumed that Maria must have finished what she was doing.

It was as he was walking back across the open area that he saw the double doors at the far end open and Malkin appear. Tom stopped as if he had turned to stone. For an instant he thought about hiding. But then Malkin saw him. He peered at him and frowned.

"What are you doing here?" he asked. His voice echoed slightly in the empty spaces. He started to move across the floor.

Malkin was very wet from the rain outside, and Tom didn't think he had ever seen him looking so dishevelled. His tie was crooked, his top button undone. He walked without his normal swagger. Tom felt weak with shock as he searched for a lie.

"I was just on my way out, actually."

The file, which he gripped with whitened knuckles, felt as if it were several times bigger than it actually was, with large flashing lights drawing attention to the printed label on the outside, mocking Tom's feeble efforts to conceal it.

"That's not what I asked."

"I have a meeting first thing tomorrow. Off-site. I was out in town and I remembered that I needed some papers. I've come to collect them."

"But you work downstairs now. What are you doing in my department?"

Tom noticed the smell of alcohol on Malkin's breath. But for now both this, and the upsurge of hatred he had felt the moment he saw him, were pushed to the back of his mind by the effort he was having to make to find answers.

"There was a book I needed as well. One of the lawyers up here has signed it out so I came to look for it."

The two men stood staring at each other, saying nothing. Then Malkin's mobile phone rang. He found it in his top pocket and smiled when he looked at the caller display. He gave Tom a withering look and went into the nearest office to take the call.

As soon as the door shut behind him, Tom put his head down and walked as quickly as he dared to the exit. He glanced in Malkin's direction as he left – he was talking animatedly and seemed to have forgotten about Tom – and then ran, down the stairs and back to where he had left Maria. She was waiting for him, the pile of papers beneath her arm.

"Quick," he said. "We have to leave now. Malkin's here."

"You're joking!"

"No. You've got the case? What about the disk?"

He looked over his shoulder as he spoke. Maria didn't answer, but ran to Tom's desk to retrieve the disk.

"Come on," she said. "Let's go the back way."

They ran to the door and then down the stairs, Tom carrying the case with the money, Maria's heels clattering noisily on the uncarpeted surface. From the bottom of the stairs they had to work their way through corridors and storerooms to the staff entrance. Tom took Maria's hand to pull her along with him and as they careered round a corner, he saw that she was laughing.

"What's so funny?"

"This. It's a scream."

"I'm glad you think so."

They reached the entrance and let themselves out into the rain. Maria made to head off towards the car, but Tom stopped her.

"Come this way," he said, and led her towards the side of the building. "He won't be able to see us."

Still holding hands, and with Maria shielding the papers beneath her clothes, they made their way by a circuitous route back to the street where they had parked. They climbed into the car. Maria leaned on the steering wheel trying to regain her breath.

"Come on," said Tom. "Let's not hang around anywhere near here. Come back to mine, if you like."

At Tom's house they turned the key quietly in the lock and crept up the stairs to his room. Tom placed the case on the floor, Maria put her papers on the desk and they stood looking at each other. Then Maria held out her arms and they hugged.

Tom slept very little that night. Maria lay on his bed and eventually dropped off to sleep. Tom sat at his desk and pored over the documents, reading everything several times, working out who was who. Occasionally he stopped to rub his eyes or to stretch his arms, and as the darkness of the night showed the first signs of giving way to another day, he collected all the papers together and put them away.

He walked over to the bed and looked down at Maria. She had worked her way under a blanket so that only her face was visible. She looked peaceful and safe, and with an aching wonder he thought about how hard she must have to try each day to keep hidden so much pain.

He also wondered if she had even the slightest idea how much impact every little thing she did – the way she smiled, the way she frowned, the way she spoke – had on him. *I can't do much*, he thought, *but I'd try anything for you...*

He picked up his alarm clock and set it to go off in a couple of hours. Taking care not to disturb his sleeping friend, he climbed onto the bed and lay next to her. She stirred without waking and eased herself towards him, making a little noise of contentment. He put a tentative arm around her, then pulled her gently closer. He fell asleep to the rise and fall of her breathing.

FORTY-TWO

Overnight, the river began to flood in earnest. Soon after the rush hour began, the city was in chaos. Roads in outlying areas were closed, forcing motorists to find different ways in to work. Businesses on low ground began to think about implementing emergency procedures, and drivers stuck on gridlocked riverside routes eyed the swollen waterway with a mixture of wonder and concern.

And still the rain fell, relentless and persistent from unchanging skies. The forecast was for more to come – things would be worse before they were better. Close to the offices of Dobson White, Alec Shaker's body lay face down and undiscovered in a puddle that deepened by the hour, his absence of frantic concern to Samantha, but as yet of little interest to anybody else. The blood that had seeped from the wound on his face the night before was now indistinguishable from the dirty brown water in which he lay.

In Tom's little room, Maria woke first and took a moment to recall where she was. She became conscious of the arm draped across her and the presence of the body behind her, and she moved round to look at Tom. He was fast asleep, and she watched him for several minutes, with her head propped up on an elbow, seduced by the gentle rhythm of his breathing, as her eyes became accustomed to the half-light.

The alarm sounded and Tom's body jerked into a panicky wakefulness. Maria leaned over him and pressed the button on the top of the clock, then stroked his hair and calmed him. He opened his eyes. He looked a little sheepish.

"I'm sorry," he said. Then after a pause, "You don't mind, do you?"

"Mind what?"

"Me lying here like this. It seemed a lot more appealing than the floor."

"Why ever would I possibly mind?"

"I don't know. I just thought..." He craned his neck to look at the clock. "What's the time?"

"Seven-thirty."

"We need to get moving. I'll make us a drink – we can pick up some breakfast later."

Ten minutes later they were sitting on the edge of the bed, each cradling a mug of hot coffee.

197

"Well then, what happens now?" asked Maria.

"We have to go into the office as normal. We'll need to collect some work clothes for you at your place."

"So we're not going to the police, then?"

"Not yet. I haven't got the whole picture."

"But what about the money?"

"That's the trouble. I don't know who it belongs to or why it was hidden there. I'm fairly sure that it's part of the money that RevCom paid to Monte Cristo Software. Why store it with these papers otherwise? It's about ten per cent of the amount of the claim – I don't know if that's relevant."

"So it could be some sort of commission?"

"Possibly. Or it could be money that's going to be paid to somebody else. And something else that's strange – the documents on the disk fall into two categories. The first are all the sort of thing you would expect to see – in fact many of them are also on the file in Malkin's cabinet. The others are different – letters to Alec Shaker from his client – private things you wouldn't expect Malkin to have."

"So what are we going to do?"

"First I want to speak to Alec Shaker again. And if that doesn't lead anywhere, I want to start looking through any other files that might be connected."

"It doesn't sound very hopeful."

"We're not giving up yet. I may not be able to work it out at the moment, but partners in law firms do not go hiding amounts of cash like this in deed packets unless something serious is wrong. Especially partners who are in the habit of framing their colleagues as child abusers. And all the other stuff."

Maria put her cup down on the floor and reached out to stroke Tom's hand.

"I appreciate you doing this for me. I really do. But don't go taking any risks on my part. It's not worth it."

"Yes it is. It's totally worth it. And there are no risks here."

"Toby Malkin is a dangerous man. He saw you in the office last night."

"But he has no reason to connect me with all this."

"I hope not."

"And anyway, we'll be in a building full of people."

Tom squeezed her hand, and then let it go, his appearance thoughtful.

"There is one other way you could get level with Malkin," he said. "Something a lot more straightforward."

"What's that?"

"Take the money. Just keep it and take it with you to Australia. He'll never know, and if he's stolen it himself he may not even be able to tell anyone it's gone. I reckon he owes you that and far more besides."

Maria stood up and straightened her clothes. She pursed her lips.

"We're meant to be the good guys."

They drove to Maria's flat, and Tom waited outside whilst she went in to change.

"You look nice," he said when she came out five minutes later in a blue skirt suit and white blouse. "I like that outfit."

"I hate it. It makes me look as though I'm pretending to be a solicitor. I haven't got anything else ironed."

They left the car parked at the end of Maria's road, and walked to the office. As soon as they arrived, Tom went to the Deed Room with the pilot case. There was nobody there, and he took out the plastic envelopes containing the money. He went not to the shelf from which Maria had removed the files the day before, but to another rack in a corner of the room on the lower level. He made a note of where he had left them. Then he shoved the case underneath a table nearby.

When he arrived at his desk there was an e-mail from Maria telling him that there was no sign of Malkin. He picked up his phone and called her number. Speaking as quietly as he could he told her where he had put the money. She said that she had run the whole of the correspondence file through the photocopier and had the duplicate hidden in one of the drawers of her desk.

Working in an open-plan office was often difficult. Today it threatened to make things impossible. Tom needed to be somewhere private – he couldn't afford any conversations he might have with Alec Shaker to be overheard. Although he was reluctant to commit himself to writing, he decided to begin with an e-mail. He sent Alec a simple message, asking him to call.

All around Tom the normal business of the office continued, interrupted by more conversations about the weather than usual. From time to time two or three people would congregate at a window, frown and pass comment on what they saw outside, then walk away shaking their heads. Lawyers talked into dictating machines, telephones rang, keyboards clattered. Tom tried to concentrate on his work.

Twenty minutes later, his phone rang. It was Maria again.

"Have you spoken to Alec Shaker?" she asked.

"No. I'm waiting for him to call."

"It's all happening up here. Lewis Cooper from RevCom has been on the phone for Malkin. He's almost as pushy as Shaker was yesterday – insisted on having his home number. And his address."

"Really?"

"And Ruth Braebrook wants to talk to him as well. She looks dreadful. She says that Malkin has done something terrible, something unforgivable. When she heard that he wasn't here she went home. Do you think that she's got something to do with it?"

"I've no idea," said Tom. "I'll speak to you later."

Instinctively he had written the names of Lewis Cooper and Ruth Braebrook on a pad in front of him. Now he stared at them both. Cooper's name made some sort of sense, but he didn't really know what. Ruth Braebrook didn't seem to fit in at all. He had a perception of a net closing in around Malkin, but he couldn't understand why. He needed to speak to Alec Shaker.

He dialled the number of Dobson White and asked for Alec. He was put through to a secretary who offered to take a message.

"I really do need to speak to him urgently," said Tom. "Can he call me back soon?"

"Yes, I hope so. I'm expecting him any minute. I can only imagine that he's been held up by the flooding. I'll give him your message as soon as I can."

Tom called twice more in the next hour, each time with the same result. He could sense that his calls disturbed the woman he was speaking to. She avoided the normal secretarial obfuscation – by the second call she admitted quite openly that she didn't know where Alec was. Her anxiety was apparent.

Tom leaned forward and put his head in his hands. This was as frustrating as playing a game where nobody had told you the rules.

The news of Alec Shaker's death – his body discovered by a tramp looking for somewhere to shelter – reached Yates and Wood late that morning. Maria heard it when she left her desk to fetch a drink and found two other secretaries in a huddle by the coffee machine. One of them was weeping – she had once worked at Dobson White and had known Alec when she was there – and it took Maria a couple of minutes of frantic questioning to make any sense of what she was being told.

"It's definitely Alec Shaker?"

"Yes. I spoke to the office manager."

"And they're sure someone killed him?"

"He was found face down in a pool of water. He'd been missing all night."

She hurried back to her desk and called Tom.

"It was Malkin," she said in a whisper. "It must have been. Alec Shaker obviously knew something, and Malkin killed him to keep him quiet. You said he was in a real state when you saw him last night. And this must be what Ruth Braebrook was talking about. Are you still there?" she asked when Tom didn't reply.

"Yes. I'm trying to think."

"You don't need to think. It's obvious."

"It may not be. And we agreed – we're doing this my way."

Maria's string of whispered invective was cut off mid-stream as he put the phone down. In the past Tom had hesitated or counselled caution because of an unwillingness to get involved. He was pausing now because he so desperately wanted to be right. What had driven him to work through the night, what was keeping his brain buzzing now, were the images he had in his mind of Malkin forcing himself onto Maria, of Malkin's thug kicking Guy Leighton when he was on the ground. Shocking images. Images of things he had never believed could happen to people you knew. It was abhorrent to him that somebody should go through life just taking whatever he wanted, doing unspeakable things to people whose only wrongdoing was to be in his important way. Tom wanted to be the one who stopped him. But for the life of him he couldn't work out what to do next.

Ten minutes later his decision was made for him. As he sat huddled over his desk, willing himself to think harder, his phone rang again. He considered ignoring it and letting it go through to voicemail, but then he picked it up.

"Oh thank God you're there," said Maria's voice. "Leave the building now. Go by the back stairs and get out. Call me later."

"What's going–"

"Just leave. Now."

The insistence in her voice was impossible to ignore. Tom took his jacket from the back of his chair and walked quickly to the stairs, and then down to the ground floor, following the route to the staff entrance he had trodden with Maria the night before.

Once he was outside, he headed up to the Market Square where he found a payphone. He called Maria. She made it clear from her vagueness that she couldn't speak and asked for his number. He waited in the booth for ten minutes, glad to be out of the rain.

"What was all that about?" he asked when she called him back.

"Malkin. He was here. Looking for you. He was on his way down to see you when I called."

"Why?"

"I think he wanted to talk to you about being in the office last night. He asked me if you were in the habit of wandering around the building at midnight."

"I knew he didn't believe me. Where is he now?"

"He's gone. Couldn't get away quickly enough. He told me he's taking the rest of the week off as holiday."

"How did he seem?"

"Difficult to say. Fairly tense. He pretended to be surprised when I told him about Alec Shaker. It was so transparent. And before he went, he asked me about those files – checked that I had put them away like he asked."

"You didn't tell him we've moved them?"

"Of course I did. I drew him a little map to make it easier for him to find them."

"Don't, Maria. Funnily enough, I'm not in the mood."

"Well don't ask stupid questions. Anyway, what are you going to do now?"

"I don't know. I just don't know."

He put the phone down and punched his palm in frustration. Then he turned to leave the phone booth. As he did, he noticed a little dog-eared business card with a cartoon of a motor car, left by a minicab company as an advert for its services. It offered cheap rates for airport trips. It may have been the cartoon which caught his eye, it may have been the colour of the card. Whatever it was, suddenly Tom knew exactly what he was going to do next.

Half an hour later, he met Maria in the foyer of a hotel in the city centre and collected from her a briefcase containing the photocopied version of the Monte Cristo file. He explained his plans, and overruled her protests.

"Listen," he said. "We have to be so careful now. The guy is capable of anything. There's no way either of us can go back to the office – I'm obviously on his radar screen, and he knows that you and I are close. I've booked you a room here..." He handed her a plastic key. "...and I want you to stay in it. Don't go near your place or mine, don't contact anybody at work. I'll be in touch later, but it may not be until later this evening."

"Tom, wouldn't it just be easier to go to the police?"

"Oh come on, Maria. This is personal. It always has been for you, but it is for me now as well. We will go to the police, but wouldn't it be so much better to go with the whole story, not just a few scraps of information? Don't you want the satisfaction of that?"

She looked anything other than persuaded.

"Trust me," he said. "Let me try, at least. It can't do any harm. If it doesn't lead to anything, we'll talk to the police tomorrow. I promise."

"Are you sure it's not dangerous?"

"Positive. I'll be fine. But I have to go now. I've not got much time."

He pressed the key into her hand and begged her with his eyes.

"Go up to the room now. And, Maria, if our friendship means anything to you at all, please stay there. For once in your life, do as you're told."

She stuck her tongue out at him, and before she had the chance to ask any more questions he stood up and left the hotel.

The journey to the airport was slow because of the weather. When the minicab dropped him off outside the main concourse, Tom thrust some notes at the driver, took his case and ran. He skimmed the departure screens and saw that he had just forty minutes. There was only one position open at the airline's ticket desk, and a queue of three or four people. With uncharacteristic assertiveness he went straight to the front and interrupted the girl behind the desk.

"I'm sorry, everybody. It's an emergency."

Ignoring the muttering behind him he bought his ticket and then raced through passport control and security. The flight had already boarded and the staff on security were suspicious, questioning his lack of luggage, and examining the briefcase in detail, putting it through the scanner twice and asking him to remove his shoes.

"It's a last minute thing," he said, looking at his watch. "A business meeting."

Eventually they let him through and he had to be escorted across the tarmac to the waiting plane. Minutes later he was in the air.

FORTY-THREE

Tom had planned to find a cheap hotel in Nice and then take a train to Cannes the next morning, but he couldn't face the prospect of doing nothing now that he had come this far. He changed some money and climbed into a cab. As he travelled along the coast past villas and little tideless bays in the fading light, he looked out at the stillness of the Mediterranean. Feeling upbeat about being somewhere where it wasn't raining, he pondered the various approaches he might take with Monte Cristo when he arrived, if there was anybody still there to talk to at this time of evening. Best probably to stick to something close to the truth – explain that he was a lawyer and not be too precise about his brief. He felt confident that he would know what to do and what to say when he arrived.

He asked the taxi driver to drop him in the middle of the town, near the seafront, and went into a bar. He bought a beer, checked his appearance in the men's room, and asked for directions in his passable French. The waiter explained that the road he was looking for was less than two kilometres away, and so he decided to walk. Passing impressive hotels and municipal buildings he made his way away from the sea. It was now dark, and with his English suit and his Marks and Spencer shoes he felt a little out of place in this rich man's playground.

The road on which the Monte Cristo offices were located was not what he expected. He had imagined a smart new business zone, with well spaced-out, low-lying units. What he found was a typical French street – narrow pavements and tall buildings with little balconies. There were shops and cafés and trees, the odd legal office or estate agent, cars parked haphazardly in the tightest of gaps. He stopped in a doorway and crouched down, resting his briefcase on his knees so that he could open it and check the address. There was no mistake. According to the Monte Cristo letterhead, this was the right street.

He walked on a little further, stopping from time to time when a number on a building was difficult to read. The air was still and it was pleasantly warm. A group of youths on motor scooters passed very close to him. After a while he saw a T-junction up ahead. That seemed wrong. There were less than twenty doorways before the end of the street, but there needed to be many more – the address of the Monte

Cristo office was another hundred or so numbers ahead. He wondered if perhaps the street continued round the corner at the junction.

But it didn't. It ended a long way short of where it should have done. There was no building with the number he was looking for. He needed number 235. The numbers on the buildings stopped at 152. He opened his briefcase again and tore the letter out of the file. Clutching it in his hand he strode across the traffic, checking the names of the streets, and then standing and looking around in exasperation.

He was starting to feel tired and light-headed with hunger. He breathed deeply a few times and tried to make a plan. There must be some way of making sense of this. He had come here sure that talking to Monte Cristo Software would give him an answer. He couldn't afford for the journey to be wasted. He went back to the top of the street where the office was supposed to be and walked back down its length, this time on the opposite pavement, checking each building that looked anything at all like a commercial property, looking hard at numbers 135 and 35 and anything else which might be the right place if the address on the letterhead were a misprint. Then he did the same on the side of the street he had first walked up. But all to no avail.

Not knowing what else to do, he finally went into one of the premises near the junction that shouldn't have been. It was a wine sellers, with a wooden floor and racks and racks of bottles. At the counter he showed the proprietor the letterhead.

"I'm looking for this address," he said. "But there seems to be some sort of mistake."

The man looked perplexed.

"The number," said Tom. "There isn't a number 235."

"Of course," said the man, suddenly understanding. He smiled amiably.

"I'm confused. This is very important. Have you ever heard of this company? Do you think the street name could be wrong?"

The man shrugged. "Wait a minute, monsieur," he said.

He went through the doorway behind the counter. Tom heard voices and a minute or two later, the man emerged with his wife. She was carrying a thick directory.

The book was a listing of local businesses, and they spent the next ten minutes searching through it. Tom quickly became resigned to the fact that they wouldn't find anything. He was right, there was no mention of any company called Monte Cristo, and he was longing to be on his own to try to work out the implications of this discovery. But the couple had the bit between their teeth now, and the woman had gone off to telephone her son who had some vague connection with the computer industry to see if he could help. Tom waited for her to come back, tried to appear surprised that this had yielded nothing, thanked them both for their efforts and left.

He walked back in the direction of the sea feeling despondent. Not far from the front he found a quiet bar, where he ordered *steak frites* from a pretty waitress who reminded him vaguely of Maria. He knew that his friend would be waiting to hear from him, but at the moment his embarrassment made him reluctant to call. He was sure that this would have worked out differently. He had so wanted to be phoning with some triumphant revelation.

While he waited for his meal he took out the Monte Cristo file, and in an effort to hold back the tiredness and despair which were threatening to overcome him, he started to make a list of events and dates.

It was just as the waitress came back with the food that he realised that there had been no need at all for him to make this journey and to waste this time. The information he needed had been with him in his briefcase from the moment he set off.

In the hotel room in Nottingham, Maria was going up the walls. She had tried everything to pass the time – watching television, taking a bath, lying on the bed with her body curled round the phone. Like Tom, she was hungry and she thought several times about calling down for some food, but didn't dare in case she did so at the moment Tom decided to make contact. Mostly she paced the room and stood by the window looking out at the uninspiring view of another wing of the hotel.

It was just after nine o'clock when finally Tom called.

"I feel so stupid," he said. "It's really so obvious."

"What are you talking about?"

"This whole Monte Cristo thing. I just need you to confirm one detail. When you let yourself into Malkin's flat, when exactly was that?"

They spent a couple of minutes working out the date, linking it to one of Tom's visits to Caroline and Malkin's trip to Dublin. When they were sure they had the right day, Tom asked Maria to repeat to him what she had seen Malkin doing.

"You saw a lot of detail about the Monte Cristo claim, then?" he asked when she had finished.

"Basically, yes."

206

"Maria, the date of the first letter on the file, the very first time that Malkin would have known anything about the claim – or would have done if this was any normal claim – was several weeks *after* you were in his flat."

"And?"

"There's only one way that he could have had that information – if somehow he was able to control what they were going to do. And I think he was able to do that because I don't think Monte Cristo Software exists – not in any real sense. There's certainly no evidence of it here. I think it's an illusion that was created to defraud Reverie. I think the whole claim is a fiction."

"That can't be right. I've typed letters to them, done file notes of conversations Malkin had with Lewis Cooper about them. I've even spoken to somebody from Monte Cristo on the telephone."

"That doesn't mean any of it is real. Alec Shaker may have been in on it as well. A guy called Eddie Tomlinson's definitely involved – he works for Reverie on the computing side, so that would make sense. But however it's been done, somebody's managed to get away with nearly two and half million pounds."

"Good God. That's unbelievable."

"I know. But I'm convinced I'm right. It explains why there were so many documents on that disk that you wouldn't expect Malkin to have. One of the mistakes I was making was thinking he had only stolen the cash we found – the two hundred and fifty thousand. That must be there as a slush fund or possibly to pay somebody off. I think Malkin has taken the rest as well."

"And what about Alec Shaker? Do you think it was Malkin who killed him?"

"I can't answer that. It looks highly likely that he's involved. But don't forget, he likes using paid thugs to do his dirty work. And it's always possible that it could have been Eddie Tomlinson, or even this man Ritchie Ripley."

"It was Malkin. I just know it was Malkin."

"Maybe it was. But that's not our problem. We've done as much as we can now. The police can sort out the rest."

"So what do we do?" asked Maria.

"We both need to get some sleep. I won't be able to get a flight until the morning. First thing tomorrow, you go and pick the money up from the Deed Room. Be careful – don't go to your desk, keep away from Malkin and make sure there are other people around. Once you've got the money, take it straight to RevCom. Try to get in to see Lewis

Cooper, and if you can't, just insist on seeing the most senior person you can – I'm sure you'll think of a story. Tell them everything you know about this whole thing, and stress that Eddie Tomlinson's involved – they may want to make sure he doesn't get the chance to destroy anything. Once RevCom understand what's happened, they can tell the police and it will all look so much more convincing."

Maria said nothing.

"Are you still there?" asked Tom.

"Yes."

"What's the matter?"

"Nothing. I just can't believe that we've done it. Well, *you* have. You're a star."

"I couldn't have done it without you."

"I'm sure you could. But you don't think there's any chance Malkin will have ... I don't know, left the country or something?"

"I don't think so. Not if he was around this morning. And anyway, he's not likely to go anywhere without the money, is he? Are you going to be alright on your own there?"

"Of course."

"I'm going to find a hotel here. I'll call you again in an hour or so, to let you know where I'm staying."

FORTY-FOUR

When Tom called back, Maria didn't answer. She didn't answer because she wasn't in the hotel room. She was standing on the pavement outside the offices of Yates and Wood, looking up at the lights on the floor in the middle of the building where the night-shift typists worked. She glanced at her watch. They would be there for another thirty minutes or so. Although she didn't intend that they would see her, their presence was a comfort.

She let herself in and took the lift up to the Corporate Department. She stopped by the entrance and looked in. The whole area was in darkness. As she moved through the door her presence activated the sensors and the lights flickered on. Maria walked quickly to her desk and picked up the jotter in which she wrote down messages. Leafing through it she found the note she had scribbled earlier that day, and tore the page out. The moment when Tom had told her where he had hidden the money seemed like weeks ago now. She glanced around her at the empty desks and the quietly humming machines, and then left by the same door she had used to come in.

The lift took her back down to the reception area, and from there she walked through to the door of the Deed Room. At this time of night it was locked, and she had to punch a code into a touch pad on the wall before the handle yielded and she was able to pull the door open. She shut it behind her, and walked across the upper floor of the storage area on echoing heels, before descending the spiral iron staircase into the tomb-like vault of the basement.

At the bottom of the stairs she paused. The silence was total. With its dust and dim lighting, this was never a place she had enjoyed visiting, and yet she was conscious now of the imposing presence of the past. This was probably the last time that she would ever be here amongst the wills and the title deeds and the transaction bibles – all this physical evidence of the transfer of wealth and property that would endure long after the lawyers who had grown rich on it had become ghosts. Although the place made her feel uncomfortable she felt a little tinge of pride at the contribution she had made to the contents of the room. She had served Yates and Wood well.

She shook her head to disperse this kaleidoscope pattern of nostalgia, and made her way up a narrow aisle between two racks of shelves to the far corner of the room. Without checking the instructions, she went straight to the place where she expected to find the money. There was nothing there. She unfolded the paper and looked at what she had written. Realising her mistake, she checked the number on one of the storage racks and peered through a gap in the files in front of her to the place where she should have been looking.

It was then that she heard the noise. A small scraping noise which sounded as though it had come from the floor above. She stood still and listened again. Nothing. For a moment she wondered if she might have imagined it, but no, she was sure that she hadn't. Moving with deliberate, measured steps she went back to the foot of the iron staircase. She peered upwards for a long time, squinting against the light above her, listening intently. *Come on, Maria*, she said to herself. *No need to be so jumpy. Just find the money and get out of here.*

Twisting her neck one more time to look up the stairs, she shrugged and went back into the racks, this time to the right place. Even now it wasn't easy to find the files – Tom had hidden them well behind a set of leases which would otherwise have lain undisturbed for years. She moved the leases to one side, and lifted the blue plastic parcels out. Then she replaced the leases as she had found them, and lifted the files to test the weight of the money.

Preoccupied with the grime which dirtied her fingers, Maria had taken several steps forward before she noticed the outline of the person leaning against the rack at the end of the aisle. Her first reaction was curiosity as she tried to make out who it was. Her second was horror as she succeeded.

"Well, well. What a stroke of luck. I've been rather short on that today. Until now."

Maria couldn't think of anything to say. No excuse would sound remotely plausible.

"There I am, sitting in my office, wondering why on earth Maria Cracolicci – a worthless tart I should have rid myself of years ago – has signed out some rather important papers of mine, some papers that have absolutely nothing to do with her, and which I actually need in a little bit of a hurry. I'm trying to work out whether it would be better to go to wherever it is she calls home and ask her about them this evening, or whether I can risk waiting until the morning. It really is a dilemma. I'm weighing up the pros and cons, trying to look at it from all angles. But then suddenly, there she is, right in front of my eyes. There's my answer. For once in my life I'm actually pleased to see her."

"I didn't see you in your office."

"If you sit still for long enough, you silly girl, the light goes out."

Maria glanced over her shoulder, but she knew already that Malkin was blocking her only way out. He stood up straight, then took a step towards her.

"Now look, I have a couple of options here." His words were suddenly more clipped and business-like. "The only possible reason for you being down here is because you know what's in those files. Am I right?"

Maria hesitated.

"Do not waste my time!" said Malkin. "I warn you, do not make me angry! You know what's in those files. Yes?"

"Yes," she said, bowing her head slightly and looking up at him.

"And so, having stuck your nose in where it really, really is not wanted – and I cannot imagine what could have possessed you to do that – you decided to help yourself and run off to Australia with my money. Correct?"

Maria's mind was racing. She was battling with a sense of her own stupidity in forgetting that she had signed the papers out in her own name. And what was the right answer now? What should she say?

"Yes," she said eventually. "I didn't think you'd find out."

"That's stealing. It's not your money. It's mine."

"So what's it doing hidden down here?"

"That's any concern of yours?"

She pursed her lips, looking embarrassed.

"I guess not."

"You guess right."

Malkin folded his arms and regarded her for a while. All the time Maria watched him, not daring to look away. Tom might have his doubts, but she knew that this man had killed for this money already. It didn't matter what he tried to do to her, she would make it as hard as she possibly could. He couldn't surprise her now. She would fight him with everything she had.

He took another step towards her.

"You really don't deserve this, but today is going to be the luckiest day of your life."

"Don't you dare come any nearer. Don't you dare lay a finger on me."

Her every instinct was to retreat, to step away from him. But she knew she had to hold her ground, face him down if she could. She pulled the files closer to her, as if somehow they could protect her.

211

Malkin looked away and sighed in an obvious effort to exercise restraint.

"Are you listening to me?"

"Fuck off."

"Oh for Christ's sake. As ever, Maria Cracolicci gets it all totally and spectacularly wrong. Is it any wonder that your life is the miserable mess that it is? I have no intention of touching you. I'm offering you a deal."

Maria continued to stare at him, her face impassive.

"What sort of deal?"

"Half the money. There are two files there. One of them has money in it. One of them has money and a disk. Give me the one with the disk, and you can keep the other."

"You must think I'm stupid."

"I know you are. But I'm hoping that just for once you're going to do the right thing. I'm offering you more than a hundred thousand pounds in cash. Where else is someone like you ever going to see money like that?"

"Why on earth should I trust you?"

"Who said anything about trust? Trust would be if I told you that I'll pay you the money tomorrow. You don't have to trust me. It just so happens that it is far more attractive to me to do this with your co-operation. All you have to do is to give me one file and keep the other."

"There must be a catch. There always is with you."

"No catch. Just keep the money."

Maria wished that her brain would work quicker. There were too many things to think of at once. Something seemed to be telling her that Malkin was being genuine, but that was a concept too far removed from anything she had ever known to be true.

"Well? I'm offering you a lot of money. Think about it. No tax to pay – it could keep you going for years in Oz."

"Which is the file with the disk?" She looked down at the packages in her arms.

"I can't tell from here. I need to see inside them."

"You can look inside one," said Maria. "Then we can swap them if we need to."

"So you'll do the deal?"

"I'm thinking about it."

Malkin smiled. "Fair enough."

Maria looked hard at him again, and then stepped forward. When she was just out of his reach she stopped. Keeping her eyes fixed on him all the time, she bent her knees and lowered herself. Then she leaned forward and let the top file fall to the floor. It landed with a thud. Slowly she straightened herself up again and took half a step back.

"Look inside."

Malkin went to the file and crouched down. He began to tear back the plastic cover. Maria took her eyes off him – just for a second – to glance at a short pair of wooden steps which were used to reach the higher shelves and which were leaning against the rack next to her.

Malkin lifted the file and felt inside. He had to look down to do this. Maria's hand started to move towards the steps.

"This isn't the one with the disk."

She let her hand drop. He didn't seem to have noticed.

"We need to swap them then."

"No," he said. "First I need to be sure that the disk is actually inside that one. How do I know that you haven't removed it?"

Maria considered this. Malkin pushed the file he had already examined along the ground towards her. Maria bent down and put the other one on the floor, then moved it in his direction with her foot. Malkin felt the outside of it before pulling at the plastic wrapping and looking inside.

When Maria hit him, she didn't manage to take him completely by surprise. She didn't grab hold of the steps as cleanly as she meant to, and she knew that she needed to raise them as high as possible to give maximum force to the blow. In the extra half second that it took to do this, Malkin looked up and raised his hands in front of his face to break the impact. Nevertheless, she made a decisive contact. There was a crunch, and he fell forward. Maria let go of the steps, dropping them on top of him. She stooped to pick up the files. As she stepped over him, she saw that Malkin was already fighting his confusion, groping with his hands to push himself up. She ran.

At the bottom of the iron staircase, she stopped to kick off her shoes. When she reached the top, she heard Malkin shout out her name, calling her back. She cursed. At the moment when the stepladder had crashed into the side of his head, she feared that she might have killed him. Now she realised she hadn't hit him hard enough. It was stupid to think that she could outrun him. Her skirt was too tight, the files too heavy.

She ran to the outer door of the Deed Room. She could hear Malkin moving across the floor downstairs. The door was so heavy and awkward that she had trouble opening it, and she thought that she would have to put the files down. But then she managed to grip the handle. She pulled the door towards her. Without passing through it, she shut it again, pushing hard. It banged as it closed. A metallic sound told her that Malkin had reached the bottom of the stairs and was starting to climb. Maria turned and moved into the shadows behind one of the racks of shelving.

Seconds later, Malkin arrived at the door. Maria heard him open it and go through.

She stood still for a minute, clinging on to the files whilst she tried to bring her breathing under control. Malkin would surely realise what she had done, and would be back. And this time there would be no offer of a deal. She needed to find somewhere better to hide.

Thinking that she might have chosen differently from her wardrobe that morning if she had known where the day was leading, Maria stood on tiptoe and balanced the files on the highest shelf she could reach. Then she started to climb up the rack. Her skirt hampered her movements, but she managed to pull herself up so that she was level with the highest shelf. Holding on to the wooden frame as tightly as she could with one hand, she manoeuvred first one file and then the other up onto the top of the rack. They were heavy, and her arm quivered with the effort. She stopped for a moment to catch her breath, then pulled herself up into the narrow gap between the top of the rack and the ceiling.

There was even more dust and filth up here than on the shelves below and she had to close her mouth tight to stop herself from coughing. She lay down flat and pressed her cheek against the cold wooden surface.

She lay there for a long time, like a body in a morgue, listening to the silence. She had no watch and no idea of just how long she waited. She expected that at any moment the door would open and Malkin would return. After a while, when he didn't, she began to wish that he would, so that at least she would know where he was. Eventually she came to the conclusion that he wasn't coming back, and that she would have to move.

Now she felt a little silly perched on top of the rack of shelving. Stopping between each movement to listen for the sound of the door, she climbed down with one of the files, and then went back up to retrieve the second. On the way down this time she snagged herself on a protruding screw, ripping her blouse and tearing the skin beneath. She gritted her teeth and held her breath until the pain receded. With the files in her arms she went to fetch her shoes. After taking a couple of deep breaths and with great trepidation, she stood in front of the door and opened it slowly.

There was nobody waiting. She shut the door quietly behind her, and flitted across the reception area like a shadow, looking anxiously up at the main staircase. She made her way down to the staff entrance, and out into the night.

So far it had all been a lot harder than she had expected. She hoped that the rest of what she needed to do tonight would go a little more smoothly.

FORTY-FIVE

The weather had worked itself up into a gale. Clutching the files close to her, Maria battled against the wind as she made her way up to the Market Square. There was a bus waiting at her stop, and she climbed on, paying no attention to the look the driver gave her. She chose a seat at the back, and looked at her reflection in the window. She was like a tramp who had found a designer suit in a dustbin, her hair dishevelled, her face washed clean of any make-up. She looked down. There was a bloodstain on her blouse just above the hem of her skirt, and she was filthy from the grime in the Deed Room.

She got off the bus a stop before the one she usually used and followed a series of twitchels between rows of houses, before scurrying across the shadows of the little park, conscious of her own vulnerability, hoping that the weather would have persuaded all the muggers and thieves to stay at home. She came up an alleyway which led to the end of her road and there she stopped, lingering in the darkness. It was obvious that Malkin would have come here to look for her. Although her own car was parked not more than twenty feet from where she was standing, she needed to be careful. She looked closely at each of the cars she could see until she picked out the Jaguar, parked facing away from her at the far end of the street.

Straining her eyes against the darkness, Maria fancied that she could make out a shape sitting in the front seat. She crouched down and started to edge along the pavement. Although she was soaked through now, the effort of concentrating on what she was doing kept any thoughts of discomfort away. When she reached her car she put the files down and felt in her pocket for the keys. From her crouching position she opened the door, lifted the files inside, wedging them behind the driver's seat, and scrambled in herself.

She peered into her wing mirror, and looked at the Jag again. With her head down as far as possible, she put the key in the ignition and turned it. The engine started first time. She moved the gear stick forward and took hold of the handbrake. Then a light in the mirror caught her eye – Malkin's car had turned and was coming up the street. She flung herself down, across the passenger seat. How much more of this was she going to have to take? Surely he couldn't have seen her.

The Jag seemed to go past, but then a reddening of the glass in her windscreen told her that it had stopped just beyond her, its brake lights on. She imagined that like some rooting creature the car itself could sense her presence. Part of her felt like climbing out, handing the files to Malkin and walking away from all this.

But then the red disappeared and with a roar that was audible above the sound of the engine of her own car, the Jag was gone. For the second time that night, Maria stayed lying in discomfort, waiting and listening, before she dared to acknowledge that her tormentor was truly gone.

She pulled out of her street and turned her car in the direction of the ring road. From there she headed onto a dual carriageway which took her away from the city. Warmed now by the car's heater, she was rehearsing in her head the story she would tell Tom. She hoped he would understand why she had to do this.

Five miles out from Nottingham she turned off the main road and passed through a dormitory town and then onto country lanes. The driving was more difficult here. The rain was falling in heavy globular droplets that were blown by the gale into the light of her headlamps, hitting the road and racing on like beads of mercury. The trees in the hedgerows danced like demented banshees and from time to time Maria had to grip the steering wheel in a moment of heart-stopping panic as the car was knocked off course by its impact with a deep and unseen puddle. Wary of the floods, she had chosen a route which kept her away from the Trent for as long as possible, but as she neared the riverside village for which she was heading she caught the occasional glimpse of fields submerged in water.

Maria knew by heart the address of the house she was looking for because she had often been asked to send papers there to be looked at over a weekend. She didn't know its exact location – she had never been to the village before – but it was on Main Street and she didn't think it would be difficult to find.

In fact it took her two trips from one end of the little settlement to the other, peering at house names through the rain, before she saw the entrance lying between two imposing stone pillars. She turned in and made her way up a dark gravel drive flanked by rhododendrons. At the end, her headlights picked out the ground floor of a solid stone house with large sash windows and creepers growing up the front. To her relief she saw that some of the lights were still on.

She parked next to a large saloon. She took a few deep breaths and made a pointless attempt to bring some order to her hair, before climbing out of the car and removing the files containing the money from behind the seat. Her shoes sank deep into the gravel as she walked up to the front door, which was sheltered by a porch supported on large stone columns. She pressed a bell-ringer encased in a brass fitting and heard the distant sound of chimes inside the house. She pressed again. A light went on in the hall and a large figure, made fuzzy by the frosted glass panels through which she viewed it, walked slowly towards the door.

"Hello, Mr Cooper," she said, when the door opened.

The man was dressed in a white double cuff shirt and designer jeans, and his hair was untidy. He moved his large head forward to look more closely. She was struck by the fact that he was clearly not much older than her.

"Who are you?"

"I'm Maria Cracolicci – I'm a secretary who works with Toby Malkin. We've spoken on the phone loads of times. There's something I need to talk to you about. It's urgent."

Cooper stared, and then looked over Maria's shoulder into the darkness beyond.

"*Malkin* sent you?"

"No. Not at all. I know this looks odd, and I apologise for the state I'm in, but if I could just come inside I can explain. We don't have much time."

Cooper didn't move. Maria could sense his unease. She hadn't expected this, but told herself that it was understandable – she didn't suppose that senior directors of media companies were used to receiving late-night visits like this.

"Mr Cooper," she said, "what does the name Monte Cristo Software mean to you?"

His eyes widened.

Maria continued, "You probably don't realise, but Toby Malkin has stolen a lot of money from you." She raised the arm supporting the files. "I've got it here – well, some of it."

He studied her for a little while longer, his expression almost pained.

"Mr Cooper, would you please just let me come in? I can explain."

"You're on your own?"

"Yes."

"And what do you want from me?"

"I just want you to listen."

218

After hesitating again, and with another glance into the night, Cooper stood to one side and let her in.

Closing the door behind her, he led the way across the wooden-floored hall, past the bottom of a sweeping staircase to the doorway of a study. It was a high-ceilinged room, lit by two standard lamps. Against one wall stood a solid oak desk with green leather skiver and computer. There was a smell of smoke from the open fire burning in the hearth. A bottle of brandy stood on a side table, with a single glass next to it.

Cooper stopped and looked at her.

"I'm sorry if I seemed a little rude back there," he said. "You took me by surprise."

"It's not a problem. I can appreciate that this is unexpected."

He stared at her again and then indicated that she should sit in an armchair on one side of the fire. She put the files on the floor beside her and watched as he parked his own bulky frame on the chair by the desk. She felt a little hurt – there was still nothing warm or welcoming about him, no sign of any gratitude.

"Can I make sure I've understood this?" he asked. "Who's sent you here?"

"You're missing the point. Nobody's sent me. I've come here to tell you what Malkin has done. It's so important that you understand and that we do something about it tonight."

He considered this.

"OK then. You'd better explain."

Maria leaned forward with her knees together. She took a moment to collect her thoughts, and then started to tell as much of the story as she knew, explaining how Monte Cristo Software didn't seem to exist, how she and Tom had found the money hidden in the basement, how Alec Shaker had been murdered.

"So Monte Cristo was just made up?"

"Yes – I think so."

"And you think it was Malkin who killed Shaker?"

"It must have been."

"This guy Tom. Who's he exactly?"

"A trainee solicitor – he worked for Malkin for a while."

"And he's in France now?"

"That's right. He's flying back tomorrow."

Interpreting Cooper's manner and questions as evidence of scepticism, Maria picked up the files, and walked over to the desk. She pulled the folders out of the blue plastic envelopes, now almost as bedraggled as she was, and laid out in front of Cooper first the money, and then the documents she and Tom had printed off from the disk. He watched her closely, then picked up one of the wads of banknotes.

"How much is here?"

"A quarter of a million."

"That's extraordinary. But we paid out a lot more than that."

"I know. I know you did. I can't tell you what he's done with the rest. But does it matter? Surely we've got enough evidence here to go to the police with?"

In the poorly lit room, it was difficult for Maria to work out the expression on Cooper's face as he sat pondering this comment.

"The police?"

"Yes. That's the whole point. Now that you know what's happened, we need to call the police. They'll listen to you. And we need to do it quickly."

"Are you sure that's the best thing to do? Wouldn't it be better if I took this up with the senior partner at Yates and Wood tomorrow? It's basically a financial matter."

She looked at him in bewilderment. "Mr Cooper – we're talking about murder as well as fraud. It's not something you can sort out with a quiet chat. What's the matter?"

"Nothing. But like you said, this is all a bit of a surprise. I have to think about Reverie Communications' reputation. There's a couple of people I'd like to call. Let me do that, and then we'll decide what we do next."

He stood up and left the room, and Maria thought she heard him climbing the stairs. He was gone for a long time. So long that after a while she began to wonder if she should go to look for him. But it was comfortable in front of the fire, and her tiredness was starting to take her over. She sat drowning in the depths of the armchair, drifting close to sleep.

Then she was aware of somebody standing over her and she blinked heavily. From this angle, Lewis Cooper seemed even larger than he had before.

"You're right," he said. "We should contact the police. But I think it would be better if we went to them. You know what it's like – if we call them they may not come until the morning. And we should go to Nottingham. There won't be anybody in any of the police stations round here who'll be able to deal with anything like this."

Maria thought about this for a minute.

"OK. It's a good idea."

She stood up, putting her tiredness behind her, and walked to the desk. She started to collect the money and the papers together. Lewis Cooper watched her do this, and when she turned to look at him she thought he still appeared troubled.

"Are you sure everything's alright?" she asked.

"Positive. I'll fetch something to carry that in."

He left the room and came back with a green canvas bag. Maria took it from him and put the files inside.

"Right," she said. "Ready to go."

"Ready to go."

In the hall he stopped to collect a wax jacket, and then disappeared back into the study briefly. When he returned, he took what seemed like an age to zip up and then button the jacket.

"Your boyfriend, Tom," he said. "He told you to come here?"

"No – that was my idea. And he's not actually my boyfriend."

As they made their way across the gravel outside with heads bowed against the weather, Cooper stopped her by putting his hand on her arm.

"I'll lead the way in my car," he bellowed above the sound of the wind. "You follow."

FORTY-SIX

The storm was showing no sign of abating. They travelled by back roads which Maria didn't know, driving through the occasional village and past farmhouses which she had never seen before. There was no other traffic. They seemed to be following the course of the river, and at one point they had to turn round when a sign told them that the route Cooper wanted to follow was closed by flooding. Soon after that the road started to climb.

At the top of the hill, they rounded a bend and Cooper's car slowed down. The brake lights lit up red, and then there was the flashing yellow of his left indicator. Maria pulled up behind him. She watched as he emerged from his car and came running through the rain towards her.

She wound her window down just enough so that she could hear him.

"Look," he shouted, "I didn't realise it was as bad as this. I think this road will be closed as well." He pointed behind him at the hedgerow. "There's a farm track here – it connects to another road that takes us away from the river. Just follow me."

Before she had chance to reply he was gone, running back to the shelter of his car.

Maria leaned forward and looked into the rain, and saw Cooper's headlights sweep slowly across the road and pick out a gap in the hedge. The solid back end of his executive saloon began to rise and fall as he headed onto an unmade track.

She sat still for a moment, not following. Nothing this evening had gone the way she had imagined it would. Cooper seemed so agitated. His car was now about forty metres away and she could see that he had stopped. Presumably he was looking back and waiting for her. Should she just drive away and leave him? Something told her that was the sensible thing to do. But if she did then she would have failed, she would have messed it up, letting Tom down and Malkin escape. She would give Cooper one more chance. But she needed to be careful. She needed to keep thinking. And if there was any more strange behaviour then … well, she would have to think of something.

Without the benefit of Cooper's expensive suspension, Maria's car bumped and groaned over every ridge and pothole as she drove down the track. She followed him round a long bend and then another.

Suddenly she was in a little parking area, with her car next to Cooper's. This wasn't right. The track didn't seem to lead anywhere.

With sharp little movements of her head like those of a frightened animal, Maria looked first at Cooper and then behind her. She put her car into reverse, but before she could move, Cooper had reversed himself, putting his car behind hers. What was he playing at? She looked ahead of her and put her headlights on full beam. In front of her was a wooden fence, and beyond that a steep grassy slope leading down to a drop into the swollen river.

The passenger door opened and Cooper climbed in beside her. He moved the canvas bag and put it on the floor.

"What the hell's going on?" she asked, bristling with Cracolicci anger. "You said this took us away from the river."

He didn't answer. Instead he looked out, studying the scene in front of the car as Maria had just done. With a growing sense of alarm, she noticed the strong smell of alcohol.

"Hello," she said. "I asked you a question."

Cooper turned his face away from her, then slumped forward and put his head in his hands.

"Why did you do this?" he said, his voice taut with emotion. "Why the hell did you have to get involved?"

"What's it got to do with you? I've got a better question – why don't you tell me why you're behaving like this?"

Even as she said these words, Maria realised that this was the time to stop arguing and be gone. She felt for the door handle, and there was a blast of wind and rain as she released it. But then she couldn't move. With one large hand, Cooper had gripped her seat belt at the place where it fitted into its holder.

"Sorry. You've got to stay here. Close the door."

She tried to struggle, but the belt was tight across her chest. She couldn't move. Cooper just kept looking ahead, holding onto the seat belt, waiting for her to obey. For a long time he stayed silent.

Her mind was racing as fast as her heart, edging towards conclusions that were too awful to contemplate.

"What's going on?" she said. "Please tell me."

"I don't have any choice," he said. "You do understand that, don't you?"

He turned to look at her, and as he did she realised what she should have realised before she agreed to make this journey. She felt wasted by her own stupidity.

"You were the last thing I was expecting," he said. "If you'd just phoned or something first it might have been different. But I can't risk the police. Not tonight."

From his jacket pocket he produced the bottle of brandy she had seen in the study earlier, and taking care not to release his grip on the seat belt, he undid the cap and drank from it. Down below them she watched half a tree appear briefly in the beam of her headlights, before being swept along by the current.

"Why would you do something like that?" she asked. "It doesn't make sense."

"I didn't mean to. It all just got out of hand."

"Well won't the police understand that?"

"No they won't. And don't try to talk me out of this. I've thought about it. There really is no other way."

Maria felt the seat belt tighten across her chest again as Cooper pulled it and reminded her of her confinement. She felt as though she were falling into a chasm of nothingness, but as she fell she managed to grab onto one sensible thought – if there was any way out of this situation she had to buy some time to think.

"I'm not trying to change your mind," she said. "But you may not be seeing this straight. Tell me what happened – it won't make any difference now."

He reached for the brandy bottle again, and this time he used both hands to make unscrewing the cap easier. Staring straight ahead, Maria moved her own hand down to the seat belt holder. She gasped as she felt his fingers close around hers.

"Shaker called me yesterday evening," he said. "It was late. He told me he'd been trying Malkin all day. He said there was something wrong with the Monte Cristo claim."

"What was wrong?"

"He'd seen somebody he'd been told was dead. It didn't make any sense to him. I agreed to see him and we sat in his office for an hour, going through everything. It was late. There was nobody else there. We could see that something was wrong, but we couldn't work out what. We agreed to talk again tomorrow. But just as I was leaving I saw a letter on his desk – a letter from Monte Cristo Software that had an address in Cannes on it. And that's when I realised."

He was silent for a while. Maria's fingers were starting to feel numb from the pressure of his. She didn't know whether he hadn't realised that her hand was there, or whether in some bizarre way he was taking comfort from the contact.

"But why would that make a difference?"

"Because it showed that Malkin was lying. He told me when the Monte Cristo thing started that it was Cannes, but later, when I said I wanted to visit them, he told my PA it was somewhere else. If Malkin was lying to me, something was very, very wrong. I told Shaker this, and although he found it hard to accept we worked out that it was all a fraud, that Malkin must have stolen the money. Shaker wanted to call the police there and then, but I told him to wait. Even though I was furious about what had happened, I could see that this was the most unbelievable opportunity. It wasn't *my* money Malkin had stolen – it belonged to Reverie Communications. And if we wanted, we could take it all. We just had to let Malkin know that we knew, and he would have to hand it all over. It would be perfect – Malkin would have done the crime, but we could have the proceeds. It's not as much fun being a director of a company as everyone seems to think, and this was a way out."

"But I suppose Shaker didn't agree."

"I don't understand how some people can be so stupid. He wouldn't have it. And then he got all high and mighty – accusing me of being in on the fraud, making out that he was so much better than me. I didn't think he'd understood what I was saying – I just wanted him to listen. But he started packing his things away, and then he pushed past me. He said that he would give me until this morning to think about it, and then he was calling the police. I couldn't believe it – I'd had one fucking lawyer make a total fool of me, and now this one was making it worse. They're all the same. I followed him out of the office, I tried to make him listen. But he wouldn't. He just wouldn't."

Maria didn't want to hear any more. She didn't want to know in any detail what the hand which was touching her own had done.

"So now you think you have to kill me as well?"

"I don't have any choice."

"But you can't get away with it. Tom knows about Monte Cristo Software. He'll be back tomorrow. You can't kill him. You can't just keep killing anybody who gets in your way. You have to stop somewhere."

"Tom doesn't know you're here. Nobody knows you're here, remember. The only reason you are here is because you wanted to stand in the spotlight. When Tom comes back tomorrow and finds you gone he'll tell the police, but if they speak to me, I'll be prepared. But they may just think that you ran off with the money."

225

He turned away from her and was silent for a while. Maria looked at the profile of his face – there was a world-weariness there, but a grim resolution as well. He unscrewed the top from the brandy bottle again, and took a long swig, wincing at the effects of the neat liquid. He wiped his mouth with the back of his hand.

"Now you need to know what happens next."

In the twenty odd years since she had left junior school, Maria couldn't recall having ever hit anybody. Now for the second time this evening, she struck out, swinging her free arm round and catching Cooper hard in the face. She surprised him, and in the confusion which followed she managed to release the seat belt and open the door. As she struggled to escape, she felt a large hand take hold of the neck of her jacket. She wriggled and squirmed, hoping that she could work her way free, and leave the garment behind. Then another hand took hold of her hair, and pulled. It was brutal. She screamed and carried on fighting, but there was no point. Taking an even firmer grip, Cooper hauled her back. He reached across and pulled the door shut, and then pinned her against her seat with his arm, breathing heavily and pressing hard into her windpipe.

"OK," he said. "Enough. Time to stop talking. Just remember, nobody asked you to get involved in this." With a nod of his head he indicated the scene in front of them. "Half a mile downstream, this river goes over a weir. Nobody could survive being in there tonight. When I tell you, you are going to drive down this slope and over the cliff at the bottom."

"Oh right. Anything you say."

Without any warning he jerked his forearm up, smashing into her jawbone, pushing her head back as far as it would go. She gagged for breath.

"Now you are starting to piss me off!" He shouted the last three words and carried on shouting. "You don't want to do it that way? Not a problem. If I have to, I will kill you and throw you in anyway. But it will be much less unpleasant if you do what I ask. Now choose, please."

226

The thoughts inside Tom's head were like something disturbing on the other side of a closed door, or a worrying pain that you hope will go away. He knew that they were there, but it was some time before he found the courage to acknowledge them.

The first few times he had called Maria's hotel room and received no answer, he put it down to something innocent. She had fallen asleep, she had taken a shower, the receptionist had tried the wrong room. After a while, these ideas lost all plausibility and his thinking turned to concern. Was she in trouble? Could it somehow be that Toby Malkin had found out where she was?

The fact that this was also unlikely tipped him next into anger. He had specifically told her not to leave the room. *Specifically.* He couldn't have been clearer. Sometimes Maria's having-a-mind-of-your-own thing went far beyond anything remotely endearing. Why couldn't she have done what he had told her to do? It wasn't difficult. His plan for what she should do in the morning was simple, and it would work. She just needed to follow it.

But in the end he had to concede that he was dwelling on these feelings to stop himself from confronting what he knew to be true. Maria had obviously considered what he had said that morning, and had taken the money. He couldn't blame her. He might have done the same in her situation, and although strictly speaking it wasn't Malkin's money, taking it from him was in some way a righting of his many wrongs. *Good luck to her*, he thought. It was the least she was due.

Far harder was the realisation that he might never see her again. Throughout the long, sleepless night in his Riviera hotel, he fought to persuade himself that it was for the best. If the truth was that Maria couldn't see him as anything more than a friend, then his own feelings didn't matter, and surely it was better for him that she should be out of his life. It was just a shame that they wouldn't have the chance to say goodbye. But Maria had decided to think about herself, and he should do the same. Returning to Yates and Wood with Malkin there and his money gone would be impossible, and he started to think about what else he might do. Go and stay with his parents for a while, probably. Give some thought as to whether the law was really for him, and if it was peopled as widely as it seemed to be by individuals who shared at least some of the characteristics of Toby Malkin, he had his doubts. He would need to fit in a trip to see Caroline at some point as well.

He rolled over and buried his head in his pillow. *Maria, why? Why such a mess? Why did we do so much to stop it from working?* It was like fallen blossom – so intense and perfect on the tree, but now just faded and sad. He had tried so hard to make it turn out differently.

On the riverbank, Maria stared ahead of her, down the steepness of the incline. The beams of the headlights picked out the surface of the river, running with smooth, irresistible force, the movement which she could see only hinting at the power which lay beneath. It was as though the water were waiting for her, like an animal waiting to be fed.

Cooper's arm kept her pinned against the seat. How could anybody be expected to make this choice? She had no doubt that he meant what he said – one way or another he intended that she was going to end up dead and in the water. It was as simple as that. He was drunk and beyond reason, and suddenly she was so very, very tired of all this, so nearly ready to stop fighting, so nearly ready to give in to these people who only ever seemed to want to do her harm.

Nearly ready. But not quite.

"It doesn't have to be like this," she said. "Wait until tomorrow – it will all seem different."

"No!" Cooper was screaming. "Don't say these things."

"OK then, you bastard. Let's do this."

Her foot found the accelerator and she revved the car hard. At the same time she reached for the handbrake and released it. They were both jolted back in their seats as they shot forward. Making the best effort she could to steer, Maria smashed through the flimsy wooden fence and accelerated again. On the slope, she felt the car start to slide, down and irreversibly down towards the water.

Cooper's arm was no longer across her neck. She was aware of him groping blindly for the bag with the money, and at the same time reaching for the handle of the passenger door. The car seemed to be slowing in its river-bound progress, and she put her foot to the floor once more. The engine protested and the wheels spun. She heard mud hitting the windows and the bodywork. She looked away from the scene in front of her and at what Cooper was doing. He was trying to open the door. Her face became contorted in desperation. *You've let me down so many times before*, she said silently to the door, *please, please let me down again now.*

The door obliged.

"It's jammed," yelled Cooper. "The fucking thing's jammed."

He was yanking at the handle with one hand, beating on the window with the other. The slope was steeper at the bottom and they were hurtling towards the edge of the cliff and the drop into the water. Maria could feel the car starting to pitch, as if it were about to overturn. Cooper was still fighting with the door handle, his movements ever more frantic. Now was her chance.

She pressed her foot to the floor again. Then she opened her own door. It was a struggle. The car was leaning more and more precariously, and she had to battle against the force of the wind outside. The door blew back in her face, and at the same time Cooper reached out and tried to take hold of her blouse near to her neck. Acting by instinct, she sunk her teeth into his hand and bit until they were close to meeting. Cooper roared and suddenly his arm was gone. Maria threw herself with all her force against the door, pushing it open again. She felt Cooper's hands on her, trying to take hold of her leg this time, but now she was starting to work herself free. She touched wet grass with her hand and she gripped hard. Then the other hand was holding on as well. She pulled as hard as she could and it seemed that she would make it. A split second later, it was all taken away as her foot became caught in the seat. She screamed out in pain as she felt herself twisted and dragged along by the car, heading for the edge.

Then suddenly she was free. Her leg was in agony, and it felt as if it had been snapped in two. But she was free, hanging onto handfuls of grass for her life, her face pressed into the sodden ground. She raised her head and looked over her shoulder. She saw the car as it reached the edge of the cliff. It appeared to stand still for what seemed like an age. Then it toppled over the edge and disappeared.

Maria passed out.

FORTY-EIGHT

She may have lain there for a minute, or she may have lain there for an hour. She had no idea. When Maria began to come round, reality reached her by degrees. The pain in her leg was crucifying, but she was also so very, very cold. Clammy and wet, her clothes clung to her as she clung to the grass. She lay with her cheek on the ground, looking up at two shining lights. It took some time for her to work out that these were the headlights of Lewis Cooper's car.

She tried to stand. Her mind was groggy, her movements clumsy, and as soon as she put any weight on her right leg it gave way. The pain intensified. She fell to the ground, and she retched.

She pressed her face into the hillside, desperate for the agony to go away. She wanted to curl up and stay there, to wait for morning and for somebody to find her, somebody who would lift her up and carry her to a warm place. But she also knew that waiting was madness. She may have escaped death at Lewis Cooper's hands, but not yet death itself. Heaven only knew how serious her injuries were. Somehow, she had to get to the car.

Raising her head, she looked up at the headlights again. She was so far from reaching them that they might as well have been moons in the sky.

Come on, she said to herself. *No giving in. It isn't allowed.*

This time, she tried another way of raising herself, bringing her good leg up beneath her as far as she could. That was easy. The hard part came as she tried to kneel. Her arms shook violently as she pushed herself away from the ground, doing all she could to keep any pressure off her right side. But this was wrong. She was asking her body to twist in a way that it couldn't. With a shouted expletive she let herself collapse.

She beat the ground in frustration, but she knew that she had to keep trying, had to do something before the pain eroded to nothing her willingness to keep going. The trick might be to twist first, put all her weight on the good left side before she tried to lift herself up. With both legs stretched out behind her, she rolled onto her side, and then eased herself up so that she was sitting at right angles to the slope. This was better. Then she looked behind her and let out an expression of horror. She was much closer to the cliff edge than she had realised.

The toes on her useless right foot were only inches from the drop into the water.

She shifted herself round so that she was kneeling. The only way to try to stand now was to push her bottom up and back, towards the river. Blocking out any thoughts of what might happen if she over-balanced, she did this, and suddenly it all became difficult, the pain in her right leg almost overpowering. But she forced herself into a half-standing position, like a sprinter waiting for the gun. Her brain told her that this was stupid. There was nowhere to go from here. If there had been anything above her to hold onto, she might have been able to move herself forward. But there was nothing. Out of sheer desperation, she began to hop. After three painful movements the inevitable happened and she was back where she started, face down in the grass.

Still she refused to accept that she could be stuck here. If she couldn't manage anything else, she wanted at least to move away from the cliff edge. Battling against her anger, she reached forward with both arms as far she could up the slope, taking hold of handfuls of grass. Then she pushed her hips away from the ground and pulled. By doing this and wriggling her lower body, she managed to move herself forward a foot or two. She repeated the process, then again, and again. She kept going. The grass was wet and slippery, difficult to keep hold of, and sometimes she lost her grip, or it came away from the soft earth in handfuls. But she was making progress. By the time the weakness in her arms forced her to stop and rest, she thought that she had covered maybe ten metres. The sound of the river had grown a little fainter. She felt exhausted.

But she also felt a little warmer from the effort, and as she looked up at the lights of the car again, she told herself that she could make it. There was no need to rush. Covering the ground steadily would be fine.

The rain kept on falling, and the wind kept on blowing, and Maria kept up her progress, arm's length by excruciating arm's length. Halfway up the slope she came across brambles, which tore her face and her clothes. When she was about twenty metres from the car, the ground became much steeper. There was less grass here, and although she clawed at the earth with her nails, she couldn't make enough purchase to support her weight.

She stopped, momentarily defeated. But she was calmer now, thinking more clearly through the pain. She waited until she felt a little strength return. Then with great care she repeated the manoeuvre which had failed at the bottom of the slope, now with more purpose, pushing herself up into the sprinter's position. She steadied herself. Then she flung an arm upwards and outwards. She struggled to make the contact she wanted, felt her arm slipping. But her determination forced her on and suddenly she had enough of a grip to support herself. Refusing to give in to the pain, she moved the other arm up and took the weight off her legs. Then she hauled herself up onto the place where she had parked earlier.

She lay on the ground, panting for breath, and looked at the car. It was as powerful and solid as its owner had been. She couldn't believe that she had ended up in this situation. She was clearly just as trusting and naive as Alec Shaker, and it had nearly cost her as dear. She wondered whether there was anything she could have done to have altered the chain of events and saved Alec's life. Probably not, but at least now she could tell the world the truth about what had happened to him.

She started to make her grimacing, cursing away across the parking area to the door of the vehicle, pausing before each movement to steel herself for the pain she knew it would bring.

It didn't occur to her until she was almost within touching distance that the car might be locked. She worked her way up into a sitting position, and looked at the door handle. She didn't dare try it. If it didn't open, the disappointment would crush her. The effort of trying to drag herself up the track to the road would surely be too much. She felt so helplessly weak. When she had been struggling with Lewis Cooper earlier, even when she had been propelling her own car down the bank, she had somehow known that she would survive. Now that certainty was gone. For the first time, the thought that she might well meet her end out here on this windswept hillside seemed very real.

She closed her eyes and said a prayer. She wiped the water from her face with her filthy ragged hand. She willed this door to open with all the fervour that she had willed the door on her own car to stay locked earlier that night. She reached up to touch the handle. She let her fingers linger on the cold metal without applying any pressure. Then she squeezed.

FORTY-NINE

At first nothing happened, and Maria prepared herself to cope with the worst. She squeezed a little harder. With a resonant click the door opened. Her sense of relief was so strong that she lost her grip on the handle and slumped forward, like an exhausted pilgrim reaching some distant shrine. After a while she recovered herself, and looked into the interior of the car. It looked so comfortable, so safe. She pushed the door open as wide as it would go and, clinging first to the steering wheel and then the handbrake, pulled herself up into the driver's seat, dragging her useless leg in behind her. Somehow the pain seemed more bearable now. She shut the door and locked it, hearing the central locking system secure all the other doors as well.

It felt as though she had been out in the rain for hours, and to be here in some sort of comfort created a rush of relief which washed over her for several minutes. As it began to fade, she realised the state she was still in. Her leg was a mess – by the car's interior light she could see a sickening and unsightly lump above her knee, presumably the result of a broken bone. She swallowed hard and looked away. Her clothes were in tatters and she was beginning to shiver in a way which threatened to become uncontrollable. She couldn't afford to lose her concentration now. But at least she had made it to the car.

Pulling her sodden jacket closer to her, Maria considered what to do next. Lewis Cooper's mobile phone was sitting in its hands-free cradle, and she saw that the keys were still in the ignition as well. She switched the engine on, hearing its efficient purr, and turned the heater up to its maximum strength. She looked at the phone again. If she called the police, would they take her seriously? She might have to wait for hours for them to find her in this place which she could describe only in the vaguest of terms, and she wondered about trying to drive the car. Even if she only managed a mile or two, that might be the quickest way of finding help.

Although she knew that working the clutch and the accelerator with one foot would be impossible, she tried nevertheless. It was only after the car had stalled violently for the third time, with its rear end now lodged in a hedge, that she accepted defeat. *Come on*, she told herself. *You need help. There's no shame in not doing it all by yourself.*

So she picked up the phone and called the police. The woman she spoke to was immediately concerned and promised that they would start trying to find her straightaway.

"Somebody has drowned in the river," Maria added. "It's the man who murdered that lawyer in Nottingham."

She talked to the woman for a little while longer, then rang off. Although she felt weak and sick, she was at least warmer now. The shivering had stopped. The warmth in the car made her eyelids start to droop. Her head began to nod, and again she lost all sense of time.

When she first saw the figure in the headlights she was confused. Her mind brought up jumbled images from earlier that evening, images of a man standing over her as she dozed by the fire in the study. It didn't make sense. She hadn't seen any lights or heard any sirens. Then, as the figure took a step towards her, she realised that this was no policeman, this was no friend. She recoiled in her seat. She was looking at Lewis Cooper.

How? How could he have escaped the death he had so confidently predicted for her? His large frame seemed more powerful than ever as he placed his hands on the bonnet and leaned forward, peering in. Her only thought was to keep still. It was just possible that he hadn't seen her yet.

Then she heard banging and watched as Cooper pounded his fist into the car. He was shouting and gesticulating. Maria revved the engine as hard as she could. Cooper reeled back and to the side, and now she couldn't see him. But then his face was at the window beside her, snarling with hatred. He pulled at the door handle, and he beat the window with his palm. Maria picked up the phone and showed it to him as she started to dial, but it only served to increase his rage. She pushed hard on the horn and revved the engine again.

Amid all the noise she could hear him kicking at the side of the car. But then the noise stopped and he was gone. She looked round, peering into the darkness, desperate to know where he was. A movement in front of the car caught her eye. He was there again, standing in the headlights, holding something in his hands. He lifted it above his head, and then hurled it at the windscreen. Instinctively Maria put her hands up to protect her face, and waited for the sound of glass shattering. But all she heard was a dull thud as the rock bounced off the car. She looked up and saw Cooper move away and then back into the light again, another large object in his hands. This time, in his fury, he missed the car altogether.

When he returned he came back to the side window. And this time, instead of throwing the rock, he kept it in his hand and hammered first at the door lock and then at the window. The alarm went off.

She pressed the phone to her ear and screamed at the person who answered.

"He's going to kill me ... he's going to kill me ... please, please send somebody now."

There was a dull crunch as a window at the back of the car smashed, then the noise of Cooper making the hole he had created bigger. Maria tried to wrench herself round so that she could see where he was and what he was doing. But it was difficult. Her leg restricted her movements. Twisting her neck as far as it would go, she saw a hand come into the car. She thought it was reaching for her, and she pulled herself back. But then she realised that he was reaching for the button lock.

She had run out of ideas. This time she was finished. Knowing that it was pointless, she put the car into gear and rocked with it as it stalled. Cooper's face appeared beside her again and the door opened. With nothing left to resist, she sat and waited.

Cooper reached towards her, his hands bloodied from the broken glass. His actions were business-like. He was in no mood now for talking. He took hold of Maria's hair and yanked her head away from the seat. He put his hands round her neck.

Maria felt his grip tighten. With an almost lazy movement she waved a hand at him, but there was no force in this last resistance and he brushed it aside. His face was only inches from hers, and she saw that he was totally absorbed in what he was doing, his eyes narrowed to slits.

He grunted as he tried to exert more pressure. All Maria could think about now was Tom. Her thoughts were wild and unconnected, but through the melee came one lonely hope – that one day Tom would understand how she had come to be here and how it had all ended like this. She hoped he would think well of her. Then even this thought started to fade, washed away by waves of blackness passing across her consciousness.

There was blue as well. Intermittent blue. At first she didn't register and it went away. She felt a hammer blow of agony as Cooper kneeled on her broken leg to give himself a better grip. Then it was back again, clearer this time. She opened her eyes and saw first one, and then two flashing lights. There were vehicles coming down the track, not far from her now. Either because he hadn't noticed, or perhaps because he had, Cooper carried on squeezing. Then there was another noise, a loud constant noise above them which was becoming unbearable. This wasn't how she had expected death to be. Cooper stopped, looked up and became bathed in white light. He let go of her, turned and started to run, a lumbering, awkward run in the direction of the river, every movement lit up from above.

Another blue light appeared and now there were people everywhere. Maria lay slumped back in her seat. She became aware of somebody else peering in at her, another pair of hands reaching towards her. She looked in confusion, not understanding the gesture the man was making. Did everybody want to hurt her?

"I just want to turn the alarm off, duck," the policeman shouted. "There's enough noise from that thing up there."

They made her warm and they talked to her and it was a long time before they moved her. The noise of the hovering helicopter faded slightly, and then was gone. There was shouting and people were running and she could hear the crackling of radios. Vehicles were moved to make way for an ambulance. The rain kept on falling. A young policewoman sat in the car next to Maria and held her hand.

When finally she was inside the ambulance, somebody told her that they had caught Lewis Cooper, and only then did she believe that she was safe. A paramedic sat with her, talking to her all the way to the hospital to keep her mind off the pain.

Maria liked this man. He seemed kind and he called her his darling. She had no idea of the connection and neither did he. But on another stormy night, almost three years earlier, this man had sat in more or less the same place in an ambulance saying more or less the same things to another patient with more or less the same injuries – on that occasion a frightened teenager who had thought her life was over at the moment when the car driven by her over-tired, over-worked father emerged quietly from the rain and smashed into her doll-like form.

FIFTY

When the rain finally stopped, it was followed by several days of perfect early summer weather. The floodwaters receded and at the hospital sunlight streamed into the private room which Yates and Wood provided for Maria. After a difficult first few hours she began to recover. She chatted to her visitors, she read magazines, she gave careful statements to the police. With her usual determination, she began to take her first steps towards putting the events on the riverbank behind her. And she wondered why Tom didn't even call.

Soon the day came for her to leave. Again Yates and Wood had sorted everything out – finding her a city-centre flat in which she could recuperate until she was strong enough to travel, paying for her ticket to be delayed and even arranging some temporary work with a law firm in Sydney for when she arrived. She knew that it was all born of guilt, but she was happy to accept it.

"You'll soon get the hang of walking with the crutches," said the nurse who had had most responsibility for her care. "Now, you're sure you've got everything?"

"Yes. I'm sure I've got everything."

"Good. And don't you go forgetting about us. I'm expecting a postcard when you finally get there."

"I won't forget."

The nurse bustled about, tidying the side table and checking Maria's notes.

"I don't know why you're sitting there like that. Mr Kelsey wants to see you before you go. He hasn't finished his round yet. He'll be at least twenty minutes."

When she was gone Maria sat on the bed, looking round the room. She had left some of the flowers her friends had given her for the next occupant, but they were starting to fade. In all other respects the room was already stripped of anything to do with her. She could happily have stayed there much longer. Leaving meant a loss of order, and she wasn't sure if she was quite ready for that.

The room was on one of the upper floors of the hospital, and from the window she could see familiar landmarks, the Council House, the Castle rock, the buildings of the Lace Market all clearly visible. She tried to imagine the things she would soon see in their place – Opera

House, harbour, ocean – and she tried to conjure up the enthusiasm everyone assumed she must be feeling.

"Hello," said a small voice behind her.

She turned round, her mind still on the other side of the world.

"Oh my God," she said. "You came."

Tom was looking sheepish, dressed in jeans and a sweatshirt, carrying a plastic bag from an electrical shop.

"I'm so sorry," he said. "I had no idea what had happened. I thought you'd … done something else."

"Where have you been?"

"At my parents' house. I couldn't see any point in coming back here. Then I went to see Caroline. I got a call last night from the police. They wanted to check a few details. They told me where you were."

"Come here," she said.

He sat down on the bed and they embraced. She clung on to him, and although she told herself she was mistaken, she could feel that it wasn't as she hoped it would be. He was holding back. It was as if something had died.

"Tell me about it," he said, disengaging from her. "Start from when we spoke on the phone."

She told him it all, but she didn't have her heart in the story. It didn't seem to matter now.

"What happened to Malkin?" he asked when she had finished.

"Nobody knows. Ruth Braebrook came to see me the other day – there was something going on between him and her, but she had nothing to do with Monte Cristo. After I saw him driving away from my flat, he went to see her. There was a massive scene, apparently. He was running away and he wanted her to go with him. She refused. He tried to drag her out of the house in front of her husband, and there was a fight. And then Malkin left and nobody knows where he's gone. But he's gone."

"You're sure?"

"He must have done."

"What about the money?"

"The cash went into the river with my car. Cooper managed to get himself out, but not the bag with the files in. The rest of it's been hidden away in various bank accounts – they've found some of it, but not all."

"But we were right – Monte Cristo didn't exist."

"*You* were right, Tom. You worked it out. The police were impressed – they explained it all to me the other day."

238

"Tell me – I'm fascinated."

"I don't really want to talk about it."

"Come on. It will always bug me if you don't tell me."

She sighed. "Apparently it wasn't Malkin's idea in the first place. He just came across something called a ghost supplier fraud. It's where somebody inside a company invents a supplier and sends in invoices which they authorise themselves. Quite common apparently, but very difficult to detect. Eddie Tomlinson at Reverie Communications was doing it."

"And so Malkin took it to another level?"

"That's right. He blackmailed Eddie Tomlinson, and built a whole story around his scam. He set up a website and phone numbers, got hold of forged documents and he arranged for some crook he knows to pretend that he worked for Monte Cristo. Between them they completely fooled Alec Shaker – they even took him to Rome and staged a meeting there. They tried to set him up with a prostitute so that they had something on him if they needed it. The police arrested this man, and they think that it was seeing him that made Alec Shaker suspicious – the plan was that he was meant to disappear off to Ireland with the money Malkin paid him, but he couldn't resist coming back for one last celebration with his friends. It's all so sordid."

"But you have to admit it was brilliant. Bringing a claim in the name of a company that didn't exist. The way he did it meant that Malkin was effectively negotiating with himself. Presumably sending e-mails to himself."

"I don't have to admit anything of the sort. Somebody died, Tom. Somebody with a family. And there's Guy Leighton as well – Yates and Wood have admitted that he was set up, but he's a broken man now. They offered him his old job back, but he can't face it."

He looked down. "Sorry. You're right. But anyway, how are you?"

"I'm OK, I guess. There are times when I just feel so stupid. I can't believe that I got so obsessed about Malkin. I should have put it behind me and moved on years ago."

They sat in silence for a while. Maria examined her fingernails and straightened her skirt several times.

"How's Caroline?" she asked, the words said so quickly they were almost inaudible.

"Fine. As far as I know."

"Meaning?"

He paused. Looked away.

"We've split up. That's why I went to see her."

239

Maria's heart jumped.

"Why?"

"Oh I don't know. I suppose I just realised that it wasn't right. We were kidding ourselves, believing in something which didn't exist. I think it probably started to dawn on me when you said that ... you know, you didn't feel attracted to me. Typical of you to be so honest. But you're right. And it made me look at me and Caroline in a different way. There's absolutely no point trying to build a relationship if an important part is missing."

She had turned away from him slightly, and she said nothing.

"But anyway," continued Tom. "Enough heaviness, as you always say. We've had enough of that to last us a lifetime. I've bought you something to take to Australia. Something to remember me by. It's about time your music system was dragged out of the seventies, even if your tastes stay there."

He reached for the bag, and out of it produced a micro stereo system, and a handful of Carpenters CDs.

"You'll never believe the sound quality you get out of something this small." He looked round the room and then peered out of the door. "Come on, let's give it a go."

His enthusiasm made him momentarily unaware of her as he unpacked the system and arranged it on the side table, then stooped beneath it to plug the lead in. He emerged, pressed a switch and took the first CD from the pile. He placed it in the machine.

Maria was still looking away.

A simple chord on the piano played three times. And then, almost falling on top of the third one, the voice. That unbelievable Karen Carpenter voice. Deep and wide and restrained.

The song's about songs, and the memories they hold. The voice goes low, swooping down, like a swallow on the river. A little bit of tremolo. A little sustain. But still holding back. So much more to come.

Tom looks for approval in her eyes. He mimics a line from the song. Maria smiles, but it's an effort. Thank you, she mouths. It's very sweet.

I think I should go now, he says.

The piano reaches a half-conclusion. A bass guitar slides in. And then suddenly, as the song dissolves into chorus, all the power of the voice is released. Forget the rest. Just hear the voice. As lonely as ever it was.

You can imagine her singin' it. Little woman, enormous presence. Slightly awkward lookin' in a pale green dress. A flick of the eyes to the band. Come on, guys, bring it on. Whatever you've got, I've always got just that little bit more.

Tom ruffles Maria's hair – like that night at Christmas on the riverbank. Here there are no players, no lights, no stage. But he's awkward as well. He shifts his weight from one foot to the other. He smiles. Then leaves.

The backing track hits a peak and falls away, making space. Maria bites her lip, screws up her eyes. She knows the song too well. Because for a moment, it's no longer about memories. It's about a girl with a breaking heart.

Malkin knew that he had to ditch the car. It didn't matter what he did to disguise his own appearance, people would remember the car. He had bought an English newspaper the day before, and had been shocked to see his own face staring out from the pages, a picture of him standing in front of the Jaguar which they must have found in the flat. And somehow they suspected that he was in France.

He peered at the map on the seat beside him and tried to work out his route. Although it was still early in the holiday season, he knew that he should avoid the Dordogne – there were too many expats living there all year round. He would skirt round it and then head east towards Italy. From there he would travel to Greece, because he was sure that he remembered hearing once that the Greeks didn't extradite for fraud. But what should he do about the car? Was it too risky to sell it? Should he just dump it and hire another? He could certainly do with something bigger – sleeping in the car was almost impossible.

Every decision seemed to be so much harder than it should be. He leaned forward against the steering wheel and put his head in his hands. Maria Cracolicci, of all people. How had *she* managed to reduce *him* to this? What was wrong with her, that she had to take such an interest in everything he did? If only he'd seen it, he could have scared her off, or bribed her or something. It wouldn't have been difficult. He despised her and every other half-witted secretary he had ever come across. There wasn't one of them who had ever really known how somebody like him should be treated, who had ever properly understood the meaning of respect.

He looked up. Across the car park, near to the entrance of the hypermarket, was a crowd of kids, teenagers hanging around. He was sure that they were looking at him, just as he thought that everybod

241

looked at him wherever he went. Automatically his hand reached out for the ignition key, preparing to drive on to the next town. But there would be kids there as well, or old ladies, or mothers with babies, and they would all be looking at him. He needed water. He was hungry. There was no point in putting this off any more.

He went into the store and moved quickly through its air-conditioned aisles, not looking properly at the items he pushed into his trolley and avoiding eye contact with any of the other shoppers. At the checkout the assistant said something to him he didn't understand, and as he packed his purchases into plastic bags a family group joined the queue behind him. He glanced at the total amount payable when it was displayed on the till, then fumbled for the notes in his wallet with trembling hands. As he did he lost concentration and the next thing he knew his wallet had fallen to the floor, scattering its contents. Then he was on his hands and knees scrabbling around for cards and cash whilst the children from the family joined in, jostling each other in their eagerness to help this hapless stranger.

When Malkin got back to his feet, he found that he was looking into the clear blue eyes of the children's father. The man's stare seemed to go right though him, and there was an awful pause until Malkin realised that he was holding out his hand.

"This is yours, Monsieur…" The man looked down at the credit card he was holding. "…Malkin."

He panicked. He grabbed the card, left his shopping and ran. When he reached the car he climbed in and drove off as fast as he could. His heart was still racing when he hit the *AutoRoute* five miles up the road.

It was more than an hour before he pulled into a parking area. It was starting to get dark. He was still furious with himself for making such a stupid mistake, and he felt so alone. He knew that he had to keep on running, but he wasn't sure if he even had the strength to make it through the night. It wasn't so much the tiredness, it wasn't so much the fear. In reality it wasn't even this night itself that concerned him – it was the lifetime of nights of running and hiding that stretched endlessly ahead after that.

FIFTY-ONE

The airport was busy, but Maria barely heard the voices of the people around her. She checked in her luggage, having to use all her strength to heave the cases onto the weighing machine. Her leg still hurt, but at least she could walk freely now. She bought herself a magazine and went upstairs to Departures.

There she hesitated. She had plenty of time before the flight was due to leave, and she felt compelled to delay the moment when she passed through the security gate. To her that seemed to be the moment when the decision to go became final.

She wandered the shops, then sat in a fast-food outlet drinking coffee. Everywhere she looked there were couples holding hands, or family groups laughing and having fun as they waited for holiday flights – it seemed that she was the only person in the whole airport on her own. She told herself not to stare, and flicked through her magazine.

After another coffee, and a lifetime's worth of troubled thought, it was time to be gone. Maria stood up and checked her ticket and passport for the hundredth time that day. Picking up her rucksack, she made her way between the gaps in the tables. She wondered if flights were being delayed, because the building seemed to be becoming ever more crowded – there were queues everywhere and her progress was slow. She stopped in front of an information screen for one final look at the flight details, and as she peered upwards something in the distance caught her eye. She blinked and looked round, not sure at first what or where it was, knowing only that it was something familiar, something precious.

With a rising sense of anxiety, she carried on searching with her eyes, fearing that this thing would be lost to her for ever. But then, in a heart-stopping, life-changing moment, she knew what it was. Across the crowded area in front of her, she could make out a dark-haired figure sitting at a table at the top of an escalator. Although he had his back to her, she knew with an overwhelming certainty that this was Tom. She was also in no doubt that he was waiting for her. How he had found out the time of her flight, she had no idea. But it was him, and he was here, and that was all that mattered. It was wonderful.

Before she went to him she paused, letting the first trickle of the happiness that would be hers for the rest of her life flow into her heart. When she crossed the space between them, the crowd seemed to part to make way for her and it felt as though she were floating, and as she neared him, he began to turn round, as if he were propelled by the same magical force as her. She reached out her hand to touch him, anticipating the emotions she would see written into his face – the joy, the surprise, the relief, the desire. With a tantalising slowness, he moved round further. She could almost imagine that the airport's piped love-songs were being played especially for them. And then Maria froze.

Not through embarrassment, through fear: this wasn't Tom at all; it was somebody she didn't know, but somebody whose dark, dark eyes were identical to those of Toby Malkin.

"No!" she screamed as she recoiled from this person. "You cannot do this to me. You cannot make me so unhappy."

She felt like a child railing helplessly against the injustice of a stern parent's actions, but the more she shouted, the more the man seemed to smirk and sneer. He was looking at something over her shoulder, inviting her to do the same. She turned, and immediately, at the furthest extreme of the concourse she picked out Tom – another Tom, the real Tom. He was walking away from her and she knew that no matter what she did, no matter what she said, there was no way of making him turn back.

Maria's head rolled forwards and she woke. She blinked, and for a few fleeting seconds she felt the primeval panic she always felt when she woke from sleep snatched during the day. As she took in the scene around her – the functional hospital room, the nurse writing something on the notes at the end of her bed – this feeling subsided, and she remembered why it was that she was still here. The consultant had said that he wasn't happy for her to go home yet. She hadn't been able to muster the will to argue.

She watched the nurse, and as her heartbeat slowed she tried to forget her dream. It was difficult. Before Tom had arrived earlier that afternoon there had been the hope that he would come, that finally, through some action or giveaway phrase, they would see, they would finally see that they wanted the same thing. However tenuous that hope had been, it had been enough to sustain her, to allow her to ignore the deflating reality of her situation. Now the rainbow was gone and she had only a painful memory of a glimpse of its end. An overwhelming understanding of her future confronted her. As ever, she was honest enough to face it. But it was terrifying.

It seemed that Toby Malkin was destined always to be a presence in her dreams, because the revenge she had sought so fervently and for so long meant nothing at all to her now she had achieved it. Why hadn't she said something when Tom was here? Why hadn't she explained? If only they had talked...

She eased herself back against the pillows. Life had knocked her down so many times before, but she had always dragged herself up – in the way she had dragged herself up the riverbank. She doubted that she would manage to do that this time. Her future would be measured out by grubby encounters with married men at sordid office shindigs. That was it. The weather might be different, the accents not the same, but beneath the surface it would all be so familiar.

The nurse finished what she doing. Outside there was the distant sound of an ambulance making its way towards the hospital along one of the main roads out of the city.

"Was I asleep for long?" Maria asked.

"Were you asleep?" said the nurse, making as if to leave. "I thought you were talking to your friend. Anyway, it looks like you're going to be with us for another day or two at least. Would you like me to see if I can find you a TV?"

"Yes, that's very kind."

"Do you think that this weather will last?" The nurse stood with her hands on her hips looking out of the window. "I'd like to take the kids out for a run round the park when I get off. It's just so nice to have a bit of sunshine for once."

"Isn't it."

Somebody in the ward outside called out the nurse's name, and she made her way to the door. Maria stopped her.

"What you said just now. About me talking to my friend. Which friend?"

"You know, the gentle one with the eyes."

Maria frowned in confusion, and looked up at the clock on the wall.

"But he left nearly an hour ago," she said. "Before the doctor came."

"No, he was here just now. Standing by the door there. He left when I came in."

"Are you sure?"

"Of course I'm sure."

As Maria considered this further, she began immediately to think of reasons to explain away why Tom might come back and then leave again. It was a little odd, but perhaps he had forgotten something, or else he wanted to clarify another detail of the Malkin scam. When he had seen her sleeping he had obviously decided not to disturb her. Yes, that must be it. Or something like that. It couldn't have been anything important. With unnecessary care she smoothed the creases from the sheets in front of her and stared at the wall.

OH COME ON, MARIA! shouted another voice inside her. *Get real. Believe in yourself. If ever there was a now-or-never moment in your life, this is it.*

For a moment she looked taken aback. Then with an action in which determination rapidly overcame hesitation, she reached for the crutches. She almost fell as she took her first steps away from the bed, and she managed to grab hold of one crutch only as she pushed past the nurse. Her actions jerky and awkward, she went out of the door and across the ward to an opening onto one of the hospital's main corridors.

It was busy with staff and visitors, and it stretched for a long way in each direction. Maria stood turning her head first one way, then the other. She saw a sign on the wall indicating the way to the exit, and set off in that direction, stumbling from time to time, trying to look round or over anybody in her line of vision, hoping he hadn't gone some other way.

She picked him out right at the end of the corridor, about thirty metres away, just about to pass through a door. Unlike in the dream, this was really him. But she wasn't going fast enough. She needed to stop him.

"Tom Elliott," she yelled. "Tom, you useless twat. Stand still!"

Everyone else in the corridor seemed to stop and look at her. But Tom disappeared through the door.

She put her head down and hobbled on again, forcing people to step aside. She reached the door, and saw that it led to a walkway which passed along the edge of a large canteen. This was even busier than the corridor and she looked round frantically, thinking that almost everybody she saw was him. She felt dizzy and put her hand out to support herself on the edge of a chair.

Just as she was starting to think that he had gone she saw him again, about to disappear round a corner.

"TOM!" she shouted, even more loudly than before. "PLEASE."

This time he stopped, as did almost everyone else around them. Some people started to fidget and look away, fearing a scene.

Tom stood where he was, looking puzzled and a little awkward.

"I didn't mean it," she said, her voice still raised. "What I said on the Market Square – I didn't mean it. Don't you understand?"

She hopped a few steps forward and saw his brows crease.

246

"I said it because I didn't ever think you'd choose me over Caroline. It's pathetic, but I didn't want to be rejected. I couldn't dare to believe that someone like you would ever be interested – properly interested – in someone like me."

Again she moved nearer to him, and rested her crutch on a chair.

"And before you go anywhere, please be clear about just one thing. What I really feel is totally the opposite of what I said."

"I don't understand."

"What's there to not understand? You do it for me, Tom."

Still he seemed not to comprehend, and frustrated by this she searched for another expression.

"You...float my boat."

"Sorry?"

They were now very close to each other. His embarrassment was forgotten, his expression intense.

"Is this some sort of Maria-style joke?"

"NO."

They looked at each other for a long time, saying nothing. People around them started to move, and the noise level grew. Eventually Maria's eyes dropped and she stared at the floor.

"So now you know," she said. "I just thought it might make a difference. You'd better go."

Wishing that, as with so many things, she had done this differently, Maria reached for her crutch. It took her two or three attempts to grip it properly. The look she gave Tom as she turned away was almost accusing.

She felt his hand on her arm.

"What did you just say?" he asked. "*I float your boat?*"

"That's right."

"And what's that supposed to mean?"

"You know exactly what it means."

"No I don't – you'll have to make yourself clearer."

She moved her head forward slightly, looking for confirmation that she had understood.

"You know ... I feel for you in every way."

He shook his head.

"Still don't understand. I'm having trouble hearing you."

His face remained serious but she could see little signs of laughter creeping into the corners of his eyes.

"Tom Elliott," she said, raising her voice. "You float my boat. Light my fire. You ring my bell." Now she was shouting. "You really,

really, really turn me on. You get me going. If it's OK with you, I'd very much like…"

He silenced her by raising his hand and resting it on the side of her face.

"And that's on top of everything else," she whispered. "There's so much else besides."

The look she gave him was suddenly full of longing for this to be real, for her to be given just one chance in her life to show how she could love. And although the look he gave her in return had in it an undeniable knowing that there would be many, many times when she would infuriate and madden, those feelings were now, and would always be, softened and made small by his boundless adoring.

"Why the hell didn't you say so earlier, Cracolicci?"

With infinite care he took her crutch from her and laid it down. Then he pulled her to him, and held her, and for the first time ever both of them could give everything to the embrace.

Acknowledgements

Heartfelt thanks to Robert and to Elizabeth for little words of encouragement which went a long, long way, to Ian Collinson at Weathervane for letting this happen, and to Muriel, Ben and Jonathan for their enduring love and support.

Michael R. D. Smith is a lawyer and writer who lives and works in Nottinghamshire. *The Deed Room* is his first novel.

Cover design by Jon Roscorla
www.jonroscorla.co.uk

Lightning Source UK Ltd.
Milton Keynes UK
UKOW03f0315200614

233772UK00002B/6/P

9 780956 219374